T0285389

Shanghailanders

Shanghailanders

Juli Min

S&G

Spiegel & Grau, New York
www.spiegelandgrau.com
Copyright © 2024 by Juli Min

All rights reserved. No portion of this book may be reproduced, stored in a retrieval system, or transmitted in any form or by any means—electronic, mechanical, photocopy, recording, scanning, or other—except for brief quotations in critical reviews or articles, without the prior written permission of the publisher.

This book is a work of fiction. All characters, names, incidents, and places are products of the author's imagination or are used fictitiously.

Jacket design by Charlotte Strick, adapted from the original UK design by Luke Bird
Interior design by Meighan Cavanaugh

Library of Congress Cataloging-in-Publication Data Available Upon Request

ISBN 978-1-954118-60-7 (hardcover)
ISBN 978-1-954118-61-4 (eBook)
Printed in the United States of America

First Edition
10 9 8 7 6 5 4 3 2 1

For my mother

&

for Haidong

Contents

All this talk was just a smoke screen.
Behind that screen, he was holding her hand.
That feeling could not be put into words.

—Eileen Chang, *Half a Lifelong Romance*

We can't go back.

—Eileen Chang, *Half a Lifelong Romance*

Shanghailanders

A True Shanghai Man

January 2040

Leo stepped onto the platform for the magnetic levitation train. The maglev was making its 2,025,659th trip into Shanghai. Back and forth, to and fro, airport to city center, city center to airport. Eight minutes for each one-way trip, every day of the year. Leo did the quick calculation after a confirming glance at the train's schedule and hours of operation. He liked to update the number every time he rode. More often since 2036, when his middle daughter, Yoko, had begun attending boarding school in Boston—followed soon after by her older sister, Yumi, for college—flying halfway around the world and back twice a year.

He was occupied with thoughts of his wife and their daughters, whom he'd left behind at security. They'd be arriving about now (he checked his watch) at the lounge, registering their boarding passes for gate 26B, PVG–BOS. As soon as the girls set down their matching silver suitcases, Yumi would go shopping. Yoko would head to the buffet. When she was nervous, she ate. His wife, Eko, would be fussing with her phone, low on battery, always close to dying. He imagined the three of them, quietly, separately doing their necessary tasks. A map of the terminal, with its gates, shops, and moving walkways, crystallized in his mind.

The maglev pulled into the station and waited, humming. It would be one more minute, Leo knew, before the doors beeped and opened. Just inside, a young but not too young train attendant stood facing Leo. She was, however, not looking at him. She was thinking about her not-so-youngness, her not-so-thinness, as she pulled down her too-tight vest. And he was not looking at her. He was thinking about how he had not wanted Eko to accompany the girls. He had picked the fight, he knew. But his wife had escalated it. Her fault, then his, then hers. An old, boring story.

"The girls can do it alone," he'd said. They'd done it so many times. Yumi and Yoko, they didn't need their mother to fly them to school. They didn't need her to make their extra-long twin beds. He expected better than that. Were they really so unextraordinary? So childish? At their age, Leo had already been on his own for years, for nearly a decade.

Eko, though, inexplicably, stubbornly, had insisted on it, on leaving him home alone with Baby Kiko. She even insisted that he say his goodbyes to them at the airport. She had pushed on this, said that if he didn't take them to the last possible point of separation, the girls would feel his lack of love, his lack of effort, his lack of care. She went on and on, speaking on their behalf like that, making him feel guilty. About what? Not going with them every step of the way? Maybe it was Eko herself who wanted to be accompanied, who wanted her hand held to the end. Her Japanese side—it required gesture. Unnecessary, irrational gesture. But she had said the words, made the accusation. And once they were said, out in the world, he had to go, hadn't he? Because if it was even just a little bit true, how could he live with that?

As Leo found a spot on the train, he imagined Yumi and Yoko settling into their seats, both window seats, the first and second rows of the plane, the ones he always reserved. They would watch Shanghai melt away. They would see the city below, its expanse, its rivers, the water that had been seeping across its land borders slowly for the past two hundred years, then quickly for the past twenty.

The city's verticality, its three-dimensionality, it was only growing higher. Into the clouds. Water everywhere, like melted iron, snaking through the clusters of buildings. His people, his ancestors had built this city of swampland. His blood was in the soil.

The DNA test he did ten years back with Eko and the girls revealed barely any other origins; his ancestors were all speckled pink dots concentrated around Shanghai on the world map. It was anticlimactic, really. The only thing revealed was his male-pattern baldness type—halo—and his high probability for memory loss late in life. Eko had for the most part Japanese in her, some Chinese, some Korean, Siberian. She would remember everything, forever. Except how to keep her cell phone charged.

Their girls, pan-Asian, their results from the DNA test predictable, along the spectrum between his and Eko's. Leo corrected himself: not girls, young women. He knew the term infantilized them. Especially since he was the one pushing for them to grow up.

"They have their freedom, their independence," Eko had said.

"Ah, but those are two different things," Leo said. "Precision of language, please. They do what they want, but you treat them like children."

"They are still young, Leo," she said. "Not everyone has to grow up as fast as you did. And did you ever think that maybe I want to be with them too?"

And then she'd had the nerve to tell him that he was the one who needed to let go. All he had been doing his whole life was letting go.

SHANA WAS THE oldest attendant on the maglev. And maybe she was the fattest as well. Her former boss had let her back on after she explained her situation to him. Her husband dead, her child sent to his grandparents in the countryside. It had been a kind of relief to come back. For as long as she had dreamed of married life, of raising a baby, it had all proved so difficult. Her husband, who'd grown up in France, who was smart, who had been a child prodigy—he had never managed to give her the life they'd imagined.

She'd met him on the high-speed between Shanghai and Beijing. Back then, ten years ago, she was twenty-two and beautiful. She walked the aisles of the train, handing out hot towels to the passengers, and she'd receive stares, compliments on her hair, thick and long and pitch-black. Men would actually turn around to watch her go after she walked past. She'd see them from the corner of her eye as she delivered cloth after steaming cloth down the line.

"What's your name?"

"How long have you been working on the train?"

"Where are you from?"

Shana. Four years. Kunshan. Nelson, so much older but playful, flirtatious, had kept peppering her with questions beyond the standard ones she got from time to time from solo male passengers. And then he lingered on the train when they reached Beijing. He said that he never wanted to get off as long as she was on it. He'd leave only if she came with him. He made a big scene, holding on to his seat's armrest while his friend pulled him away. She met him later that night, and he convinced her to leave her job and move in with him. Within six months they were married. They waited the requisite two years before trying for a baby, to rid her body of any potential radiation poisoning from working on the train. Michael came to them right away.

Her boss was unhappy when she contacted him a few months ago, looking to get back on the train. There were no more spots left on the Shanghai–Beijing first-class, he replied. "And the slow-speed?" she asked. After a long pause, he finally said, "There's a spot on the Pudong Airport maglev." The airport maglev was not a premier job. It was a fast trip, just back and forth to the city center. It wasn't flashy like the Shanghai–Beijing maglev or the Shanghai–Hong Kong maglev, the recently built two-hour rides. It was the old version of the technology; it felt archaic now. It was a useless train, really—a tourist trap, a test case. Everyone was laden with big suitcases, confused as to what to do.

Shana was heavier now. There were beautiful girls working every car. Their vests sat lightly on their minuscule waists. Hers was tight and short and kept scrunching up into her midsection. She missed her life before Nelson; she missed some of her life with Nelson. Now she was back to work again. Now she was a train girl again. She adjusted her blue hat and pulled down her vest as travelers filed past her, boarding the car.

What was the real reason Eko had to go? In the end, she had agreed that their daughters were no longer children. They flew all the time—to Kyoto, to Tokyo, to Paris; they were seasoned travelers. What was she hiding, then, the true motivation for going away? Leo asked her once, twice, thrice. He knew with each ask that the likelihood of a straight answer was decreasing. She dug her heels in like that. But so did he. She was always dancing around the truth, yet Leo would fish it out, dig it up from deep below.

The idea dawned on him as he sat on the maglev: a sliver of an idea that was mean and ugly but that he would face head-on, without fear. She was not really going to help their daughters. She was going to get away from him. Maybe to find something new. Maybe even something, or someone, that was not so new.

The panic and the anger rushed through him like a current, and he closed his eyes and counted to ten, focusing on his breath, as his new therapist, Dr. Zhu, had told him to. *And so what?* Another question he'd learned how to ask. *How would life be so different?* And what evidence did he have? What proof?

So what? So what?

Take a pause and focus on the present, something happy.

The maglev, its faded blue seats, would go back and forth, back and forth. For all time? Until it was decommissioned, put to rest. Leo thought of his old horse, Py, who would soon need to be put down too. The stallion was living at the hotel next to the house on the land, the farm they'd bought back in 2032, when he was at the height of—what had Dr. Wen liked to call it?—yes, the height of his "manic paranoia."

He had no regrets, though. The farm, the house in the mountains of Vancouver, the boat docked off the shore of Changxing Island, the village house in Zhejiang with its cellar full of water and bars of gold, the ponies, the vineyard in France—he still felt, in the back of his mind, that the world was going to shit, any day now. All the structures holding up life as they knew it would completely and suddenly collapse.

He, and they—the girls, Eko—would have to survive. They were too important. "To whom?" Dr. Wen had asked. To himself, of course. And who knew? Maybe to the world, to the future of mankind.

The maglev was filling up, and a young woman walked in and down the aisle to the seat across from Leo. Her hands were fidgeting with a red hat that matched her red coat and—as Leo sensed rather than saw through a quick glimpse—her red lipstick. She was nervous.

It was Mary's first time on the maglev, and her first time in Shanghai. In fact, this was her first time away from home at all. She was on her way to meet a man—someone she'd first connected with over WeChat a year ago. He had sent money for her plane ticket and for the ride on the maglev. As if it were some kind of treat, to take this fast train from the airport into the city, where he was to pick her up. She didn't care about the maglev; she'd rather he had sent over some spending money. And wouldn't it have been nicer for him to meet her directly at the airport? Already she had a sinking feeling. She glanced around her. A handsome man in an expensive-looking cashmere coat sat on the other side of the aisle. Thick wavy hair speckled very lightly at the temples with white. A true Shanghai man!

The maglev doors beeped, then closed, and the train began to move, its acceleration smooth and quiet and displayed on a screen at the front of the car in digital numbers that ran up quickly from 1 to 400km/hr. Despite her anxiety about the entire trip, she couldn't help but feel impressed by the speed.

Shanghai zoomed by outside the window. It went by so fast it was just a blur of colors. Mary could not see much. She was waiting for the tall buildings, the rush of cars, the fancy people holding hands along the Bund.

But they were still in the outer regions of Pudong. Mary saw a familiar landscape—the houses, the plots of farmland, the tiny anonymous farmers walking in the distance. It was the same as in her hometown, where her parents tended cabbages to go to market, some traveling as far as Shanghai. She had often had the thought, while packing the cabbages in their little boxes: *Even these cabbages are going to see Shanghai before I do.*

Mary was going to see the tallest building in the world. She was going to take photos on the Bund. She was going to ride the floating bubble down the Tranquility Tower. She was going to put on a mermaid suit and swim with the turtles in the aquarium. All the things she'd paid tokens to see and feel and do on the screen—they would be real very soon.

Her desire to leave had existed forever. It had been born in her, as intrinsic and as extraordinary as her beauty. And she had cultivated both. When they'd gotten their home screen from the government five years ago, things had just gotten worse. Since then, she'd spent hours with it each day, walking along simulation Shanghai streets, sipping virtual coffee, chatting with strangers over drinks at bars along the Bund. In Shanghai no one would care that she was twenty-five. She heard that in the city, women even got married at forty. Fifteen years—she could live another entire lifetime in fifteen years.

Mary had left a voice note to her parents on their family screen. Her parents had never learned how to read; they barely knew how to use the screen. They would see its flashing green light, though, and know to press the button. Mary's voice would spill out, unemotional, strong. *Ma, Ba, I'm going to Shanghai. Don't look for me. I'll send money home.* She packed a small bag full of her prettiest clothes.

Mary was just a girl from Anhui, but she knew she was striking. She was short, but her face was nearly perfect, as long as she fixed her eyes. She only had to cut thin strips of clear, dissolvable tape and attach them to her mono lids, and her eyes would fold and grow double in size. Over the years she'd perfected the angle and placement of the tape, to create the right shape—she liked a squarish, rather than a round, eye. Mary looked out the window in glances, noting the train's fluid motions. Oh, now they were making a turn, and she could feel the train lifting to her left, angling into the turn. She felt she might almost fall over into the aisle. Would the handsome man help her back into her seat?

Mary looked at herself in her compact mirror. Her eyes were good today. She had good eye days and bad eye days. Every night before bed, she washed off the sticky remnants of her eye tape, her thick skin slowly pushing the foreign creases out of her lids. Mary had read about cases where years of tape had effectively trained a person's lids to stay creased forever, but by morning she always peered out at herself from her own small, hooded eyes, their natural expression fittingly unamused, dull.

Mary hated mornings, in part because of how she looked, her original self. She was too frequently late to her job at the hotel, but she always made time for her tape. In her small bathroom, the mirror, surrounded by a ring of light, was festooned with little pieces of tape that hadn't made the cut. When turned on, it looked like a sun with many rays. Or a lion with a thick mane. Or a peach, being burrowed into by an army of worms.

When she arrived in Shanghai and finally met Xin, it would be a while before they spent the night together. She'd decided to get her eyes done at the Ninth People's Hospital, famous for plastic surgery. No more tape—freedom from tape! The idea thrilled her, even more than the thought of meeting Xin. She glanced over at the man next to her. She could even shoot higher.

When she next looked out the window, the landscape had changed. They were now rushing by tall blocks of apartment buildings, some of them still under construction. Cranes lifted their metal necks into the sky.

SHANA RECOGNIZED THE MAN in seat 14C and hung back. In all her years working the trains, there had been the occasional friendly regular, but no one she knew from her personal life. She pulled her vest down and smoothed the wrinkles that cut into her skin. The man's face was familiar, but his name evaded her. Then, suddenly, she remembered how she'd met him. He was a friend of Nelson's, from university. They had set off from the same starting line, but Nelson had fallen off the track, and then he'd gone and died. She watched the man as she made her way down the aisle. He was older, but still handsome. As she passed him, she quietly turned her face away, wanting to remain hidden. She remembered Nelson talking about this man. Leo. Yes. Now it came back to her, the name, everything. Leo had lucked out as an early investor in real estate. He had bought several apartments when Shanghai was still cheap. His Japanese French wife, aloof and pretty, always speaking French, their three little girls. The whole family had come over once for dinner—to the house on Anfu Lu, the handsome stone-and-brick house that Nelson had rented when they'd been granted the seed money for Café Je t'aime. It was their house and also the office. The home had been shady and secretive, someone always coming out of a room, turning a corner, finishing a meeting, lounging on the patio. It smelled at all times of freshly brewed coffee. Grinds were packed into every crevice of every table, every desk, between cracks in the computer keyboards.

Leo and Eko had brought their girls over for dinner. What Shana remembered noticing that night was the hand-holding. Husband's and wife's hands were always in contact, fingers rubbing against one another. But it hadn't been grotesque; it had been lovely. Because the wife's hands were lovely: elegant and long and prettily manicured. And Leo's hands were lovely, too, large and square. She could imagine their embrace—warm, dry, soft. The girls were charming, with precociously beautiful faces atop the bodies of children. They traveled as an entourage. Their presence radiated wealth. Already at that point, two businesses down for

Nelson, Shana was starting to get a sense of her own man's limitations, how he could never give her what this family had.

At the end of the night, after they'd all said goodbye, Shana was on her way out to throw away the trash. That was when she heard them, Leo and Eko, and saw them standing under a streetlamp a few buildings away. Leo was yelling. Eko was glaring at him. Their faces were clear, illuminated by the light. Where were their children? Shana remembered those faces, remembered her concern for the girls, saw it all now in her mind's eye.

LEO LOOKED OUT THE WINDOW; they were passing over a bridge. Leo was going back to an empty home, and he hated an empty home. For so many years, business trips had ended with bursts of energy and brightness—him spilling through the front door and his daughters running, colliding into his open arms, the squeals of delight when he pulled small presents from his coat pockets. His wife's warm kiss on his cheek, despite the inevitable days' growth of beard.

But he knew what awaited him now. The older girls away and Yukiko out with her friends or simply too cool to stay up for him, a plate of cut fruit left wrapped in plastic on the dining table by their housekeeper and a cold Pepsi in the fridge. The sugary cola, his one nightly indulgence, his welcome-home party.

Better, then, to be out, walking among the people, solving problems in his head. Work issues, management issues, his least favorite—then math issues, his reprieve, his solace. Though it was just a hobby now, he still spent quite a lot of time on math. Several years ago he had begun revising the foundation of his intellectual framework. He had become convinced: the rise of intuitionism, the nondeterministic nature of the universe, our inability to conceptualize infinitude, the inevitable collapse of relativism . . . the past could no more predict the future than the future could foretell the past.

He had Yoko to thank, or maybe to blame. She, his middle daughter, had been the only one interested in numbers, in theories. When he gifted her *A Brief History of Time* for her tenth birthday, she had inhaled it, just as he had when he was young. Yoko was cut from the same cloth. She had reignited in him a long-forgotten passion for all those fundamental questions. The arrow of time, the limits of our understanding, the question of infinity. He had worked with her just last summer on parsing through Euclid's *Elements*.

He had been considering, recently, reframing his own specialty, in engineering and physics, through an intuitionist lens. Because it was becoming clearer that classical mechanics did not represent the truth of the world, the universe. Everything he'd believed about infinite precision needed to be rethought. Then, he might understand how information is created rather than revealed, and how to predict, or even how to give up on predicting, change. When Yoko was younger, she worked on her middle-grade problems in his office, while he tackled his own. When the others walked in on them, sitting silently side by side, they joked, "Dad and Yoko, forever thinking about infinity."

Now she was back to school, where she was studying with masters, on her own. He felt the pang of loss. His Yoko, she was something special. They all were, sure. But she—maybe she would figure it all out.

Who was staring at him? Leo felt too old for these games. And yet. The fatigue slipped from his mind. He couldn't help but look at the plump red lip, the lined eye, the lean legs, uncovered, that extended out from under the short skirt and red coat. Women. So many women in this world. They made eye contact, then both looked away. Outside his window, a landscape of steel, iron, sky, and clouds. He flexed his palms and clenched his jaws. The old animal in him—he enjoyed being watched, appreciated. He was still attractive in his late middle years. To a certain type of girl. Not a young girl; a woman still youthful. A woman with ideas about herself. A worldly girl.

Leo turned his gaze back toward the aisle. But the red girl was not watching him. She was staring out her own window. In a flash, another maglev passed on her side. Their train jostled in response. She startled, looked around in panic.

Her eyes met his again, fear across her face, a question: *Is this right? Is this the way things should be?* So it was her first time on the train. He smiled, a calm, reassuring smile.

The maglev was fast and soon they would be packing up, shuffling onto the platform, balancing bags down escalators and elevators. In movement, the river of people, the electricity in the air would dissipate.

But then, unexpectedly, the train was slowing down. Leo watched as the number on the monitor decreased. It dropped and dropped until it was in the single digits, and finally it came to a rest at zero. The passengers looked around at one another. This was not right. Leo stood up to peer down the aisle. Others, too, were looking around and through, out the windows. A murmur began to crescendo. "What's going on?" The thought crossed

Leo's mind that this was it, the war that was going to bring every country to its knees. The start of apocalypse. The end times. But he pushed the thought away. The end times had never arrived, and he'd decided years ago to put them out of his mind.

Leo had the urge to snap a photo of the scene. He wanted to document this moment, the way he'd liked to do in the past. He wanted to show and tell his wife about it. He wanted to talk. He always wanted to talk. The problem was that Eko no longer listened. He had been talking past her for years. Eventually, he'd stopped talking to her nearly altogether. It wasn't that he was punishing her. She had lost interest, and he had lost interest in return.

Should they have gone back to France? Should they have spent more time in Kyoto? Who would have imagined that he—that they—would still be in Shanghai after all these years, would be living out their lives in his home city? For his work, ostensibly, yes. But had he kept them all here to no end? Would they have been a different family in France, in Japan? What kind of family?

SHANA MARCHED DOWN THE AISLE, avoiding the heads that were sticking out along her path. She squeezed into the conductor's cabin. There were already several attendants crowded in.

"We hit something. We were going too fast to see."

"Well, what was it? On the tracks?"

"It couldn't have been a person, right?" Shana asked.

After a pause, the conductor shook his head. "I don't think so."

"But you didn't see it."

"What did it sound like?"

"Like a small pop."

"Who's going out to check?"

The conductor got on the phone with the transportation authority. They were on their way. They would have to inspect the train before it could move again.

Shana had never been in an accident on the train before. When she was first working as an attendant, they had regularly practiced for these kinds of situations, but she had participated halfheartedly. She'd never been the most diligent. She'd been young and beautiful instead.

All those trainings seemed like a lifetime ago—before Nelson, before the hard restart of his death. Her heart was racing. She was excited and nervous and also scared. She would be in control of her car, though. She felt the way she did whenever her son ran over the rocks studding a river, crossing to the other side. "Ma!" he'd call out, and she'd hold her breath, forcing herself to jump from rock to rock with a similar confidence. She did not want to teach her son to be afraid of anything.

"Everybody calm down," she said, coming back into her car. "Everything is fine. We're going to do a quick system check, and we'll be up and moving in no time. Thank you for your patience."

She saw Leo glance up at her, then down at his watch. He had not recognized her. She saw the young girl across the aisle from him nearly shivering with fear as she looked around her, wide-eyed and helpless. *Help me*, the girl said wordlessly. She was someone who had received help her whole life. The girl was pretty. No, she was beautiful. She looked like a little doll. It exhausted Shana to look at her. She was exhausted all the time now.

. . .

WITH THE TRAIN STOPPED, Leo imagined the doors swinging open. He could get out, climb down from the elevated tracks, into the grass. He had not been happy for years. He thought about taking the pretty girl and escaping from the train. He remembered again the old house on the outskirts of the city—farmland, the glass angles reaching up into the sky. The weekends with the animals, the board games, riding the ponies with his girls on the mountain.

Leo imagined running through the fields, settling in. His daughters were practically grown. Eko made her own money now. Those days on the farm had been his happiest, and he could re-create them with someone new. He still had the land, maintained by a local farmer who sent a large box of vegetables to their house in Shanghai every week.

He would hide, out there. How long would it take for them to find him? Would they make a concerted effort? He would raise a kid, a son, of course. Homeschool, everything. He'd do things right this time. He could do it all over again. A new, totally sustainable life.

The young girl rummaged through her bag and pulled out a small mirror. She reapplied her lipstick and used her pinky nail to poke at her eyelids, stretching her skin in strange motions that made her look unnatural, inhuman. Leo saw it all clearly, then: the young girl, the insecurities of youth. How tiring, the first years of partnership, of adjusting and negotiating and ultimately relenting. That was Leo's problem. He had to do things completely, totally, correctly. It couldn't be just sex. It would have to be a life, a child, a farm, an entire system unto itself. And he would never be able to forget: who he was, who they were, and how they'd shaped him. With his family, now, the ties were intractable, gravitational. In the end, he loved them, all of them—he was still in love. Eko still drew him, with her secrets, her silences, her unrelenting beauty.

The train began to move. The numbers on the screen climbed slowly, and then quickly. A woman with an infant began to make shooshing sounds; her baby was getting agitated. A young man wearing shorts and sandals stretched his long legs into the aisle. An elderly woman and her even older mother continued chatting; they had never stopped. All the people on the train settled back into their seats, glancing around before returning their attention to their windows. Now they were almost there, almost home.

Rouge Allure

January 2040

At the duty-free, the girls stood side by side, their backs to their mother, as if working on some difficult project or telling each other secrets.

Something had changed about Yoko, something Eko couldn't place. A new self-consciousness, maybe. Her second daughter was different somehow.

But what did she expect? Living on one's own—of course things would change. Hadn't she herself changed after leaving for college? And then hadn't she changed again, after reaching Shanghai? Eko felt like she had, for so many years, shape-shifted and adjusted and improved, pushed the limits of her personality, the outlines of her personhood, so much so that she was stretched and had become shapeless. Thin. Amoebic. A thing could be formed and re-formed, but what was its essence, its core shape? Maybe only a mother could ever know.

She hoped her daughters would find men who loved and cherished—sharpened—their essential shapes. Who didn't make them change. Well, maybe Yumi could use some adjusting. She could be less mean, less abrasive.

When had Yoko started wearing makeup? What had happened to her over the last semester at boarding school, between the summer and the winter months? Was she finally starting to take an interest in boys? Yoko had always been so unaware of her own beauty. She was the most beautiful, though Yumi tried the hardest. This, Eko thought, might have been the source of all Yumi's cruelty over the years.

Eko wanted this moment to last, hoped it was an image of the future—her two oldest girls, getting along. Now they turned and looked back at their mother. Yumi and Yoko had applied the same shade to their lips, an intense, bright red. The two shocks of color made Eko gasp. For a moment, the girls looked nearly identical. It caught Eko off guard, their sameness. Yumi's lips triangular and small, Yoko's full and round. The color, though, had overwhelmed all the differences. When she looked at her daughters, she was often busy comparing them: Yumi a physical copy of herself, Yoko with her father's high nose, Kiko lovely but always trying this and that with new trends.

Eko walked closer to where they stood, at one pricey makeup stand among many, in front of a display of red and pink and orange circles. Eko thought of a field of roses, a Seurat painting of a park bench in autumn.

"I'm going to get this one," Yumi said. She had stopped asking for things since leaving for college, since they'd given her her own credit account. The bill came once a month, extraordinary charges made up of coffees and takeout and late-night Mexican and shops on Newbury and Boylston. On one hand, her daughters' fearless spending, their sense of perpetual security, comforted Eko, even gave her a demented sense of pride. Look what they had. Look at the freedom. On the other hand, she sometimes wondered if she had done it wrong, if they were ruined, if she had made a terrible mistake.

Yumi scanned the code to pay, and Eko felt a pang of sadness, seeing her girls like that, independent. Because it meant that soon, she was going to leave them. She'd made up her mind. They were old enough. Yes, with their red lips and their own credit cards. They didn't need her anymore. But it would be sad, wouldn't it, for Eko and Leo to have to split the holidays and the flying—and, later, the lives, the families, the grandkids?

Eko had connected—no, that was not the right word; she had reconnected—with an old friend. Well, an old friend that she'd dated her first year of college, before she'd ever met Leo.

David. She had done so many firsts with him. Tequila shots and dancing till she blacked out, the small tattoo of a circle that she kept hidden on the back of her neck. He was the first boy to take her traveling out of Paris. They'd gone one weekend to The Hague. Some free trip he'd bought with points on a credit card. She couldn't imagine a more boring place now. But back then, it had been grand, hadn't it?

Who had she been then? So bright, so kind, so unaccustomed to confrontation. Some people bring out the best in you. Some, the worst. Why hadn't it worked out, so many years ago? Eko had thought him not attractive enough. How fleeting, how deceptive, how unnecessary all of that, in the end.

Eko had seen David's sparse photos through the years. The woman he'd married, the son he'd raised, the gradual absence of her photos. There had been a divorce.

And then a college friend started a new group on an app that brought all their classmates, their friends, back together—chatting, reminiscing, connecting. Leo had been in graduate school, and so he had not been invited. When they'd met, when she was twenty, Leo had seemed so much older, so wise beyond his years.

David—she scrolled now through his photos and videos, read through their message history. Nothing crossed a line, but it was very friendly, needlessly so. When he'd heard she might take her girls to Boston, he offered the possibility of his taking a business trip to New York. It was settled: a friendly reunion lunch at the Museum of Modern Art.

"Mom." Yumi had purchased her makeup and was waiting. Eko raised her eyes and then her brows. *Yes?*

"I'm going to check out some shops. I'll meet you at the gate, OK?"

"Fine."

"Yoko—you coming?"

"No, I think I'll take a look at the blushes."

Yumi gave her sister a look. "You'll always be a weirdo under all that makeup anyway." And then she left, flicking her hand in the air. "Bye, weirdo."

Eko felt the familiar pang of hurt she often did on behalf of Yoko, always the butt of Yumi's cruelty. But it was nothing, really. It could be much, much worse. Yoko continued browsing through the lipsticks, opening and closing lid after lid. Eko looked back down at her phone, lingering on a photo of David on a ranch, wearing what looked like a cowboy hat. She smiled.

"Okaasan."

Eko heard it and froze. No one had called her that in years. Japanese was the language of their childhood; it had been usurped by French and Chinese, and then by English. She put her phone away and looked up, meeting her daughter's face in the mirror.

"Okaasan. Ma." There were tears rolling down Yoko's cheeks. The face in the mirror looked away and mumbled the words Eko had not expected to hear from her middle child, from any of her children, so soon: "Ma, I'm pregnant."

A drone buzzed overhead and Eko turned her back to it, putting her arms around her daughter and shielding Yoko from its camera. She couldn't remember the last time she'd held Yoko. Hugs were not Yoko's thing; in this she was unlike Yumi, who still let Eko stroke her hair in passing, and Kiko, who ran in for a hug after every dance performance, every curtain call. With Yoko, from very early on, there had been no invitation, no reasonable excuse for close contact. At times, even, Eko had felt her daughter was repulsed by her presence, moving her leg away when it brushed against her mother's on a couch, nodding tersely when Eko congratulated her on winning a place at a robotics or math competition. *Her father's daughter*, Eko had always thought. *Let him have one.*

So Eko took the time to embrace Yoko, who smelled like her older sister—coconuts and milk—they shared a bathroom, they used the same shampoo. Yoko was only mildly sniffling now. Eko had been whispering, "It's OK. Don't worry. I'll help you," into her soft hair.

The lipstick Yoko had been grasping fell onto the ground and Eko released her hold to pick it up. Chanel Rouge Allure.

"Don't tell anyone, please, Ma. Not Dad, not Yumi, not Kiko. No one, please."

"OK. No one. Let's go have a seat, hm?"

"Ma, I wanted that . . ."

"Oh, the lipstick? Sure." Eko picked up the lipstick, then another, and brought them to the counter. It was an old habit now, buying one of each for every girl. As she accepted the shopping bag, her hands were shaking. During the winter holiday, her daughter had been pregnant. At the dinner table, in the car, under the same roof. Yoko had maybe even made that devastating discovery at home. Eko took a deep breath and thought about the options. The United States? No, it would be too difficult to do it illegally. Back to Shanghai, maybe, or to Japan, or Paris. The places they knew best.

She signaled for Yoko to join her, and they walked together to the gate. There was still time before boarding. Yumi would shop until the last possible minute. Eko could imagine her, indecisive and hesitant, trying things on repeatedly, unsatisfied with this or that small detail.

"So what happened?" Eko had meant to start with something more comforting, but it just came out before she knew what she'd said. "Do you want to talk about it?" she tried again.

Yoko's eyes were a little swollen, her lips still bright red. But she was composed again, herself again.

"There's a boy at school," she began. She was looking away from her mother, out at the terminal. Eko, sitting next to her, the metal armrest between them, felt far away once more. "I don't know what to say," Yoko said, shaking her head. "We weren't careful."

Eko had never talked to her daughters explicitly about sex, about boys, about birth control. She had failed them in that regard. The speakers announced the last call for a flight to London. They both listened until it finished in Chinese, and then in English.

"Your boyfriend?" Eko asked.

"I guess, yeah."

Eko nodded, relieved. At least it hadn't been forced. "Does he know?"

"No. I don't want him to know." Yoko looked into her mother's face. "I really, really, really don't want anyone to know."

"OK. I understand." Eko wanted to hold her daughter's hand. It was what she herself would have wanted. But the moment felt gone now, the opportunity.

"Ma, where do we go?"

"First we fly to Boston. We have to drop off Yumi at school. Then we can do it, all right?"

Yoko nodded.

"It can't be in the States," Eko said. "It's too dangerous there. How about going back to Shanghai?"

"No way. No way."

"We can be secretive, hide out in Pudong or something."

"No. Not in Shanghai."

"OK. Then Paris. Yes, Paris. We can stay at the old apartment. And the flight will be easier. What do you think?"

"Sure. Paris."

"I'll call school to let them know you'll be a few days late. That you're not well."

"Is it going to hurt?"

"Not much," Eko lied.

"What are you going to say to Dad?"

"He won't know you missed any school. He'll never ask. For me, I'll just say something came up with Grandma. We can even go visit her together if you want, see her new place. It's nice there. Not far from Paris."

"I don't know. Maybe."

"Well, we'll take it easy. Decide later."

"Ma. I'm sorry."

"Yokochan, you have absolutely nothing to be sorry about."

"What about my training?"

"You'll get to go. Don't worry. I'll tell the coach you'll be there soon. You're the star on the team. No one is going to replace you."

Since the previous summer Yoko had been training for the Math Olympiad, her place on the US national team all but guaranteed. Eko and Leo had sent her to the States specifically so she'd be able to study at one of the best high school math programs in the world. A year later, Yumi had ended up joining her sister in the Boston area, at Harvard.

Eko bought them their tickets to Paris. She used digital coins, converted from her own savings from the money she made on her embroidery work. The announcement came on; their flight was getting ready to board.

Yumi walked toward them with a few shopping bags in tow.

"Maman, I got you this!" she said, dropping a small bag into Eko's lap. "It'll look better on you than it does on Yoko." It was the red lipstick.

. . .

THEY FLEW INTO BOSTON just before the airport was locked down for twenty-four hours, and just after a snowstorm had melted. As they got into their car, stepping gingerly over the puddles, they watched a surge of gun-carrying agents jog through the front doors of the terminal. Eko was reminded of just how much she detested America. After settling Yumi into her dorm room and after a night at the Charles Hotel, Eko and Yoko flew into Paris. It was early evening when they landed, Eko's favorite time of day. The city's streets were aglow with buzzing streetlamps and the yellowing, setting sun.

Eko's plan was to take Yoko to a gynecologist first thing in the morning, to set a date and time for the procedure. She had told Leo that she needed to handle some things with her mother, that Daphne was sick, so she'd make a stop to visit her on the way back. It was a horrid lie, she knew, but she could think of nothing better.

Eko and Yoko were silent on the car ride to the Fifteenth Arrondissement. Yoko was often silent. She had always been different, even from the beginning. It had been nearly impossible for her to express herself verbally until the age of five; they'd held her back from school for a year so that she could do intensive speech therapy. There was a point when Yoko, so frequently alone, had become fixated on a classmate, a girl from South Africa named Angel. It must have been in the seventh or eighth grade. Yoko had been so intent on befriending Angel, on buying her the right Christmas present, that Eko had wondered if Yoko wasn't simply gay. Angel, however, turned out to have little interest in being Yoko's friend, and it all just quietly simmered down and away.

The apartment was on the top floor of a walk-up, and as soon as they scanned their faces and entered, Yoko shut herself in the bathroom for ten minutes, making the occasional retching sound.

Eko had called this one-bedroom in the Fifteenth her home from the ages of twelve to twenty. Her mother had bought it in the early aughts, after nearly a decade of scraping by in Paris, alone with Eko and far away from everything they knew in their native Japan. She had paid for it slowly, over many years.

The apartment had not changed in a long time. It featured her mother's whimsical and eclectic style, whatever Daphne liked and bought at local thrift shops: a seventies-style mohair carpet, a Tiffany lamp set atop the glass cube of a side table, a forest-green velvet couch, a narrow bookshelf that reached the ceiling, filled with colorful high-heeled shoes. On the low coffee table, along with a crystal ashtray, were all Eko's books on nature embroidery, in all their languages.

In the corner of the living room, on its own round table, was the old Singer that Eko had used, back in high school, to make basic cotton dresses, to repair torn seams. They had kept, in a large, round hatbox, a loose pile of sewing patterns: McCall's, Vogue Paris Original, Butterick, Simplicity. They had once even, for fun, for laughs, attempted an Elizabethan gown from Reconstructing History. Eko remembered it now. Where had all those dresses gone? How did clothing seem to magically disappear?

After Eko left, Daphne had lived alone for twenty years, and then with a Japanese sculptor she had met through work for five.

After he moved out, Daphne finally retired from her job assisting the cultural attaché at the Japanese embassy, and when it looked like she would not date again anytime in the future, she let Eko and Leo move her into Residence St. Clair, in the South.

On previous trips to France, Eko had brought the girls to visit their grandmother, but they had never stayed with Daphne, preferring, instead, to stay at the Bordeaux estate. The apartment was too small, too inconvenient. But it would work well for this trip, when Eko was ostensibly traveling alone.

Growing up, Eko had slept in the bedroom and Daphne the living room, where they'd installed a pulldown bed. Eko tried it now—she had to move the small glass dining table and slide the couch closer to the opposite wall, but the bed still worked. With a creak, it was down. It was still fully dressed too. Eko lay down on it, taking in the musty smell of old sheets sprayed with old perfume. She tried to remember her own procedure, but the details remained murky. Mostly she remembered lying alone afterward on her dorm-room bed, a deep pain in her stomach. She had never told anyone. What did it matter now? She could tell Yoko. Maybe it would help. She closed her eyes for a moment.

Despite being poor, Eko's mother always liked to look rich. Daphne dressed immaculately, with a clean, powdered face. Her hair, perpetually long, was always curled softly, in what she called "the salon style." But Eko had never seen Daphne at the salon, not once. Her mother cut and colored her own hair every six months, at the start of the year and the start of the summer. For her entire childhood, Eko had long hair as well, cut and styled by her mother.

But at the age of sixteen, she'd chopped it all off and dyed it blue. Oh yes, she had been wild—with her Doc Martens and her plum-colored lipstick that stained her Gitanes cigarettes. Her mother off at work from morning till night, doing events at the embassy. Eko at home, with her instant Bolino hachis parmentier, which she always ate in the living room, her boots on the table. After she finished the small bucket of instant potatoes and beef, she always had cramps, then gas.

"I think I could have made it work with your father," Daphne said to Eko, a few times only, when she was drinking. "If I had been older, smarter, savvier."

"But wasn't he, like, abusive?" Eko had asked.

"Well, they all are, sweetie. More or less."

Eko liked things fine just the two of them, living their separate lives in their tiny space. What had made it so good? Her desperate clawing out, her vivid displays of individuality: silks on the walls; her thrift-store digs with her best friend, Elodie; posters on the walls. Eko played the Strokes and her mom was wild about Vanessa Paradis.

On weekends they cleaned and window-shopped. There was never any money, but they tried on everything and sometimes splurged when a thing was too good, *magnifique*. They would hang it up on the wall—once a leather coat that draped down to their ankles, thin as paper; once a silk blouse with trumpet sleeves and bejeweled buttons; once a green bondage Alaïa dress. Mother and daughter would look at it for days, worshipping its perfection until they could wait no longer. They took turns with the clothes. They were exactly the same size.

The wanting and saving and scrimping—Eko knew only after becoming a mother herself how hard that must have been. How far away that feeling—the fear of not having enough—had grown from her. Eko's own house in Shanghai was so full of things, so full of the children's things. What excess she lived now. Her daughters, her apartments, the clothes, the stuff. The toys—what a lifetime of toys her children had accumulated over the years. And after they were grown she'd given it all away, just like that. For free.

EKO AND YOKO waited for the doctor. Eko had been able to secure an early appointment, the first of the day. She had said on the phone that she was worried the pregnancy would be more than first-term any day now. The window was closing. The doctor had squeezed Yoko in right away.

"You haven't told anyone, right?" Yoko asked. They were the only ones in the waiting room.

"Yoko, I haven't told anyone. I won't tell."

"You swear?"

"On my life."

"And if Dad finds out I missed the first week of school?"

"I'll say I took you to Paris for a quick girls' trip. He knows I'm always trying to get you girls to be better at French."

"But he'll know you lied to him. He'll think it's weird."

"I'll lie again."

Yoko looked at Eko in her calculating way. "Have you ever lied to me?" she asked.

"No," Eko said.

"How can I believe you?"

"Maybe you can't." Eko knew better than to sugarcoat the truth, or to get into a logic contest with her daughter. "But I've tried never to lie to you," she offered.

"Do you love Dad?"

"What? Yes. Of course."

"But—"

"Do you love your sisters?" Eko countered.

Yoko paused. "Define love."

"I think you love someone," Eko said, "when you truly care for their happiness and well-being."

"That's what you think? Well, then: no."

"No?"

"Why would I? Yumi doesn't love *me*—not according to your definition. She takes my things. She doesn't return them. She's mean. You wouldn't treat someone you love like that. And Kiko doesn't need anyone to love her. She loves herself enough."

Eko sighed. "Yumi wants to change. We had a long talk over break. She knows. She's going to try harder."

"Sure. You always make excuses for her."

"What would you prefer I do?"

"Be honest! She's a bitch. I don't blame you for that. But it's the truth."

"I tried my best. I tried to teach you girls."

"Mom. It's not about you." Yoko was quiet for a moment. Then she said, "I think love is when you think you need someone for your survival. Survival, defined broadly."

"The way you *think*, sometimes . . ."

"The way I think, what?"

"It . . . surprises me. Yoko, we need each other. Family—family is all we have."

"Yeah, that's the narrative. That's what people say to get you to stay in toxic relationships."

"Where did you get that from?" Eko asked. Yoko did not reply. "When we're gone—me and your father—your sisters will be all that's left."

"All that's left of *you*," Yoko said. "They don't love me."

"They do."

"Yumi *lies*, Mom!" Yoko was getting frustrated. "You don't know the *half* of it."

"I do know, Yoko. I know her. I know all of you."

"You'll never know."

They sat in their chairs, alone in the waiting room. But they wouldn't care if someone sat nearby, or if someone was watching them from afar. They were speaking in Japanese—in their "Japanese bubble," as they used to call it, so many years ago.

"I think you all love each other, in your own ways," Eko finally said.

"So then love is indefinable, or subjective?"

"Maybe." Yoko always had to push her into a corner. She was just like her father. "Do you love your boyfriend?"

"By your definition? Probably not. I haven't thought too much about his 'well-being.' By my definition? No. I don't need him."

Eko made a gesture with her hands that said she was giving up. "And what is he like?" she asked.

"He's on the math team."

"Oh, I see. What kind of math is he interested in?"

"Mom, you don't have to try to talk about math."

"OK." Eko took a deep breath.

"He got into MIT early too. We're going to go together."

"Really?"

"Yeah. He already did a research program there."

"He's American?"

"Canadian."

"Yoko Yang?" the receptionist called. Eko was disappointed. This was the longest conversation she had had with Yoko in years. They stood up to go in. But then Yoko stepped in front of Eko and held her hand out, stopping her mother in her path.

"Mom, I want to go in by myself."

"What? Really?"

"Yeah, I'm sure."

"Oh, OK. OK." Eko put her jacket back down on her seat. "Well, I'll be out here if you need me." As Yoko disappeared through the door, another woman entered the waiting room and said a quick bonjour to Eko.

Had she really just let her daughter go in alone? Should she barge in and demand to be involved, informed? What was even the law regarding age here? Of course, Yoko was over eighteen already. Her phone vibrated. It was a message from David.

Looking forward to tomorrow.

Eko had forgotten completely. She drafted a message quickly: *I'm so sorry. Something came up with my mother and I had to fly to Paris! Can we reschedule for next time?* But Eko deleted the question. When would next time realistically be? Summer break? Better not to suggest it. She sent it off and looked around for a photo to snap, something that would prove her location. But the reception area was like any other in any other city in the world. Seats, mostly empty; racks of magazines; advertisements for in vitro fertilization and egg donation; pamphlets on the latest experimental methods of creating life out of single strands of hair; framed illustrations of the uterus.

Becoming a mother—what gruesome business. Eko's own uterus was gone, had nearly volunteered itself out. When Yoko arrived, she had come out with such speed and force that everything else had come out too. The midwife had simply cut Yoko free and pushed everything back in, using just her hands, in the hopes that the body would reaccept it all: the uterus, the tubes, the eggs, the blood. Eko had lost a dangerous amount of blood. She'd had two transfusions, was moved to the hospital for days. But miraculously—that was the doctor's word—it all somehow went back into place.

When pregnant with Kiko, Eko was always on alert. She was high risk. After Kiko came out, screaming, the doctor gave Eko a hysterectomy right away. Everything gone, no more babies.

How much a woman endured—the poking and prodding, splicing and vacuuming, stretching and sewing of her reproductive organs. To make babies, baby girls. Young girls who would become young women who would endure the same things. How had science advanced so much and yet birth and birth control remained so primitive? Eko got up and asked the receptionist to take her to her daughter's room.

Inside, Yoko was lying on the table, covered in a paper gown, her legs spread, in stirrups. She closed her knees as soon as Eko walked in.

"Mom! I wanted to be alone."

"I know, honey."

"So leave."

"No, dear."

The doctor handed Yoko a tissue and told Eko that they'd done an initial assessment: Things were still very early, he said.

A couple of pills would do the trick. She could miscarry at home.

"I'm not so sure about that," Eko said. "What about a vacuum aspiration?"

"A what?" Yoko asked, staring at her mother.

"Sweetheart, it would be faster and cleaner and more complete."

"Mom, what are you even talking about? We should listen to the doctor."

"Yoko, I know what I'm talking about." Her daughter gave Eko a doubtful glance, but the doctor confirmed it. The aspiration would be faster, though more invasive. "There could be a sedative, right?" Eko asked.

"We could do a light sedative, yes."

Eko noticed Yoko had gone quiet. She asked the doctor to give them a moment to themselves. "Yokochan. You're not the first person to get an abortion, and you won't be the last. The doctor performs them daily. You do the math. I know you're scared. You're confused. But let me help. I did something like this a long time ago."

"What? When did you do it?"

"In college."

"With Dad?"

"Not Dad. It was before Dad."

"Really? You never said."

"You never asked."

"The vacuum thing?"

"Something else. I did it later than you're doing it. I had no choice. But I know other people who have done the pill, who have done the vacuum."

"You do?"

"Yes. It's more common than you think."

It was a sad thing to be a mom. Kids never thought that their mothers could have done all the things they did, gotten into the messes they got into. Kids thinking they were writing the book on life. A mom was barely a person—she was more like a symbol, a statue, a couch.

"OK. You're right. I don't want a lot of downtime."

That was the thing about Yoko. She was utterly, extremely reasonable, unlike her sisters. Yumi wouldn't even listen. Kiko would always do the exact opposite of what was suggested.

Eko went out to fetch the doctor. When he came back, they scheduled the procedure. After blood work and some tests, later that same morning.

THAT NIGHT, back at the apartment, Eko went into Yoko's room—her old room—and put a glass of water on the nightstand. Her daughter was doing well, just a bit of soreness. Eko was glad Yoko wouldn't have to go through seeing the blood and everything else, seeing it in her underpants, in the toilet. For all that she presented herself as tough and rational, Yoko was sensitive.

Eko put her hand to Yoko's forehead. It was cool and dry. Yumi had been the one who always spiked fevers as a kid, the one who got so hot that, one time, she even had a seizure. Eko placed a pack of painkillers near the water.

"I'm going out for a walk. Call me if you need anything," she said. "I'll be in the neighborhood." Yoko nodded and rolled onto her side. In a day or two they would discuss flying back to Boston.

Eko stepped out into the night air. Paris never changed, not really, not in the way Shanghai was always changing, ripping up neighborhoods and building new things in their place. Whenever Eko was back in Paris she felt fifteen again, felt that electric sense of possibility in the air. Tonight, though, that feeling was dimmed. She was exhausted. She needed a drink.

She remembered sneaking out to the neighborhood bar—it was called Allez! She walked there now. It was still there, in the same spot, though its name had changed to Voulez-vous? She opened the door. The interior was blue now, instead of red. She took a seat at the dimly lit bar. The clientele was different, fewer college-aged girls and more businessmen. Eko ordered a glass of Sauvignon blanc and pulled out her phone.

David had sent her a reply: *No problem. I hope she's OK. Let me know the next time you're in town.* Eko scrolled again through his photos. She knew them all by heart. Her eye caught on one of him in a botanical garden, holding a plucked flower over one eye. It looked like an alpine anemone. Eko took a sketchbook from her bag and began to copy it down, removing the face behind the flower and expanding the petals and leaves and stem. Anemone was not a tree flower, but it became one in her drawing. Other flowers also blossomed on the branches. The tree had become a cornucopia, a wild bouquet.

She finished her third glass of wine. She snapped a photo of her sketch and uploaded it onto her channel. She watched the likes and votes and pinging of notifications as they came in. She ordered her fourth glass of wine.

What was David anyway? Just some idea, some dream, some happy memory from her youth. If she had chosen David, maybe Leo would have played the same role—the handsome, smart, rich man, the one that got away. What was she doing? After so many years, couldn't she simply forge ahead? Life with Leo might even change for the better now, with the girls all going away.

Yoko had not sent her any messages. Eko searched for heavy feelings of pity, regret, sadness, but found only an old wistfulness. She loved Yoko, yes, but Yoko had always resisted her, always resisted being mothered. Yoko was brilliant, had been her own person, an island, since the very beginning. Eko sometimes even felt that her middle child looked down on her. Yoko remained impenetrable.

But they will be what they will be, she thought to herself, through the numbing buzz of wine. They had the gifts of beauty and brains. Their father had provided them with money. A woman needed very little else. An abortion? It was a blip, a week in a long life.

A man took a seat next to Eko, and she felt—smelled—his predatory anticipation.

"Bonsoir, mademoiselle." His voice was deep and pleasant, with a Marseille accent.

"Oh, je ne suis pas une mademoiselle," Eko replied.

"Excusez-moi, *monsieur*." Despite herself, Eko laughed. She turned to look at him. A nice-looking French man in a tailored suit, maybe in his early fifties, around her age. He was holding a glass of amber liquid. She smiled. "Where are you from?" he asked.

"The neighborhood."

"Oh, really? You look more *exotique* than the neighborhood."

"No, there are many Japanese in this arrondissement." She gave him what he was looking for. He would dig until he got it anyway.

"Did you draw that?" He pointed to the sketch.

"I did."

"It's incredible. Just like you."

Eko laughed again. She had not been picked up in a bar in what—decades? And she, a little tipsy, was finding it funny just now.

"You are an artist, then."

"Yes, I suppose you could say that. And you?"

He held out his hand. "I'm David. Just here on business."

She chuckled at his name. What were the chances? His left hand was ringless. Eko looked, then felt that fact when her fingers slipped into his. She wore her ring on her right hand.

"You laugh easily," he said.

"You compliment easily."

"I will order you another drink, eh? What is your name?"

"Eko. But no, thank you. I have to head back—my daughter is waiting for me. And I have one, maybe two, long flights ahead of me."

David graciously bowed and raised his glass to her. "Eko. Echo, echo, echo. I will always remember you. You have an immense talent." He returned to his end of the bar. Eko paid her tab and left.

And why that David and not this David? There were so many Davids in the world, she thought, on the short walk home. By the time she opened the front door, she realized she had left her sketch at the bar.

IN THE MORNING, Eko and Yoko shared a baguette and blueberry jam that they bought at the market. Yoko was fine, she said, just tired and still sore. They spent the day in the apartment, Eko cleaning and Yoko playing video games on her phone. She was back to the girl Eko recognized: T-shirts and sweats, hair in a bun, glasses, a smattering of light freckles.

That evening, Eko saw a notification from Residence St. Clair on her phone. She opened their chat app. *Please contact us when you have a chance. We would like to discuss your mother's condition. It is nothing urgent.* Eko called the administrator's number and got through right away.

"Is she OK?" was the first question she asked.

"Yes, she's doing great," said Alexandra, the administrator assigned to her mother's care.

"So what's the situation?"

"Well, it's nothing major. Just—there have been some recent signs of difficulty in short-term memory retention."

"You mean, she's losing her memory?"

"No, nothing from long ago. Just a teeny-tiny bit of trouble with new day-to-day items."

"Like, for example?"

"Say we are in the pool in the afternoon. Her instructor will ask her, 'What did you have for lunch today?' And she might not remember having eaten lunch. Like this."

"Since when has this been happening?"

"Maybe a week or two now. Please rest assured, we are very experienced in these situations. Our state-of-the-art Memory Room is also a terrific therapy resource."

Eko listened as Alexandra went on to describe the Memory Room, its technologies, the pedigree of its developer, and its track record. Eko felt a creeping sense of dread. The thought came to her that she had brought this on—that lying to Leo about her mother's health had caused it to become real, that she was being punished, for everything.

"I happen to be in Paris," Eko interrupted. "I'll come down to visit and talk to her doctors."

"Oh! Fantastic. She talks about you all the time. She will be delighted to see you."

"Yes. In a day or two." Eko hung up. She looked around the room. Her mother's hand was everywhere.

Yoko cleared her throat from the couch. She had been gaming, listening. Yoko was always listening. "So Grandma is losing her memory? What is it—Alzheimer's?"

"Yes, maybe. I don't know, Yoko."

Yoko shook her head. "It's ridiculous. Nobody cares about Alzheimer's because the people affected are old and can't stand up for themselves. Like, they figured out the cure for prostate cancer just because the men who get it aren't senile, because they were motivated and able to fund research."

"I didn't know that, Yoko."

"Yeah. Well, we can go see Grandma. I'm feeling fine."

RESIDENCE ST. CLAIR was a high-rise in Nice, dedicated to luxury senior living. Leo and Eko had secured Daphne a spot early on in its construction—Leo had been tipped off by a friend who sold European real estate to wealthy Chinese. They signed Daphne up for a Sea View Suite for one. It overlooked the Mediterranean and had a large bedroom, a small sitting room, full closets, and a wheelchair-accessible bathroom.

Daphne had been excited to move in three years ago. Though the building housed a medical clinic and on-site nurses, it was occupied mostly by healthy retired seniors. Daphne was a talkative, charming woman who easily made friends. From the beginning, she told Leo and Eko that she loved it.

Eko and Yoko got out of the high-speed Travel-Day van, which Eko had set to Japanese. The autotrunk unloaded their bags. The speakers said, *Travel dē o shinrai shite go ryokō itadaki, arigatōgozaimasu. Tanoshī ichinichi o osugoshi kudasai*, playing the company's chiming melody, and the van zoomed down the road to pick up its next passenger.

"*Merde*," said Eko. "I forgot to bring a gift."

Yoko walked toward the high-rise's entrance, unfazed. "You have, like, ten lipsticks in your bag. Give her one of those."

They announced themselves at the front desk and were allowed up. Leo had insisted on a room on the highest floor. Otherwise, what was the point? They rode the glass elevator to the top and pressed the doorbell of 5201. Daphne opened the door with a gust of wind. Her blue silk dress and scarf whipped out into the hallway like long, beckoning fingers. Behind her, inside, all the windows were open.

"Eko! Yoko! What a pleasant surprise! I had no idea you were coming to town. You naughty girls, surprising an old woman like this." Daphne's hair, streaked with gray, was pulled up into her signature high French twist. Her face was fully painted and her eyes darkly lined.

"You're looking good, Okaasan," Eko said, moving through the door to check the apartment. Cleaning staff came every day, and the place was spotless. Eko closed the windows in the bedroom first, and then she came out and closed them in the sitting room. With the breeze trapped outside, it felt as though everything had come to a standstill.

In the quiet, Daphne was serving Yoko a cup of tea. "How do you get more and more beautiful every time I see you, Yokochan?" She placed a few yokan in a shallow bowl while eyeing Yoko's casual look. "You just put on a little makeup, you'll be unstoppable." Daphne turned to Eko. "Don't tell the other girls, but Yoko is the prettiest of them all!"

"Okaasan, they're all beautiful."

"*You* were once the great beauty. Now it's your daughters' time to shine."

"I was never a great beauty. Thanks to you, giving me these short, stumpy legs!"

"Ugh, my legs! My legs! The tragedy of my life." Daphne's legs were very normal, very average legs. Only short, and a little thick.

"Okaasan, did you eat lunch yet?"

"Oh, yes. I did. A delightful mushroom soup. Have you girls eaten? If not, feel free to order something."

"Oh, gee, thanks," Eko muttered. But she was glad, and hopeful, that her mother had remembered what she ate for lunch. "We ate on the road. You two catch up. I'll be back soon. Settle some bills, you know."

As she was heading out the door, she heard Daphne telling Yoko about her daily swimming lessons, and her handsome swim coach. "You take a lesson with me today. He won't know what hit him."

"Okaasan, you hate swimming," Eko called out from the doorway.

"No, dear. I was afraid, always. Because my father—your great-grandfather, Yoko—threw me into a hot spring when I was four years old. This was way back when, in Kyoto. In the winter!

No nice swimming pools and good-looking coaches back then. Just all the kids crowded into the water, like a big dumpling soup. Your great-grandfather, a mean old man. But nothing, nothing, compared to your grandfather, let me tell you."

Eko closed the door. She had heard the story so many times over the course of her life: an evil father, an evil husband, and the heroine who ran away from it all to make a new start in Paris.

She took the elevator down to the clinic. Aside from a few residents doing some kind of physical therapy, the place was empty. Eko peered into the doctor's office.

"Oh, Eko, come on in!" Eko took a seat and waited as Dr. Bernard pulled up Daphne's file. "So, as you know, your mother has been displaying some very preliminary, very minor signs of short-term dementia. We have been spending a lot of time in the Memory Room, focusing on storytelling exercises."

"Yes, but Doctor, how could this have happened? She has no genetic predisposition for Alzheimer's."

"Ah, yes. Well. This kind of memory retention issue is not necessarily Alzheimer's. We think it was a result of an illness a few months back." Dr. Bernard scratched his full head of red hair with his pen.

"An illness? I wasn't informed."

"Yes, hm. Daphne chose not to disclose it to her family."

"But what happened? Was it serious?" Eko shifted in her seat. She put her purse down on the floor and settled in for a longer conversation.

"Not too serious, but there was an infection and subsequent high fever for several days."

"Excuse me? Did you say *fever*? And you couldn't tell me?"

"Your mother is of sound mind. She insisted on confidentiality," Dr. Bernard replied.

"Well, what kind of infection?"

"It's not an uncommon one, for these types of facilities. Actually, many here were infected."

"Was there some kind of issue with the food or cleaning services? If that's the case, Doctor, we deserve to know—not only as paying residents but as founding investors." Eko was leaning into the desk now, her finger jabbing into the wood as she spoke. She had gotten better, over the years, at this kind of thing.

"No, please, nothing to be upset about."

"Nothing to be upset about? My mother had an infection and a fever and you didn't tell us!" Eko surprised even herself with her anger. "Don't make me go to the board," she threatened.

"OK. OK. I understand. Please wait." Dr. Bernard looked at his computer, then out the window, and finally at the closed door behind Eko. In a lowered voice, he said, slowly, "You see, it was a very common, very treatable . . . sexually transmitted disease."

Eko stared at him in disbelief. "A what?"

"A sexually transmitted disease," he repeated, an apologetic look on his face.

"Oh."

"Yes. It was unfortunate, but, as I said, completely curable. And she was better in record time. The only thing is that we suspect the illness or fever may have triggered a bit of the short-term amnesia." Eko stared out the window, across the street, at the sea, as she listened. "With the right treatments, we suspect this won't accelerate or degenerate further. It may even get better in no time. We expect full retention of long-term memories. And we've made note to our caretakers to be mindful of Daphne's daily schedule and needs in light of this."

"She told me today she had a mushroom soup for lunch."

"I'll just go ahead and confirm that for you," the doctor said, clearing his throat. "Ah, here it is. Today's menu was a seafood paella with radish salad and a chocolate mousse for dessert."

"So no mushroom soup, then," Eko said. It was less a question than a confirmation.

"I'm afraid not."

Eko pursed her lips. It was as if she could hear the roar of the sea in her ears, though the windows were closed and there was no sound in the room. Dr. Bernard waited. There would be no one else left on this earth who would remember, who would know, how it was, how it used to be. And then there were all the things she herself didn't know, all the things she hadn't been told.

"Does she know? Does my mother know?" Eko asked.

"She doesn't like to talk about it. But she seems to be somewhat aware, yes," Dr. Bernard said. "She avoids answering questions she doesn't know the answers to. She fibs."

Eko nodded. "What is the treatment?"

Dr. Bernard went on about the Memory Room, the games available to all residents, and the customized memory rehabilitation that could be provided to Daphne at an extra cost. Eko was half listening, half thinking abstractedly about David, who felt so, so far away. She agreed and signed the papers. She went back upstairs.

When she got to the suite, Yoko was seated on the couch and Daphne was busy doing her hair and makeup. Daphne had gotten Yoko to dress up in some of her old clothes. Eko recognized a vintage Dolce & Gabbana dress that her mother loved. Yoko's thick hair had gone up into an elegant French twist. Her skin was plastered with foundation.

"Maman, I gave Grand-mère the lipstick," Yoko said. Daphne was applying it to Yoko's lips.

"Come here, Ekochan," Daphne said, beckoning to her with the Chanel Rouge Allure.

"No, it's OK," Eko replied.

"Come on. Just for fun."

Eko looked at her mother and her daughter, then out the window again. There were no tourists this time of year. The beach was empty. The sea and sky were gray.

Eko sat down on the couch next to Daphne and Yoko. She closed her eyes and opened her mouth into a half smile. She felt her mother apply the slick color to her lips.

Moshi Moshi Marilyn Monroe

September 2039

Kiko had no excuse for going into sex work. If someone found out, and then told her parents, she would have nothing to say to them. There was no real reason, except for plain curiosity.

It had come up because of a rumor she heard about Takako Takahashi. The rumor was that Takako, who was in grade twelve, was seeing an older businessman who paid her in Chanel bags and rides in a Maserati convertible. Apparently, all the girls did it back in Japan.

Kiko didn't need Chanel bags or Maseratis from some random old man she didn't know. She could just ask her father for the latest bag, and—though he would hem and haw about his spoiled daughters, and who even needed a designer bag at sixteen?—he would eventually give in. And if not her father, she could always go to her mother, who would buy her the bag or pass along something vintage, and then wait quietly to see if Dad noticed. He wouldn't; he never did.

Kiko—Baby Kiko, as they called her at home—often got what she wanted. Maybe it was the boredom of this that made her want to get something in a new way, a path that felt darker and unknown—thrilling, like walking into the shadowy tent of a traveling circus.

Kiko had never seen a traveling circus. She'd seen the Shanghai acrobatics show (dull), Cirque du Soleil in Macau (cool), and SeaWorld in Orlando (sort of sad), but never a proper traveling circus, with red-and-white-striped tents set up in a trampled field. She put *traveling circus* in her diary, on a list of things she'd like to see in the future.

Before learning about Madame Sun from Takako, Kiko had had the idea for several months that she was tired of love. Or maybe she was just coming to realize that love was something that could be acted out, sold, and exchanged. She'd been in a relationship for the past three years with Peter Ozzy, the lacrosse-playing son of the director of Shanghai Disney. They were in the same class at SH Foreign, and they'd known each other for years.

KIKO HAD CHOSEN PETER. Her best friend, Jessica, had chosen Sam. They were in eighth grade when they decided to get boyfriends.

On the count of three, Kiko and Jessica parted at their lockers and went to their respective partners. Kiko announced to Peter in an offhanded way, "Peter, you're going to be my boyfriend now,

OK?" and Jessica did the same to Sam. They'd rehearsed it together the entire week. They'd even had an emergency sleepover to plan for all contingencies. If the boys refused, the girls would slap them across the face. That way, everyone would know who was boss.

Peter put away his geometry book. He grabbed a pack of gum from a shelf in his locker and held it out to her. "Want a gum?" he asked, as if he hadn't heard Kiko at all. She stared at him for a moment, unsure whether to slap him or not. They hadn't planned for this. Then he repeated the question. "Want a gum, girlfriend?" He was smiling. Kiko had made the right choice. Peter was endlessly cute.

Jessica, on the other hand, received some pushback. Upon receiving the news of the relationship, Sam looked at her unhappily and asked, "Do I have to?" She replied, "Yes!" and walked away, her face burning red, but still feeling victorious, somewhat. After two weeks of not speaking to her, Sam sent an envoy in the form of Barry Peterson to inform Jessica that he no longer wanted to be her boyfriend. She cried in the bathroom all afternoon while Kiko stroked her hair. "There will be others," she said. "There are plenty of fish in the sea." They were thirteen.

KIKO ATTENDED EVERY LACROSSE TOURNAMENT of Peter's on campus. And once she even stowed away in the back seat of the away-game bus when the team played the French school across town. When Peter was benched at halftime, Kiko would sit on his sweaty lap, her arms around his neck, her friends and his making fun of them for being codependent. Peter and Kiko would stick their tongues out at the others and sometimes kiss dramatically before the game resumed. They were happy and they flaunted their happiness in front of their friends, who were just kids who knew nothing about love. They were in it, together, to the end.

What a time to be in love! The eighth grade was still busy with weekend bar and bat mitzvahs for classmates from the United States and Israel. When their friends left the dance floor during slow songs or pretend-danced foolishly with one another, Kiko and Peter stayed on the parquet, holding each other, her head on his chest. Sometimes they were the only ones dancing. And that was OK—that was how it felt to be with Peter Ozzy, as if nothing else in the whole world mattered as much, or was as singular, as their love.

In the ninth grade, they spent nearly all their weekends at Disney. She and Peter made it a game to have sex in every hidden corner of the park. Of course, they went on rides, too, flashing their Fast Passes to skip past all the children. One weekend they devoted entirely to the park's new addition, Space Mountain, riding it over and over, coming out into daylight again and again, dizzy, blinded, and happy.

Peter lived in the compound next to Kiko's. Both compounds were gated, and only a few blocks from SH Foreign. Kiko's house and lawn were bigger—they were three sisters and Peter was an only child, after all—but Peter's compound had the better clubhouse, plus swimming pools, both indoor and out. So Kiko was around a lot.

Kiko sometimes watched Peter Ozzy Sr. He and his son looked uncannily alike, except that the elder was bigger, broader, and perpetually masked with a five o'clock shadow. He was the man who ran the park—the park that Kiko and Peter enjoyed, treated as though they owned—although Peter Sr. was always very serious. Kiko wondered what childlike qualities remained in him, this grown-up version of her boyfriend, that had brought him to work at Disney. Surely there was something there, some belief in the place's magic.

She also loved to stare at Peter's mother, Peter Sr.'s wife. Patricia Ozzy didn't *do* anything, but she always looked like she was about to go into a meeting. She wore suit jackets and pencil skirts, but the effect was really odd because Mrs. Ozzy looked like a porn star. Her breasts were enormous and her long hair was so blonde it was almost white. *So that's what Mr. Ozzy likes*, Kiko often thought to herself as Patricia walked by.

Baby Kiko was the physical opposite of Mrs. Ozzy. She was round-eyed, round-faced, flat-chested, button-nosed. She had twiggy arms and legs and silky black hair down to the small of her back. She was as pale as a sheet of paper. Kiko was cute, lovely, a baby in a schoolgirl's uniform.

THE THING KIKO WANTED MOST in life was to be a star. Jessica also wanted this. They planned diets and exercise regimes together to stay slim, and they practiced makeup on each other. Jessica, if she didn't make it, was going to become a makeup artist. For her, proximity to fame would be good enough. But for Kiko, it was all or nothing. She had no backup plan.

Jessica was not beautiful, but she was tall and lean, with sharp features. She could play any character: a villain; a seductress; a smart, witty heroine on a cable television detective drama. Jessica was mixed, like Kiko, but she was half white, rather than all Asian. Jessica set her sights on the Hong Kong film industry, while Kiko considered China's and Japan's.

Jessica already had a deal that if she graduated with a 3.5 GPA, her mom would get her a nose job. Kiko would never be able to cut a deal like that with her parents, because what she wanted was boobs. And not just a natural upgrade: she wanted massive ones. She wanted *Playboy* jugs, Mrs. Ozzy's boobs. How could she even go to her father and say that? He still called her Baby Kiko. Her mother was not sexy by any definition—she made a career of pulling needle and thread, doing intricate embroideries of flowers and small animals like chipmunks and bumblebees. She posted carefully arranged, warmly lit photos on her social accounts, sometimes getting sponsorships from companies to do branded work. She was always sophisticated, clean-cut, pretty. Kiko wasn't interested in that look, however. Kiko wanted to be a goddess, a fantasy.

As Jessica applied concealers and foundations and bronzers to Kiko's smooth skin, Kiko always made the same complaint: she was too cute. Why couldn't she have been born a little taller, a little more glamorous? Jessica replied the same way every time—so many stars were cute, when you thought about it. Marilyn Monroe, essentially, was cute. She looked and talked like a kitten. Audrey Hepburn—she had the body of a child! "But Kiko," Jessica would say, "you're more of a Marilyn, because you have the baby face."

In this way, Kiko came to the understanding that to become a true star, you had to have either the face of a child and the body of a woman or the face of a woman and the body of a child. And Kiko would look in the mirror, and she would be unhappy. Because her face was cute. Her body was cute.

Because of what Jessica always said, though, Kiko started to watch all of Marilyn Monroe's films. Her favorite was *How to*

Marry a Millionaire. Kiko thought it was funny that Marilyn would settle for a million. Everyone had one million dollars nowadays. But it was probably worth something more a hundred years ago.

For a few weeks, Kiko had tried to raise the pitch of her voice to be like Marilyn's. When her father heard her one evening, he asked quickly, "Baby, are you not feeling well?" She laughed, and changed back to her normal voice, and slapped him playfully on the shoulder. "Oh, Daddy! You don't understand!" she said, just as she'd always replied to him since the age of three. And when he seemed entertained by this, as he always was, she explained: "I'm just practicing my vocal range."

"Why not practice your algebra instead?" he said, going back to his book, not really expecting an answer. He had given up long ago on the last of his three daughters becoming mathematically inclined.

EVERY NIGHT Kiko wrote in her diary: *I'm going to be a star. I'm going to be a star.* Since Kiko first told her parents that she wanted to be an actress, when she was ten, they'd indulged her with acting classes, with stage camps over the summers. Her mother, however, warned her every now and then about the "realities" of the entertainment industry. How men preyed on young women. How girls were sometimes forced to do things they didn't want to do.

Once, when her mother said this, Kiko replied, "You do things you don't want to do all the time." Kiko often heard her parents arguing in hushed voices late at night. The next morning, their faces would be pulled tight, the expressions loosening only after two or three days. Kiko didn't know what they fought about, but it seemed clear to her that her father always won. When she mentioned this, her mother looked at her with mild shock and said, "It's different. I'm married." Kiko said, "How is that any different?" Anyway, Kiko already knew the way of things. The entertainment industry had always been tough on young women. She knew because of Marilyn Monroe.

"Fame isn't as glamorous as it seems," her mom started again.

"You know this because of your fans?" Kiko asked, more sarcastically than she'd intended.

"I'm not famous. My work is just popular."

But her mom was famous, in a way. She had almost two million followers on social media, mostly but not entirely Japanese, who religiously liked the photos of her work. She'd published three books on nature embroidery. She was constantly fielding interviews and occasionally hosted live streams of herself sewing. Kiko had twenty thousand followers, but only because she'd begged her mom to link her account on Eko's bio page. Kiko's photos were largely selfies, often with Jessica, along with some artistic snaps of Shanghai's street cats.

Peter was going to be a professional lacrosse player when he grew up. During the summers, he joined a league in the United States to train. Kiko stayed in Shanghai, with the exception of the Yangs' annual trip abroad. That first summer apart, Kiko's older sisters were both home for a stretch, Yumi doing a virtual internship before her graduation trip, and Yoko back from boarding school. Kiko should have been happy during those days, but she was despondent. She sent Peter text messages every day, as well as handwritten letters, even though they would arrive slowly. The pace made the letters more romantic, in her eyes.

Kiko's sisters teased her constantly about Peter. But they also gave her advice. Yumi said that many people went on to marry their high school sweethearts. Yoko said high school boys were so much more mature than middle schoolers. ("You'll see. When you get to high school and look back, the middle schoolers just look like kids.")

Every night they all sat down to dinner, and Kiko felt the warm fullness of her sisters being back together, the house teeming with them and their things. Her parents were so happy—she could feel it radiating off them. They held hands when they walked out in the backyard after dinner.

Everyone addressed her again as Baby Kiko, and she had to admit she loved it, loved looking at her sisters, who were so beautiful, so sure of themselves. But Kiko, who spent her days going to theater rehearsals in the morning and dance classes all afternoon, felt that life was incomplete, even with everyone at home. Peter, Peter had shown her that there was more than just being Baby Kiko.

It was during the summer that she and Jessica became really crazy about Marilyn Monroe. Movies featuring Marilyn gave way to books and documentaries and biopics about Marilyn. Kiko learned about every moment of her life: born Norma Jeane Mortenson, Marilyn was originally red-haired, stub-nosed, petite. There was a mother she didn't connect with, a husband who held her back from her dreams. Kiko admired Marilyn's willingness to do anything for fame. Her desire was enormous. Kiko felt she had that same outsize desire. Kiko, too, would eat up anyone and anything on her path to fame. Any of those men she'd married and maybe used—they were all footnotes in Marilyn's life story. She was still a legend.

Jessica told her that Peter would think Kiko's new obsession was silly, that she shouldn't tell him about it, for now. Kiko saw that Jessica had been feeling left out, so she agreed. Marilyn would be their thing. She knew that Peter wouldn't mind. Yes, she wanted to tell him everything she'd learned about this beautiful and tragic woman, but there was no time anyway. Peter was far away and busy. And Kiko saw no harm in sharing with Jessica an innocent secret, at least for a few months.

But the secrecy became a habit, and at the end of the summer, when Peter came back to Shanghai, she did not tell him the extent of her studies. He saw the new Marilyn poster in her room, and so he knew that she was a fan. He knew that she loved theater and acting. That was all there was to it, as far as he was concerned.

As TIME WENT ON, Kiko started to see parallels between Peter and Marilyn's second husband, Joe DiMaggio. Peter was the nicest boy she knew; he would be the type to bring roses to Kiko's grave every year after her death. But Peter was also—like Joe—prone to jealousy and possessiveness.

Kiko, already well-versed in ballet, tap, jazz, and modern dance, had recently taken up swing. She'd become interested while listening to all that music from the 1950s. Her school didn't teach swing, and neither did her dance academy, so Kiko went to another studio downtown in the former French Concession.

Peter didn't have time to join, and in any case he wasn't interested. But he didn't like the idea of Kiko—then fifteen, then already his girlfriend for two years—going around and dancing with one man and then another.

Kiko, however, loved it. She loved the feel-good music, the fast and loose dancing, the way she could smile and laugh out loud, limbering and relaxing into her lead—so unlike the structure of ballet, and so unlike the seriousness of modern. Tap, jazz, they felt like manufactured joy. Swing felt authentic.

Peter was right to feel jealous, in the end. Kiko denied it, but moving from one partner to another—grabbing one pair of hands, spinning away, and landing with a different pair—what a pleasure it was. Dancing with a partner was like sharing a kiss: intimate but not involved, friendly, flirty, easy to walk away from.

YOU COULD SAY they broke up because of Marilyn. It was after their third summer apart. Peter had been particularly jealous, always texting to ask where she was and what she was doing. Kiko even had the suspicion that he'd set up an app to send her periodic messages about it. She was constantly receiving variations on *What's going on, Kiks?* or different spellings of *I love you.*

Kiko was busy—doing rehearsals for a show with the Shanghai Conservatory, swing dancing (she'd since given up ballet), and researching the Japanese celebrity scene. She was constantly surprised by what she found. For example, in Japan, more than in any other place she was looking into—China, Hong Kong, or Hollywood—it seemed as though girls came up into the movies from lots of unexpected places: hostess bars and cafés, even porn. It was as if, once they became stars, everyone forgot and forgave them for their past careers. They got a clean slate.

Even their profiles were different. In the United States, there was more Real Content: dogs, friends, boats. In China, it was often High Glam: events, ball gowns, fashion shows. But in Japan, it was Exposure Content: half-naked shots, legs splayed in a bikini, bending over a car and looking back at the camera. Who was taking these pictures? Kiko followed the comments and tags and came up with a list of photographers, all in Japan, who worked with the "hot girls," the influencers. She collected their contact info in her journal.

Kiko created a new, secret profile for herself, since she could not use the one linked to her mom's account; followed all the photographers, models, and actresses; and began to style herself in similar poses, setting up her phone in her bedroom. With the right tags, she gained a small following, breaking a thousand in a few weeks. Sometimes she sent the photos to Peter. Fire emoji was what came back most often.

When Peter returned from lacrosse league, he visited her place. There was, as after every summer apart, the initial awkwardness of getting reacquainted. Kiko had to imagine, as she did now whenever she was in an ambiguous or difficult situation, that she was Marilyn Monroe. She imagined the actress on set for a movie, confidently performing a scene with her costar. So Kiko sat on her bed, Peter lying with his head on her lap, and ran her hands through his hair. Peter's grimy lacrosse stick and ball were on the floor, always within reach. He was looking through the selection of sexy photos Kiko had sent him over the summer. He sat up suddenly, grinning, and hid his screen.

"What are you doing over there?" Kiko asked.

"You'll see," he said, his fingers flying.

"What is it? Show me!" Kiko tried to swipe the phone away, but Peter lunged sideways and protected it against his chest.

"OK," she said. "I'm not going to play lacrosse with you on this." That was what they said whenever they got into a joke-fight. But Peter's face had fallen. He was not smiling anymore, and Kiko could see his eyes scanning quickly—left to right, up and down. He presented the screen and asked, "Is this you, Kiko?" He had found her secret profile. She had 5,557 followers. All the photos she'd sent to Peter were on the page, and more.

"How did you find that?" Kiko thought with fear of her parents, or her sisters, finding the profile.

"I was drafting this"—he showed her the post: a relatively tame bare-shoulders shot of Kiko with the caption *My girlfriend!*—"and my bot gave me a replica warning. So I clicked and got here. Kiks, is this you?"

At first Kiko said nothing. She just looked at Peter holding the phone, the screen filled with a grid of the sexy photos she'd taken all summer. Seeing them side by side—Peter and her profile—made her realize just how incompatible the two were. She had to explain herself. But shouldn't she be with someone she never had to explain herself to? The guys in her comments—the ones who liked every photo and told her she was The Most Beautiful—they would all line up to date her. And here, Peter was angry.

"What the hell is this?" he asked.

"I don't have to explain myself to you," Kiko said. She was beginning to feel a change within her—a cool detachment, as if Peter had suddenly become insignificant, as if she were floating farther and farther away from him, from the scene, as if she were merely watching them having this conversation.

"What were you thinking? Are you doing this for the likes? Kiko, this is *insane*. Your boobs . . ."

He scrolled through the photos. He stopped at one that showed her bending over, her legs spread, peeking back at the camera. Her bed—on which they still sat—was in the corner.

"Delete this, Kiks. It's beneath you. And . . ." He paused. She was watching him; she felt as if she hadn't blinked once since he'd started. She'd become a statue. "I thought these photos were for me."

She finally unglued her lips and said, "I'm sorry."

He was reading through the comments now, though most of them were in Japanese. He was shaking his head.

Kiko watched him read, and with every shake of his head she hated him more. His simple life, his hard lacrosse ball that was like an extension of himself, the way he knew her, or thought he did. She felt the words bubbling up slowly from her stomach, rising with fear and power and a velocity that could not be stopped.

"Peter, this is not going to work out," she said. She felt victorious yet she was also aware of an inexplicable chill coming over her, her teeth chattering so that she had to clamp down to stop their dance. "I don't love you anymore."

Peter put his phone down and stared at her, unbelieving, until doubt crept in. "You don't mean that, Kiks," he said. "What, because of this? Just delete it. I don't think anyone we know has seen it. I hope not. Just delete it. I'm sorry—I didn't give you much attention this summer, right? But I'm back. Kiks, let's just forget this ever happened. I forgive you. I love you."

"No, Peter. I'm not going to delete it. It's my career. We're over. I'm sorry."

"Your career? What, to be a whore?" He was upset now, picking up the grimy lacrosse ball and squeezing it in his hands.

Now she knew. It was a choice between her profile—her career—and Peter. "Why would you say that to me?" She imagined a nude scene in a future movie. What would Peter say then? That was why actors had to date actors. She could never completely belong to him. "You know I'm going to be an actor. This is what girls do in Japan." Marilyn had posed in all kinds of photos, Kiko thought. In the United States. So long ago. Things had always been the same. The price had always been the same.

"You don't have to get there by being a slut," Peter said, standing up, packing his things.

"I've only ever slept with you," Kiko said. "If you think that makes me a slut, so be it."

Peter laughed. "Your head's not right, Kiks." He walked to the door. "Take some time to think about what you're doing. And call me once you've decided to do the right thing." At the threshold he bounced his lacrosse ball three times, as was his habit.

Kiko listened to him walk down the hall. She pictured him turning left into the living room, going past the library and out the front door. The guards at the gate all knew him. He'd walk over to his compound and ignore his mom on the way to his room. All the while bouncing his ball angrily.

Kiko stood up and shut her door. She would never have to hear that three-thump of the ball ever again. She took off her pants and set up her phone. She spread her legs and held her middle finger in front of her crotch, waiting for the flash to go off.

. . .

Shortly after the breakup, Kiko was in the bathroom at school, reapplying her lipstick. The toilet flushed and she heard the click of heels coming her way. It was Takako. She gave Kiko a quick smile and said, "Hello." She put her black Chanel backpack on the ledge of the mirror. Kiko watched Takako's reflection. She wore long fake lashes and her nails were filed to points, the shape of spades, gel-hard and dark purple. The nail on her left ring finger was pierced with a sparkling little hoop.

"Can I help you?" Takako said, abruptly, looking up into the mirror and meeting Kiko's gaze. She smiled again, and Kiko felt suddenly as though she were in a movie. Two women having a conversation in the bathroom.

"I like your nails," Kiko said, in order to say something. But really, she wanted to ask for Takako's truth—she wanted to know what Takako knew, what she wanted from life. She wanted, in other words, to be her friend.

Kiko put her lipstick away. She wanted to explain to Takako why she'd never reached out after Takako transferred to their school in the eighth grade. They were the only two Japanese there; most went to the Japanese school in Pudong or the one in Gubei. Kiko wanted to apologize for not making more of an effort. Her life had been so full, with Jessica and Peter. Kiko watched Takako powder her face.

In Japanese, Kiko said, "Takako, what do you do on the weekends?"

Takako kept her eyes on herself and sighed. In Japanese, she responded, "I know there's talk about me."

"Oh." Kiko began to wash her hands, unsure how to reply. She'd already washed them once, before Takako came out of the stall.

"I don't do what I do because I need to," Takako said. She met Kiko's eyes in the mirror. "I like it."

"You're not scared?" Kiko asked, forgetting to pretend she didn't know what Takako was talking about.

"Everything is vetted," Takako said. "Besides, I don't really care what happens to me."

Kiko didn't know what to say to that. She'd finished washing her hands and pulled out two sheets of paper to dry them. She dried them slowly and thoroughly, not a drop of water left. "People care," was what she finally said. Kiko couldn't very well say *I care*—she hadn't cared much about Takako until today. And she couldn't say *Your parents care*—she knew nothing about Takako's life.

Takako scoffed. "So, like, you interested or what?"

Kiko felt like she'd been pushed back by two strong hands, even though she was still standing in front of the sink. She realized with embarrassment that her armpits were slick with sweat.

"I don't know," she said. But Takako was already rummaging through her backpack. She pulled out a Louis Vuitton pouch and snapped it open, her fingernails scratching against the hard leather. She removed a completely white business card with embossed letters rising from its surface. Kiko took it and held it under the light to read the ghost of a name: *Lily Sun*. There was only a phone number underneath. Kiko rubbed it as if it were braille.

Takako slung her backpack over one shoulder and flipped her hair away from her face. "I won't tell anyone," she said. "Just do whatever you want."

. . .

Kiko didn't know how many rings to wait because she hadn't talked over the phone in maybe five years. But she waited a long time. It was almost fun, listening to the ring of a phone, waiting for a call to begin. For Kiko, it made the whole thing more exciting. At last, the ring broke and a wispy, soft voice said, "Moshi moshi."

Kiko identified it right away as Marilyn's voice—if Marilyn could speak Japanese. Without thinking about it too much, she softened her own voice and answered back in the same language. "Hello. I received this number from Takako."

Even though Lily Sun sounded like Marilyn, she looked nothing like her. She was stick-thin and wore all black—a sweater that climbed up her neck and down her arms, black pants, black heeled boots. She had on what looked like no makeup and her left hand had a diamond ring on every finger. Each one was different: a small band on her pinky, a large square on her ring finger, a dangling pendant from the middle, a thick gold band inlaid with tiny studs on her pointer, and another band for her thumb with huge diamonds all around. Kiko thought to herself: *I wouldn't want to get slapped in the face with that hand.*

They sat down in the tearoom, where running along the bottom of the wall was the room's only window. Visible through the long horizontal strip of glass were moss and plants and a small running stream. It looked like something Kiko's mom would embroider.

"Do you prefer Chinese or Japanese?" Lily Sun asked.

"Either is OK," Kiko said, surprised by the question.

"I'm half Japanese and half Chinese."

"Really? I am too. There aren't too many of us around here," Kiko said. "Besides my sisters, obviously."

"Yes, it's not the most common mix." Lily's parents, she said, had met when her father was studying abroad in Tokyo. She went on to share more details of her life, explaining that she had begun working as an escort while she was a college student trying to make ends meet. It was better than any office job she'd tried. And she'd tried many.

Kiko started to relax. She had not known what to expect, but now she felt relief in hearing what Lily ("Call me Lily Sister," she'd insisted) had to say. This meeting was not an evaluation or some kind of test. It was just a getting-to-know-you chat.

"Do you know many Japanese men?" Lily asked. Kiko shook her head. "Men are the easiest creatures in the world. Japanese in particular."

"Why?"

"The thing about a Japanese man is that he has his fetish. It's not something they keep secret or discover organically one day. The men, they search and pick one, they develop it and identify with it, like a hobby or a career. You know, it makes my work easier. Japanese men will always tell me their fetish, during vetting."

"What kinds of fetishes do they have?" Kiko felt the words marble in her mouth, foreign and awkward.

"Schoolgirl, cosplay, food play, feet, orgies—you know, mostly standard stuff. Sometimes they want to role-play. Sometimes they want specific locations. Very few are into violence. And we try not to cater to those types, anyway."

“I’m an actress,” Kiko offered. She hadn’t done anything especially unusual with Peter, but the term “role-play” had stood out and made her want to offer something up to Lily.

“Oh, that’s good to know,” Lily said.

“I’m currently playing Ophelia in our school play.”

“Ophelia, eh?” Lily asked. Kiko could see the gears in her head turning. “What else can you do? Any good imitations?”

“I can do almost any accent,” Kiko said. “The rain in Spain stays mainly in the plain.” She did it in Cockney.

“Oh!” Lily clapped her hands in surprise.

“In Hartford, Hereford, and Hampshire, hurricanes hardly happen.” Now Kiko was doing it proper.

Lily laughed. The sound tinkled out like bells, and Kiko longed to continue.

“And I can do a great Marilyn,” Kiko said, in a breathy voice. Now she was smiling. Now she was showing off. Now she was singing, “Happy birthday, Mr. President.”

KIKO DEBATED TELLING JESSICA. But something in her wanted to do it by herself. She did not want any advice, or interference, or—worst of all—for Jessica to copy her.

Lily sent her a message after their meeting that she’d had a brilliant idea. She would auction Kiko’s virginity to the highest bidder. If Kiko was willing to play along, she’d give Kiko a higher cut—fifty-fifty—but this time only. Next time, it was back to sixty-forty.

But I’m not a virgin, Kiko reminded her.

Men won’t know the difference. Anyone will be too excited to really think about it.

Kiko only replied *OK*. She didn't care about Lily's plan. She didn't even care about the money. Actually, if she thought about it, faking it would be like performing in a movie. She looked at herself in the mirror and made what she thought was a virgin's face, a face that looked like losing her virginity. A face of pain.

KIKO WAS IN REHEARSALS for *Hamlet* when she got the call from Madame Sun.

It was happening. Next Saturday evening, at the InterContinental. The highest bidder had paid two hundred thousand.

Kiko didn't even have a bank account in which to deposit the money. Where would she keep it all? Her heart raced. She was going to have her own money soon. She was going to do it. She had told herself that the money didn't matter, but when she heard that number, it made things better. Money did matter.

Kiko put her phone away and went back on stage to practice. She felt she was poised to lift off and fly right out of the theater, far past campus, up above Shanghai, to meet her greater fate. She was above and beyond *Hamlet*, beyond high school.

ON SATURDAY, Kiko took the elevator to the lobby, on the ninety-second floor, her ears popping along the way. She had spent a long time over the past few days thinking about what to wear. She'd finally narrowed it down to three items: a pretty white sundress that scrunched in at the waist, a black miniskirt with a gray blouse, or a bright red dress that just grazed the floor, with thin straps and a slit up to her thigh. It had been Yumi's junior prom dress.

She sent a photo of the three outfits laid out on her bed to Lily. *White*, was the reply.

The early evening air was warm, and Kiko told their housekeeper that she was going out to meet some friends on the Bund. Her parents had been always overprotective of Yumi, setting all kinds of rules about when and how she could go out. But they were more lenient with Yoko, and they never set any rules for Kiko. They were busier, too, as Kiko grew up—her father opening another office for his firm and her mother frequently on tour in Japan, doing publicity for her embroidery work.

Kiko thought about asking Mr. Fu, their new driver, for a ride, but decided it wasn't worth the risk of him telling the housekeeper. She called a car on her phone and set the destination for Lujiazui.

In the lobby, Kiko looked out through the walls of glass at the cloudless night. Soon the sky would be filled with a full moon. She thought of how, when she was a child, she and her sisters would howl at the full moon. After she told this to Peter, he'd started howling at moons too. Her thing had become Peter's thing. She smiled at the memory, but then she felt a twinge of irritation—Peter had always been taking her things.

WINSTON YAMASHITA HAD the look of a boy. A tall, lanky boy who was well into his forties. When he first brought her to his hotel room, Kiko was nervous, but after a few glasses of champagne, she was feeling warm and excited. She told him about what she studied in school and what she did outside of school, her love of swing dancing. Mr. Yamashita then asked her to show him some moves, and they danced together in the middle of the hotel suite, the colorful lights of Shanghai spread out far below them. The Huangpu River was a gash of ink among the stars. He told her about his family business, in the hotel industry, and how he was planning to go into movie production.

Kiko imagined the two of them, their stars rising in concert with a hit film or two. Yamashita, as she imagined he would come to be known publicly, like Kurosawa, like Miyazaki, would eventually move into directing. And later in her career she might give it a try too. Though she would always focus on her acting. When they got into bed, Kiko was drunk and giddy with thoughts of a future with Yamashita, who was nice, and handsome, and not as old or gross as she'd expected.

But after a failed attempt, Yamashita said to her, "Sorry, this is not going to work. I thought it would, but it's not."

"Oh, what's wrong?" Kiko wanted to please—she felt her whole future stretching out from this night. People would ask, "How did you meet Winston Yamashita?" And she would say, "On set," while holding his hand on the red carpet, or after it became public that they'd eloped, evading the control of her management team, who perpetuated the myth of her as single and innocent.

"I just need you to shave. Is that OK?"

It took Kiko a moment to register what he was talking about.

"Oh, I see."

Of all the things Kiko had done with Peter—oral, anal, that awful threesome with Jessica last year—she'd never gotten rid of her pubic hair. Not that she had so much to get rid of. Peter had always asked her to keep it, saying that it made her womanly. That when they were naked together, it made him feel like Tarzan and Jane, or Adam and Eve. After so many years, she never thought about it much. Now she was being asked to shave it off.

She hesitated. Even the thought of touching a blade to that area scared her.

"I've never done that before," she said. Winston was sitting on the end of the bed, his long, lanky arms hanging down by his sides. Peter, twenty-five years younger, had a stronger, manlier build. Winston jumped toward her, excited, smiling.

"I can do it for you," he said.

"Really?" Kiko wasn't thrilled with the idea, though Winston was now getting off the bed, pulling her along with him to the bathroom.

"I'll do it in the shower," he said. "It'll be nice. I'll be careful."

Kiko felt her arm being pulled off, her body following the arm. She looked at his face—smooth and hairless—and comforted herself with the notion that he must shave his face every day, the delicate fleshy areas around the mouth. He would know how to do it. Maybe it was his fetish, shaving? But still, the thought of blood from her mutilated genitalia running down the shower drain: it made her pause. What if Winston had a violent streak, a psychopathic impulse?

"I'm afraid," she said, pulling away from him.

But he only smiled more broadly and doubled down on his efforts. Finally, Kiko agreed when he offered to let her shave off his pubic hair first. The offer made her laugh, relax for the first time since they'd started the conversation. And it made her feel as though maybe they could be partners, equals, or at least that their night together had taken a unique turn—that maybe, for Winston, this was also a first, and maybe it could be the best, the last of these kinds of nights for him. Kiko was only sixteen, sure, too young to settle. But a producer! An actress and a producer. She followed him into the bathroom and waited as he ran the water;

he had wrapped himself in a fluffy white bathrobe. The razor—a nice one with flashes of silver along the sides, presumably the one he used on his face—was sitting on the bathtub's edge. Winston removed the bathrobe, and Kiko saw that his thin penis was fully erect. Like all of him, slimmer and slighter than anything of Peter's.

KIKO TURNED TO FACE THE WINDOW. A black sky. In the window's reflection the blurry outline of Mr. Yamashita moving on top of her. It was all very boring.

She closed her eyes and thought about Space Mountain, her and Peter's favorite ride. She imagined the stars in the pitch-blackness, the way her body jostled from left to right. She knew what to expect—an even beginning, a steep incline, a fast looping, the slow middle where you could catch your breath and the stars seemed to dance with dizziness all around you. It always went by too fast.

She remembered Peter's hand, warm and soft, always holding hers. Perhaps he was the one who was really afraid, she had scoffed to herself. There were times when she had wanted to release herself from his grasp, when she'd wondered what Space Mountain would be like if she could get the seat in the front all to herself. She would hold herself, brace herself for all the bumps and turns. She would see everything more clearly, unobstructed. It might be lonely, even scary. But it would also be exhilarating.

Mr. Yamashita didn't realize it, but Kiko was silently crying. She was not much scared, now that it was almost over. Mostly, she missed Peter—his kindness, his grin, his handsome young face that had broken when she told him she didn't love him anymore.

Peter was probably sitting at home in his chair, cradling his ratty old lacrosse stick, chewing gum, and letting the grimy ball hit the wall again and again. The sound of it as the backdrop to all their conversations had become an annoyance, but now she longed for that familiar rhythm.

In the Time of Period Trees

April 2038

It was again the time of period trees. Yoko closed her darkening window to the stench. They lined the paths on campus, and every spring they blossomed, flooding the green with the smell of menstruation blood. *Pyrus calleryana*, as her mother had told her when Yoko asked in the spring of last year, her first living abroad. The smell would last just a few weeks, until the flowers fell to the ground.

Was she the only one bothered by it? Everyone else on campus seemed to be unfazed, buoyantly happy, even. The girls had pulled out their dresses and skirts. The boys were in salmon and orange and pink khaki. There came, with the period trees, a feeling of celebration in the air. Stench and joy. Springtime at boarding school. Yoko had only two more years, and then she'd be done. Maybe she would choose a college for its lack of period trees. Somewhere far away from Massachusetts.

A loud, inconsiderate moan emanated from the inner room. Charlie Canter. Senior. Crew team captain. Yoko glanced at the door, the familiar leopard-print ballet flat wedged at the bottom, creating the thinnest sliver of openings—Bernadine's way of following the school's shoe-in-door parietal policy.

Yoko had requested a single room the year before but pulled a high number in the housing lottery. She was stuck now with a new sophomore—Bernadine from New York City—in one of those awkward walk-through doubles. Bernadine had initially intrigued Yoko. She had a flippant, almost slovenly look, as if she didn't care about her beauty. At first, Bernadine had been very nice to Yoko, trailing her like a lost puppy all over campus. But soon she had attracted the attentions of similarly cool, slovenly girls. And, nearly as quickly, the attentions of boys.

Yoko kept count of how many boys came over for parietals, legal and illegal, in Bernadine's room. By the spring of this year, by this time of the period trees, the number was already at twelve. Yoko liked to read the sign-in sheet for parietal guests. It was there for anyone to see, splayed on a side table in the common room, listing the girl's name, visitor's name, date, time in, and time out. Bernadine always wrote her name in a confident cursive that took up the entire space, both vertical and horizontal. Just the first name, just *BERNADINE*. She knew she was the only one. The boys' names were scratchy adolescent things, first and last.

Yoko looked around her room, accounting for her belongings. She did that whenever Bernadine brought someone over. Yoko knew it was unlikely a boy would take any of her stuff. But one time there had been a slight impression on her bed when she came back from the library. Had Bernadine and a guest been sitting on her bed? *Kissing?* Yoko had never confronted her roommate about it. She wasn't upset, per se. She was not a prude. But since then, she'd become even more vigilant about keeping tidy and organized: everything in its place.

Yoko's bed was pushed up against the two windows, her quilt laid flat and folded over at exactly one-third of its length. It was a quilt her mother had made for her before Yoko came to Massachusetts, forest green and embroidered with red, white, brown, and purple mushrooms—spotted, short, tall, fat—all along the border.

When her mother had asked what Yoko's favorite forest creature was, she answered that it was the mushroom. She had been reading about them just then, had developed an encompassing interest in them. She was writing a report for science class on the secret language of fungi and how they connect through an underground communications network. Mushrooms, and their messages, were crucial to the health and survival of the forest. In a way, they were as alive as any animal. Eko had probably expected Yoko's answer to be something like a fox, or an owl, or a rabbit, but she didn't miss a beat. "Mushrooms it is, then," Eko said, up for the challenge. Yoko brushed the folded-back edge of the blanket, fingering a silky fly agaric. Today, no one had touched her bed.

She straightened the sign above her headboard. *Let no one ignorant of geometry enter here.* She'd bought it on their family trip to Greece five years ago. Before Yoko came to school, at home, the sign had hung above her bedroom door. But here she wasn't permitted to keep personal belongings out in the hall.

Anyway, Bernadine was bad at math, and Yoko couldn't very well exclude her from her own room, could she?

Yoko sat at her desk, where her homework was waiting for her. On the desk, leaning against the wall, were three things. There was a small ball of golden string, an inside joke with her dad. Next to it was a framed photograph of her family from long ago—Yoko was maybe four, Yumi six, and Kiko just a toddler. Their parents stood behind them. They were in front of a temple gate in Japan, and ayi was standing off to the side, just slightly apart. Ayi looked awkward, as if she didn't know what to do with her empty hands. She was old already; only a few years later, she would retire and leave them. Hanging from a corner of the frame was a bracelet made by Kiko, all pink beads except for three that spelled *SIS*. Everything was in its rightful place.

Her phone buzzed on her desk, next to her open Chinese textbook. Yoko had missed a call from Yumi. She put the phone face down and tried to focus on finishing her essay. Yoko was in the highest-level class because she could say anything in Mandarin, but her reading and writing were far behind the others'. She had been fluent by the age of five, thanks to ayi, who had spoken to her only in Chinese. Yoko glanced at the photo again, before returning her attention to the textbook. She was the only one of the three sisters who regularly kept in touch with their former nanny, now living in the countryside after retirement.

Memorizing Chinese characters—and writing them with their strokes that had to go from top to bottom, left to right, or whatever—was the bane of her high school existence. It wasn't hard, but it was time-consuming. The inefficiency was what irked her the most. Why? No one needed to handwrite anymore. She could dictate an entire essay into an app. She hated the unnecessary legacy stuff of education.

Yoko had been eager to learn ancient Greek when she arrived at school. She thought it might help her to understand the mystery of the Greeks, their particular talent, their genius streak of innovation, and their demise. But the language, at least in its elementary instruction, didn't give her any great insights, and learning Greek from scratch took time—too much—away from her math, which was incredibly rigorous here, compared with SH Foreign.

Yoko had always assumed she was good at languages, speaking four of them—Chinese, Japanese, French, and English—with fluency, and understanding a fifth, Shanghainese. But only when she got to high school did she realize how much work was required to gain even basic proficiency in something utterly foreign. She had been born, essentially, into multilingualism.

Her phone buzzed again. Yoko knew it would be Yumi, just half an hour away by train at university. Even though they were so nearby, and their family so far away, they hadn't seen each other since winter vacation back in Shanghai.

"Hey," Yoko whispered, finally picking up.

"Why are you whispering?" Yumi asked. As usual, her voice was full of disdain.

"There's someone here," Yoko said, the simplest way to explain the situation.

"So go somewhere else."

"OK. Hold on." Yoko quietly left the dorm room, making sure the outside door didn't slam on the second leopard-print shoe. In the hallway, she put the phone to her ear and walked toward the stairs.

"So . . . how are you?" she started. Over the holiday, she and Yumi had gotten into two fights. The first was an argument over college. At dinner one night, the family talked about where Yoko was thinking of applying. Harvard was on the list, and after dinner, when the sisters were watching a singing contest on TV, Yumi told her to take it off. "Why don't you just live your life and I'll live mine? Why not Paris? You could go the same route as Dad. That would make him happy."

"Yeah, but I want to go to the best program. Harvard's not even my top choice. I have other options too."

"Good. Don't, like, stick to me," Yumi said.

"When have I ever stuck to you? I went to America first."

"I was the one who suggested they send you away," Yumi said. "I couldn't deal with you hanging around me and my friends all the time."

"Whatever. I don't believe you. And I don't care what you think."

"You don't care what anybody thinks—that's what makes you so dangerous," Yumi said.

Now, on the other end of the line, Yumi kept her voice light. "I'm good. Really good," she said.

Yoko opened the door to the stairwell and sat down on the third-floor landing. The heavy fire door swung shut.

"Great. So what's up?" Yoko asked. She was biting the inside of her cheek.

"Well, I'm thinking of moving off campus," Yumi said. "Dorm life is stupid. It's restrictive. You're with everyone all the time. I need some space."

"Seriously?" Yoko asked. "I thought you guys had all the freedom in the world."

"Yeah, but it's not the same."

"The same as what?"

"As being on your own."

"Fine. But I don't think you can do it even if you want to. Harvard doesn't allow freshmen to live off campus."

"I can. No one's, like, monitoring where I am at all times. One guy from Malaysia rents a penthouse suite in a hotel in Boston."

"You want to live in a hotel in Boston?"

"No! But I could get a small place off campus in Cambridge. There's a ton."

"Um, OK," Yoko said. "So do it."

"Well, I need your help."

Yoko twirled her hair in her fingers. Then she stuck the end of it in her mouth, chewing it into a wet wad. "How?"

"I need some money."

"Don't you have a credit card?"

"You can't put an apartment down on a credit card. You need one or two months' rent."

"What about your debit card?"

"I used up my allowance."

"Already?" Yoko looked down at her watch. "It's only the fifth."

"Whatever. I needed some things. How much do you have?"

"I need money too," Yoko said.

"Yeah, I know, but you're in boarding school. Don't they give you everything?"

Yoko had a habit of ordering pad thai for dinner most nights; this allowed her to avoid the anxiety of the dining hall for one meal a day. Unlike the other students, she didn't often go downtown for Starbucks or to buy things at the local shops. Downtown also made her nervous. She went only if she really needed something that couldn't be delivered.

"They don't provide everything," she told Yumi.

"Listen," Yumi said. "It's kind of an emergency. My roommates are horrible. They're real bitches. They are so, so mean to me."

"*They're* mean to *you*?" Yoko asked, incredulous.

"Yeah. They don't talk to me. They treat me like shit. They put all my stuff in a box and basically told me I needed to go."

Yoko listened to her sister's voice. It made her feel queasy. Yumi's voice was something Yoko associated with fear and hurt. It always surprised her, then, when she heard recordings of herself, just how much they sounded alike.

"Why don't you talk to the school? Like, a housing person? They can get you a new room," Yoko said.

"No, they can't."

"Why are you so sure? You haven't tried, right?"

"I'm going to be homeless," Yumi said.

"Oh my God, you're so dramatic," Yoko replied. "Where are you now?"

"I'm in some boy's room. I'm spending the night with him."

"Why are they so mean to you? Like, all of them at once?" Delicately, Yoko asked, "Yumi, did something happen?"

"OK. Yeah . . . something did happen."

"What? What happened? You can tell me," Yoko said, wary.

"I sort of pissed them off. I sort of, like, took some of their things," Yumi said.

"What? This again?"

"I know. I know. I have a problem. But you know what? They are honestly the biggest bitches."

"What did you take?"

"Some clothes. I don't know. Shoes. Books. Pens. Toothpaste. Tampons."

Yoko let the hair drop out of her mouth. This was beyond hair-chewing. "You took things from all of them? How did they find out?"

"They found the boxes under my bed. They went looking through my stuff."

Yoko ignored the hypocrisy of the statement. "Boxes? Are they going to report you? This is, like, a *crime*, Yumi. You're an adult now."

"No shit," Yumi said. "I know." She paused. "They told me they wouldn't report me, but only if I left the room right away and never came back."

"What about the rest of your stuff?"

"They're going to pack it up for me."

"Yumi, this is not good," Yoko said. "You're not twelve anymore. You have to stop doing this."

"I know. I know, OK? I *know*."

"So what are you going to do about it? This is a problem. It's a real problem. It's a *condition*. You need to see someone about it. I don't know what to say to you!"

"See someone? Seriously?" Yumi said. "Come on."

"Yes. Like a doctor. A psychiatrist. This is an actual thing. There is an actual term for this."

"Whatever. I don't care about the term. And don't you dare tell anyone about this. I can't even believe you right now. I'm coming to you in need, in a fucking dark place, and you're telling me to go somewhere else. Thanks a lot."

Yoko waited for her sister to hang up on her, as Yumi often did at the ends of their infrequent calls.

"You there?" Yumi asked.

"Yeah. I'm here," Yoko said.

"Listen. Maybe I'll see someone. Maybe later. But what should I do now? Like, right now? I'm living out of a box, Yoko."

"Those therapy things are confidential, you know. They legally can't tell anyone else what you tell them," Yoko said.

She knew this because she'd begun visiting the on-campus shrink the past fall. After a suicide on campus, everyone in her class had been required to see him twice, and Yoko just never stopped going. To her surprise, she enjoyed the conversations, which more often than not circled around the topics of her older sister and how to handle "toxic family relationships." What Mr. Corellini told her, every week, was that Yoko did not deserve to feel wounded after every interaction with Yumi. That she had the right to protect herself. That love was not defined by pain.

And yet the hold her sister had over her, as Mr. Corellini called it, renewed itself with this phone call, the sound of her familiar voice. Yoko was drawn back in. And she felt, also, sorry for her sister, the one who had been there from the very beginning of her existence, who had shaped it violently and cruelly, manipulating it according to her nasty moods.

"Come on, Yoko. You have to help me. You're the only one in the world who can. You're my sister, goddammit."

"Why don't you just call Mom? You know she'll help you."

"Why don't you just call Dad and tell him you need a little extra this month? *He'll* help *you*."

"But even if you get the money, you still need real help."

Yumi sighed. "I don't want to tell Mom and Dad. They'll be really upset."

"They should be."

"Yeah, but you know how it will be. Dad will go on and on at me for, like, days, and Mom will cry and be like, 'What did I do to deserve this,' and then afterward they'll never want to talk about it again. It'll be so annoying and take so much time."

"Maybe they need to know."

"Listen—I'm upset too! I hate this. You think I like this situation? You think I like doing this?" More quietly, she said, "You think I like being this way?"

"If you don't like it, then stop," Yoko replied.

"It's not so simple, OK? It's like—I can't help it."

"That sounds like bullshit."

"So what? What are you going to do? Call the cops? On your own sister?" Yumi's voice was laced with anger now, familiar.

"Honestly? Maybe I should," Yoko tried.

"Come on. You wouldn't. I was just being sarcastic."

"But maybe I should. Maybe you need to feel the consequences of your actions for once."

"Yoko! I would go to jail. You would put your own sister in jail!"

"It's not like I want to punish you. But how will you ever change?"

"And how would Mom and Dad feel about that? About your betrayal of the family, huh?"

"Maybe they'd thank me later."

"They'd blame you for all eternity. The way Kiko blames you for Lucy."

They waited, each holding on to their own end of the silence. It was an old game, an old war. When they were young, when they got into a fight, one of them would run to their mother. The other would stand by, waiting. Their mother had no tolerance for fighting, or she had no tolerance for their fighting, constant as it was. “Handle it between yourselves,” she’d say in that quiet, threatening way, the voice that meant they were close to being in trouble, her hands covering her ears, refusing to hear them out. They would both stand there: the one with the grievance, silent; the one with the defense, silent. Each knowing that their mother would get angry at the first one to speak. Eventually she would wave them off. “I haven’t got all day!”

“Yoko. Please.” Yumi was nearly whispering. “Please.” And now she was crying. “Yoko. Yoko. I’m in a fucking bad place here. Yoko,” she said, sobbing. “You’re the only one I can turn to. Yoko. I’ll change. I can do it. I can be better. A better sister to you. I just need your help now. I just need to get through today. Yoko. Yoko,” she said through tears. “Yoko!”

Hearing her name called, on end, by her sister, was almost too much to bear. It was repulsive. She could imagine Yumi’s face, wet with tears, crumpled into the ugly mess it became when she wept. Yumi was the one who cried at movies, sopping up tears and snot when the credits came rolling through. “The sensitive one,” their mother always said about Yumi. To Yoko, it had always felt wrong, this label. The evil one, the bitter one, the hateful one: those would be more accurate.

“Yoko!” Yumi cried out. “Are you still there?”

“I’m here.”

“Why aren’t you saying anything?”

“So . . . living off campus is really possible?” Yoko asked. “And what about next year?”

“Who knows? I’ll figure that out later,” Yumi said.

“And how much exactly do you need?”

“How much do you have?” Yumi countered.

"Not much."

"How much, exactly?" Yumi demanded.

"I think only eight hundred or so," Yoko said.

"Fine. I'll get a smaller room, a roommate," Yumi said. "I'll pay you back when I get my allowance next month."

"Do you think that's a very good idea?" Yoko asked. "Getting a roommate?"

"It's fine."

"I mean, it clearly is not fine. Nothing is fine."

"I've learned my lesson."

"I want my piccolo back."

There was silence.

The second fight they'd had over Christmas break was about the piccolo. Yoko knew that Yumi must have taken it. Ever since Yoko had stopped playing it, after primary school, the instrument had kept its place on the top shelf of her bookcase at home. Yoko never practiced, but she liked its presence there, silver and shiny and small. It was proof that she had done something different, that she could. That she might very well once again do something other than what people expected of her, in the future.

On her last day at home, it had disappeared. She and her mother looked for it everywhere, and it finally dawned on Yoko that Yumi had taken it. Yoko confronted her sister, who, not unexpectedly, denied it. Why would she take a piccolo? She didn't play the thing. She didn't even like the sound, shrill and annoying. *Annoying.* That was what she called Yoko all the time.

Yoko rushed to Yumi's suitcase and emptied it out down the stairs of their house, the clothes tumbling out from their neatly rolled places. There was no piccolo.

Only later, after they'd returned to the United States, did Yoko imagine a hidden compartment, her piccolo stuffed along the hard ridge of the suitcase, carelessly banging along without protection. She had been too driven by emotion, too irrational, to conduct a thorough search.

"Fine," Yumi said. "I'll mail you the piccolo."

"Send it in bubble wrap," was all Yoko said. She wasn't going to push her advantage. Victory against Yumi was always tenuous.

Yoko took down the details on her phone as Yumi dictated the transfer codes for her digital currency account over the speaker. That way their parents wouldn't see where the money went.

"Just tell them you were buying some digital manga collectibles or something," Yumi told Yoko. "They'll believe anything you say."

After Yoko made the transfer and hung up, she walked back down the hall to her room. The leopard-print slipper was gone and the door was closed.

"Bernadine?" Yoko called. There was no reply.

YUMI HAD NO IDEA where the stupid piccolo was. OK, she had taken it. And then she had taped it inside the leg of one of her pairs of pants, rolled them up, and packed everything in her suitcase.

But was it still in her pants? Would she ever see those pants again? She pushed the piccolo problem out of her mind. How was she going to survive this? It was going to be nearly impossible to continue at Harvard. Maybe she could take a leave. Cut ties. Do an internship. Start a small business and never have to go back to school again. Then, later, if she chose, she could return to school with a clean slate. Or she might go to a different school. A different country. England. France.

Just a few more weeks of the spring semester. She could last a few more weeks. Yes, people would talk, but the summer would come and go, and if she was gone then the rumors would fade slowly from their minds.

Yumi left the stairwell and went back into Jay's room. He was sleeping. She got into the narrow bed with him and grimaced. It smelled like boy. Like boy who hadn't changed his sheets all semester. He wrapped his long limbs around her and pressed his face into her hair. She pulled her hair out from under her shoulder and ignored the erection that was pushing into her thigh.

The next morning, Yumi blew Jay and persuaded him to cut all his classes, as well as football practice. She explained that she had gotten into a fight with her roommates—a big misunderstanding about what was being used communally and what wasn't.

"How was I supposed to know that they didn't want to share clothes?" she asked. "My sisters and I, we share everything. Maybe it's a Chinese thing." She shrugged. "They were so mean, Jay. I just decided to get an extra place. On the side. So I don't have to deal with all that negativity. It's not like I even need their clothes. I have yours." She smiled at him. She'd arrived at his room with nothing of her own; she had been wearing one of his *Veritas* T-shirts all night.

He would help her look at a few apartments. "Can I stay over some nights too?" he asked. "More privacy for us." Jay had a single room in Adams, but the bathroom was shared.

Yumi kissed his nose. "I'd love that," she said.

Jay had told her, one week ago, that he loved her. And Yumi hadn't said it back. She knew that was a bit mean, but she didn't feel it, love. She couldn't help it. She was still reeling from her breakup with Sven. After their summer riding the Trans-Siberian, club-hopping in Moscow, and staying up through the white nights of Saint Petersburg—and then their separation to different universities and his admission two weeks after orientation that he'd slept with three other girls—her world had completely shrunk. It had changed from the size of the entire planet—Russia and China and Boston and Palo Alto—to the size of a single bed in a quadruple room in a freshman suite on Harvard Yard.

She had never felt more adrift, more unloved, more desolate than in those early months of her first semester. After she'd crawled out of her hole of despair, she spent weeks trying to catch up with her classmates, who already had favorite final clubs to party at and favorite late-night greasy spoons, who had already comped for clubs and activities. It was all she could do to hang on to the fringes of her roommates' social circle.

They were three blonde girls, all from the South. Well—one from South Florida, one from Texas, and one from Southern California. But to Yumi, it was all essentially the same. And in any case, the girls looked very much alike.

Yumi had planned to major in history, or maybe East Asian studies, but on campus that, too, had been disappointing. The students in the classes she trialed in the first weeks of school, before the add/drop deadline, were so out of touch. They were Asian Americans. Or they were white. Most had never been to Asia; some had never even studied Chinese or Japanese or Korean. Their ideas, well articulated, strongly opined, were just shallow, stereotyped things. OK, name-drop Edward Said—so what? *Congratulations.* Yumi felt like she started every statement with "Actually, in Shanghai . . ." or "Actually, in Japan . . ." Was this the best Harvard could offer?

THE FIRST APARTMENT they saw was at Porter Square, about a mile from campus. It was the perfect distance for a run. If she could run to class and back two or three times a day, she'd get a good handful of miles in. Yumi was determined not to gain the freshman fifteen. Not even a freshman five.

She and Jay knocked on the door of the apartment, in a house that had been partitioned into a couple of units. A young man of about thirty—he introduced himself as Ben—opened the door and invited them in. Jay looked around, a frown on his face.

Ben was a PhD student in sociology, all but dissertation. He had lived in the house's first-floor apartment for three years now, and had been subletting the smaller bedroom since his funding ended.

"So you're here all day?" Jay asked.

"Sometimes I'm at the library," Ben said.

The room was clean and simple: a bed, a desk, a chair. The bathroom was off the living room. It would have to be shared.

"And who lives upstairs?" Jay asked.

"Two guys, recently graduated from MIT, doing some sort of startup. They moved in half a year ago."

"OK. Got it."

"This is for the two of you?" Ben asked.

"No, just me," Yumi said. She pushed her hair behind her left ear and smiled.

"And you're at Harvard?" he asked. "I saw your email address."

"That's right."

"What department?"

"East Asian Studies."

"Oh, cool. I sometimes go study at your library. It's a good one."

"Yeah," Yumi agreed, though she'd only been once. Usually she studied at Lamont.

"How many more years you got?" Ben asked.

"Three," Yumi said. She realized that Ben had assumed she was a grad student.

"Ah, then I'll be long gone by the time you finish," Ben said. "Hopefully." He crossed his fingers in the air. Yumi laughed, bigger than the joke deserved.

Jay looked at his watch and said, "Hey, Yumi, we've got that appointment." When she looked at him, he nodded to the door.

Yumi thanked Ben, told him she'd be in touch, and walked out the door with Jay. On the street she asked, "What was that all about? He was nice."

"Seriously, Yumi? A house with three guys and you alone there? And a shared bathroom?"

"It's fine. They're harmless."

Jay scoffed. "You have a lot to learn about men," he said. Then he kissed her roughly, put his arm around her back, and said, "What else do you have to look at?"

Yumi rolled her eyes but was moved by Jay's protectiveness. He was a country boy from Iowa. He'd grown up on a farm. "There are two more. But this one was the cheapest. I haven't talked to my parents about the rent because I know they won't agree. I only have a few hundred in my account now."

Jay nodded. "But is the next one with a guy or a girl?"

Yumi looked at the note that she'd written up on her watch. "A girl. Unless Ariel is a boy's name."

"You never know nowadays," Jay said. They smiled at each other and walked to the next house.

ARIEL OPENED THE BUILDING DOOR and walked up the three flights of stairs ahead of them. Yumi caught Jay stealing glances. Ariel was Israeli and a student at the School of Education, concentrating on early childhood. Before even unlocking the apartment door, she held them hostage on the landing, spending a long time introducing herself, and then an even longer time going on about her recent stint in the Israeli army.

Yumi didn't like her. She didn't like that Jay was curious about the army stuff. She didn't like that Ariel talked only to him. But most of all, she didn't like that Ariel was drop-dead gorgeous. Long legs in a tiny miniskirt, a physique that corroborated her description of army training, barracks life, frontline combat in the war against the resurgence of that militant group—as soon as Ariel mentioned the name, it fell into the narrow, dark well of Yumi's limited knowledge about Middle East politics, and then it was irretrievable.

Ariel showed Yumi and Jay the bedroom, which was the only one in the apartment. Ariel would sleep in the living room, on the pullout couch.

Yumi took in Ariel's boyish coolness, her modelesque looks, her talkative demeanor, and she knew that this would be a recipe for disaster. Yumi could never be so effortlessly chill, so bouncy, so truly happy. Happy about war! Yumi imagined Ariel, gun in hand, smiling, fighting rebels in her miniskirt.

"Excuse me, can I use the bathroom?" Yumi asked.

"Certainly! It's right there." Ariel pointed to the door near the sofa. So Yumi would have to do all her business right next to the girl's bed.

"Great. Thanks."

Yumi went in and locked the door. From inside she could still hear Ariel and Jay talking, then laughing. Yumi went to work.

Noiselessly, she opened the medicine cabinet above the sink. She was surprised, pleasantly, to see that Ariel took all sorts of pills. She revised her assessment of the girl. Underneath the pretty exterior was a mess of a brain.

Yumi also saw a pack of birth control pills and, next to it, in a clear plastic container, what she guessed was a diaphragm. Yumi had heard about the things before, but she'd never actually seen one. She herself got the shot that was offered for free by Harvard Health Services at the start of the school year.

Yumi carefully opened the diaphragm case and examined the contraption. It was huge. She again reassessed Ariel. Yumi had never seen a penis so wide; the diaphragm spanned the width of her palm. Yes, Yumi had slim hands. But still. Ariel had quite the vagina. Yumi imagined it, with glee, hiding just under the miniskirt, like some kind of feral animal. She pictured Jay making a wrong move, tripping, falling in—whoops! She smiled.

Even though Ariel had the Largest Vagina in the World, Yumi was not happy about her boyfriend—well, maybe-boyfriend—flirting unabashedly. Yumi's first idea was to poke holes in the diaphragm, invisible to the human eye. But she couldn't find anything with which to make such holes.

So instead Yumi slipped into her pocket a partially used bottle of concealer, about three shades too dark for her own fair skin; a pair of daily-use contact lenses; and half a bottle of Ritalin. She checked her appearance—good—and, feeling much better than she had before entering the bathroom, rejoined the others.

". . . and that's when I realized that I wanted to go into education," Ariel of the big vagina was saying.

"Hey guys," Yumi said. Her hand was in her pocket. She was fingering the loose Ritalin.

"Hey lady!" said Ariel. "So what do you think?"

Yumi looked at Jay, who made an encouraging nod.

"I don't know," Yumi said. "I need to think about it. It's a bit on the pricier side."

"Oh," said Ariel, making a crying face, as if she really were sad about Yumi not being her roommate. Yumi wanted to jab her in the eye.

Jay lifted a finger at Ariel, apologetically, as if Yumi were a misbehaving child who just needed to be dealt with. He pulled her into the corner of the room.

"Yumi, this place is perfect! Close to campus, clean, and Ariel seems so cool. If it's a matter of rent, I can help you out for a couple of months . . ."

Yumi's expression softened. "Really?"

Jay put his hands on Yumi's waist. He really was handsome, Yumi thought. Cornflower blue and sunflower yellow.

"I meant what I said the other day," he whispered.

Yumi looked into his face and silently mouthed *I love you too.* He smiled. She smiled.

"But let's just see the last place before I decide, OK?" she asked. "There's only one more."

They walked back to Ariel, who had sat down on the couch/her bed.

"I may take the room," Yumi said, sweetly, "but can I confirm later tonight or tomorrow?"

"Sure," Ariel responded. "Take your time. I'll be here."

Yumi felt good as they were leaving Ariel's place. Yes, maybe she had a small problem. But it wasn't like she didn't know what she was doing. She could control herself. It was a choice. Sure, maybe not the nicest choice. But niceness only got you so far. And anyway, Yumi could be nice when she wanted. She could be the nicest girl on earth. Like how she was to Jay. Yumi squeezed Jay's hand. She was going to be nice, and happy, and easygoing for the rest of the day.

THE LAST APARTMENT was the most expensive, but only by a little; it came furnished and occupied a private floor on the ground level of a house in Davis Square. When they knocked, no one answered, so Yumi called the number on the listing.

"Hey, I'll be there in ten minutes. So sorry, I'm coming from across town. There's a key under the mat—just let yourself in." The landlord apologized a few more times before hanging up.

Jay found the key under the mat and opened the door. Before Yumi knew it, he'd picked her up in his arms like a baby and crossed the threshold. When he put her down, inside the doorway, he was smiling proudly.

"I've always wanted to do that," he said.

"I've never wanted to do that," Yumi replied. Jay's face fell, and Yumi realized that she was messing it up, ruining it all. "Just kidding," she added, laughing. "Look at your face."

A shadow of hurt ran through his eyes. Yumi ignored it and turned to look around. A small one-bedroom with a tiny kitchen along the wall. The window was lined with metal bars.

"This could be our place, together. What do you think?" She walked over to Jay, who was peering into the bedroom. She wrapped her arms around him and rested her head against the middle of his back. She used to hold Sven like that. "Our little place," she said.

Jay turned around and returned the hug. "You're mean sometimes, aren't you?" he asked, kissing her forehead.

Yumi looked down and shook her head. "I don't mean to be . . . I know, I'm not perfect. I'm sorry. I don't know why."

"It's OK," Jay said, after a moment. "I can take it."

Yumi smiled but made no reply. She bolted the front door and returned to Jay, pushing him gently into the bedroom.

THE TEN MINUTES was nearly up. Yumi and Jay put on their clothes. Yumi sat on the edge of the bare mattress, watching Jay lace up his shoes.

"I don't want to leave," she said. "I don't want to go back to campus. Maybe I'll just do everything virtual. Maybe we can just stay here for the rest of the year. Maybe we can just lie in bed all day and night and maybe even all summer. What do you think?"

Jay looked up from his shoes. Did he have to lace them up tight like that every single time? "I wish we could, Yumi."

"Then why not?" she asked. "Screw Harvard. Screw football. We don't need them."

"Maybe you don't."

"No! We could go away—far away. We work, we fuck, we live. We do things on our terms. Later, we can make some babies. Little pretty mixed babies. The prettiest babies in the world."

"And name them Susie and Tootsie and Mootsie," Jay said, laughing.

"Whatever you want!"

"California—I've never been to California."

"OK! California! Let's go! Let's go right now!"

A knock on the door. They both turned to look. The blurry outline of a woman in a dark coat could be seen through the frosted glass. "You guys in there? Did you turn the bolt?"

"No. Don't open it," Yumi whispered to Jay.

"Yumi, she knows we're in here."

"No," Yumi said. "No, no, just wait a bit. Let's see." She clung on to Jay's sleeve, preventing him from leaving the room.

Yumi and Jay sat there for a moment longer, as the landlord rapped on the door. "Hello? Hello?" Then Yumi's phone began to ring. She picked it up.

"Oh! So sorry. We were running the shower, checking the water pressure. Be right there!" she said in a bright voice. In that moment, to Yumi, the empty apartment with its bare floors and low ceiling, with its tiny kitchen, old fridge, and security windows—it felt like the last place on earth.

Jay pulled away from her and went to open the door.

Born with a Broken Heart

June 2037

I was born with a broken heart. One of the valves doesn't close all the way shut and so blood is continuously leaking from one side to the other. I only found out about it a few years back, after I fainted while delivering packages in the rain. Rainy days are always the busiest for deliveries. Nobody wants to go out if the streets are flooding, and there's always something that goes wrong: a package or an envelope soaks through, the food gets cold, the tarp covering you and your scooter starts to leak rainwater down your neck. People are also real assholes on rainy days. They're hungrier and angrier than usual. They call more often to check on the order status.

I fainted while running down the stairs of a six-story lane house on Wulumuqi Lu. The guy had ordered literally one bottle of water and one carrot. He opened his door a crack and took the bag, sunspotted arm clutching for the plastic like I was some kind of thief trying to get into his home. He slammed the door in my face. Not a word, not a murmur of thanks. I turned to head out for my next delivery. I was already running late.

I woke up on the landing between floors two and three. A granny was standing over me, holding a bag of wet garbage that was leaking onto my hand. It was either the stench of the garbage or the slime dripping into my palm that had woken me up. I vomited right away.

At the hospital the doctor told me I'd had a minor heart attack but that things were stable, and then he told me about the valve and asked if the condition was congenital. I didn't know. I couldn't say. I'd never had my heart checked. When I told the doctor that I was a delivery guy, he shook his head. "Is there anything else you can do?" he asked. "You're so young; you've got your twenties ahead of you. Take some risks." Maybe it was time to think about a career change. For my heart. When my mother visited me in the hospital a few days later, she told me that indeed there had been something going on with my heart when I was born. But I looked normal growing up, so she eventually forgot about it. We couldn't afford regular health checks anyway. I told her I was going to give up deliveries. "Fine," she said. She'd never been one to interfere with my life.

I wasn't exactly telling the whole truth to the doctor. Yes, I had been doing deliveries since I was eighteen, in addition to driving a taxi at night. It was stressful. Customers were shits. The rainy days and hot summers were dreadful. But there was something else putting pressure on my heart that I hadn't disclosed: I was involved in the night races.

The night races had been in the news a lot. Everyone knew about the masked drivers, but no one knew who they were. If I told the doctor that I was one of them, would he even believe me?

People had their theories. Stunt drivers for the movies, professional racers from Hong Kong, playboys competing for large sums of pocket money. They never guessed the real thing: a marketing ploy run by the car companies themselves, with racers plucked from the midnight garages on the edges of the city—where cabs went for off-hours maintenance and gas—and from private cars and delivery vans. Released CCTV footage of a Ferrari speeding through Shanghai in the early morning hours, slipping through a maze of streets like a silent eel, disappearing as if by magic . . . this was advertising gold to Ferrari. We made decent money racing their cars through the city. I'd saved a good chunk of change doing it too. But the stress was getting to me. I found myself short of breath at the end of a race, almost passed out, heart going like crazy.

In the night races, the key was to know where the traffic police liked to park. And then you also had to know where all the CCTVs were posted. You had to keep the license plate covered, you had to—in essence—stay invisible. The city, of course, had its blind spots. Not many, and fewer and fewer as the years went on. But you could speed down a highway and squeeze into a series of no-name lanes, rolling soundlessly through on neutral, then slip into a garage, abandon the car, change your hat and jacket, and walk back out into the night.

Someone was always waiting at the designated parking spot, to wipe the car down from top to bottom. We wore gloves and masks. No identifying DNA whatsoever. Sales of that model would jump that year. Every young, rich kid in Shanghai would be driving one. Even the masks and hats we wore would spike in sales. The masked driver effect, they called it. We weren't vigilantes, fighting crime. We were just professionals, selling cars.

But was it worth risking another heart attack? I called Li, my friend at the garage who had set me up with my first race. "I'm done," I told him. "I'm out of the game." I was decisive like that. I hung up the phone.

I quit deliveries and racing in one go and linked up with an agent who helped me get a private driving job. I enjoyed using my knowledge of the city's streets and shortcuts. I took it easy—never sped up, never cut others off. I had always been happiest behind the wheel.

I LEARNED HOW TO DRIVE in 2025, when the first self-driving cars were coming onto the market. All the car companies made proclamations: "2025 is the year of the self-driving car!" "Autonomous in 2025!" I was thirteen and I remember seeing all those statements in the news, feeling the urgency. My time was running out. See, I'd always wanted to drive. It was all those arcade racing games I played growing up; I was the best ranked in our neighborhood. It was the only thing I was ever any good at.

I spent a Saturday calling taxis, the cheapest option on all the apps. I made small trips along the Bund until I finally crawled into the back seat of a yellow Shanghai cab, old-school. Vinyl seat covers and seat belt buckles pushed deep into the seams, impossible to use. In front, beyond the scratched-up plastic barrier, sat an old man, his hands slack on the wheel. A stick shift. Next to him, a glass thermos of brown water with a layer of molted tea leaves floating on top.

"Nong hoa." I threw some Shanghai dialect his way.

"Hello, young man," he said back to me, in a downtown city accent, a mild and unhurried voice. He had a full head of white hair. He was wearing dress pants, ironed with sharp creases, a long-sleeved collared shirt. He was the kind of taxi driver I'd been waiting for.

I had him take me past the Bund to the other end of Suzhou Creek, to the shantytown, one of the last still standing back then. It was where I grew up, where I was born, and where I still sometimes visited our neighbor, old man Shi. (My parents had been given a new apartment in the city's outskirts, in Jiading.)

The shanty was being razed. It was mostly gone except for a small section in the corner where old man Shi held out in protest. He had no water, no electricity, not even glass in his windows. Just a shell of a house with tarped-up squares in the winter. Shi parked his scooter under a large tree next to his home. He'd hung a hammock from the tree's low branches and on sunny days he splayed out on it, shirtless. It was Shi who used to tell me stories about driving his truck across the country to deliver shipments of fruits and vegetables from one city to the next. He had a pack of trading cards with pictures of race cars on one side and facts about the cars on the other.

The razing was at a standstill because of him. The shanty was now, essentially, an open driving course. On our way there, I got to talking to the driver, Master Wang. I asked him how much he made for an hour driving around the city. Then I offered him the same if he'd spend an hour teaching me how to drive.

"How old are you, kid?"

I was tall and broad for my age. I told him I was sixteen. Master Wang took a good look at me in the rearview mirror, hands shifting gears all the while, and nodded.

We spent that hour driving loops around the razed neighborhood. We were driving over to the Fengs' old place. Then the Luos'. In the center had been the home of my childhood friend Ming Yi. He was now a line cook at a Western restaurant downtown. Old man Shi was away that afternoon. We drove circles around his house, and I looked into the empty doorway and windows.

I learned quickly. I loved being behind the wheel, controlling the route, seeing and then feeling the texture of the ground. Dirt bordered empty concrete foundation running up onto soft patches of grass. I loved the challenge of coordinating my feet and arms, the satisfying pushback of the stick as I shifted between gears.

Master Wang was getting ready to retire. I brokered a deal with him. I'd practice, get good, then drive his car all night, fill his gas, and give him 50 percent of the earnings. It was better than nothing, so he accepted.

I was just a kid—a stupid kid in an old night taxi, figuring out my driving style, learning about cars on my own. But no one calling a cheap taxi at three in the morning really looks at or questions the age of the driver. They're too drunk, too tired, or too in love to notice.

LATELY I HAVEN'T BEEN SLEEPING WELL. It started in the spring, when the family I've been driving for the past five years told me that their oldest daughter, Yumi, was preparing to move to the States for school. I felt like a father to that kid sometimes, or maybe an uncle, or maybe an older brother, given that Yumi and I were only seven years apart. The dreams started around then, and then the sleepless nights.

In one recurring dream, Yumi follows me around on a bicycle. It's the same bicycle her youngest sister used to have, the one I'd pack into the back of the van, along with her parents' and sisters' bikes. I'd take them to the elevated bike path in Pudong, which stretches along the river. There I'd park and watch the ferries going back and forth, until they called me to pick them up and take them back home. It was a pink bike, with streamers off the handles.

In the dream Yumi is eighteen already, as she is in real life, but still riding that kid's bike. And she is trailing behind me as I drive my old taxi. I watch her in my rearview mirror, but I have the feeling that I have to get away, get away fast. No matter how fast I go, though, I can't shake her. She stares at me through the mirror. She bares her teeth. She points at me, screaming words that I cannot hear and cannot decipher. The dream ends. I always wake up drenched in sweat.

Worse than the dreams are the visions I've started having. These began soon after the dreams. Yumi's face flashing in and out of my mind when I was in bed with Estelle. It got to the point where I couldn't make love anymore. I couldn't get things going right.

Estelle doesn't care so much. We've been together for three years. An older woman I met online, forty but in great shape, running a makeup import business on her own. We see each other mostly on the weekends, usually at her place, in a former airplane hangar on the old docks of the North Bund that's been sectioned off into expensive residences. Her apartment also serves as the warehouse for all her products. Huge walls, lofted bed, tall windows that she keeps half-closed most of the time because the sun would ruin all the bottles of lotion and toner and serum packed on shelves along the walls. She has everything you could imagine. The apartment is full of colors, like someone came in and spray-painted the room with a rainbow gun.

Her shippers come in once a day, at five in the evening, to box and label and prepare orders for automated pickup. In the mornings, Estelle makes videos of herself testing new products, applying makeup, experimenting with a hairdo. In the afternoons she does advertising, accounting, customer service. Estelle: capable, sexy, independent Estelle. Completely out of my league Estelle. My looks are the only thing I have going in my favor. And maybe the fact that I'm younger than her.

Estelle doesn't want to marry, and she doesn't want to have children. She just wants to grow her business. Lotions and bottles coming in, then going back out. Some time spent stacked and displayed on her shelves and then some time spent stacked on other women's shelves.

I go sneaking out at night, after Estelle is asleep. The bottles are glistening, the moonlight streaming in, making everything glimmer. I can't sleep well at her place. Too many things, too many colors, too many scents. I feel like my mind is swirling, sweeping along all the shiny, sparkling plastics and frosted glass and biodegradable packaging. It's like they're alive, trying to say something. A chorus of products—do they want to live, or do they want to die?

. . .

I STEPPED OUT into the heat of the hallway and down to the parking lot and into Master Wang's cab. I was holding on to the car for him. He'd retired but still let me drive. I didn't drive often; I didn't really need the money. But from the little I made from the cab, I still gave him his cut. The car smelled like him: mothballs and black tea. The gray seats had been wiped down so many times, they were hard as plastic.

At night there were barely any drivers on the road. Most of the cars I saw were autodrivers, going at the maximum speed. I turned off my vacancy sign and kept my eyes open, watching out for them. They were easy to spot. Autodrivers kept at a steady pace. I would accelerate toward them, pummeling ahead, foot heavy on the gas. I made a game of it. Speeding ahead, drifting to the left, to the right. Always, though, the cars would smoothly glide away, keeping about five meters' distance between us, like we were magnets set to repel one another. I kept thinking, *Maybe this time the car won't work, the system will break down.* The thought of a blip in the software kept me on edge. I liked moving the cars, like little pieces of a puzzle.

At some point, I started to close my eyes. Partly, I was tired. With the window cracked open, cool wind blasting onto my face, I looked out and saw a stretch of road ahead of me. I knew I could drive it for a few seconds if I kept my hands straight on the wheel. I did it once with my eyes closed, and then I kept doing it, for longer stretches. I saw in my mind's eye my car speeding along the highway, the autodrivers making way for me. I became one of them, like a robot myself, like one of those cars. I had the sensation of melting into the street, into the city. In fact, everything around me was liquefying, slow and thick, metallic, mercury.

I'd accelerate and get to where I was pressing the pedal of Master Wang's taxi until it was flat against the floorboard. On the elevated highway I'd go as fast as I could, counting the seconds with my eyes closed. Sometimes I imagined drift, collision, floating off into the sky, taking flight.

Of course, Yumi had a boyfriend. A good-looking kid named Sven. They held hands in the car. I took them to the mall. To movies. To restaurants. When he was seventeen, his family bought him a black Mustang convertible, shipped over from the States at great expense, as he liked to remind everyone.

Sven was always wanting to go out, to party, to be with other people. Yumi was, as I saw it, nearly identical to her mother. Quiet, reserved, poised. Pretty too. I knew she was studious, serious about her work. Yoko, the middle child, was like her father: science, math, robotics club on Wednesday nights. Then Kiko, bright, charming, theatrical; the dancer, the beloved.

Eko and Leo, the mother and father, seemed always to be teetering between one extreme and the other. Holding hands, Eko sitting on his lap at times, whispering to each other in French. I came close a few times to telling them: Go and get a room. On other days, a cold silence. Both of them staring out their windows. Or arguing, one-sidedly mostly, from Leo, in forceful French—always French between those two. An occasional cutting remark from Eko, in a sharp tone she never used with anyone else.

I once bought a French language course, curious to see if I might be able to follow along. But the language, its complex grammar, its sounds, eluded me. Japanese—the language between Eko and her daughters, and the secret language among the daughters when they wanted to bar their father—I had a better chance at. It was similar to Shanghai dialect in sound, with some overlap of words from Chinese. I could tell Leo felt excluded when his family went off in the language, though to my knowledge, he'd never made an effort to learn it. When the three girls were alone, they spoke in English.

I started learning Japanese by reading manga. It became my diversion, the way I spent my nights when not driving the cab or staying at Estelle's. I started out with shonen, studying the elementary kanji mixed with kana and parsing out, slowly, the story lines. Later, I graduated to seinen. *Ghost in the Shell*, *Tokyo Ghoul*.

I kept a notebook where I wrote down all the words I didn't recognize. I watched the movie or TV versions of the manga afterward, pausing after each line of dialogue to repeat what was said:

"All things change in a dynamic environment. Your effort to remain what you are is what limits you."

"There's nothing sadder than a puppet without a ghost."

"Can you offer me proof of your existence?"

YUMI AND SVEN CAME INTO THE CAR. They were talking. I usually try to keep my eye on the road, but inevitably I end up listening.

It's amazing what a driver learns. It's like the passengers forget you're there. They just keep talking. About themselves, one another, the staff. I have learned about every relationship between each of the family members, have learned the salaries and year-end bonuses of all the staff. I find I am the keeper of their secrets.

You're together with them in the same small metal box. But you've got your seat; they've got theirs. You've got to keep your face forward. You can sneak peeks, but not too many. A perceptive rider will notice the eyes wavering back and forth, in and out the rearview mirror. There's nothing more uncomfortable than meeting the gaze of your riders in that tiny window. Eyes on eyes, just the brows and the sockets and the tense, flickering balls, all magnified, curious, unwelcome.

You can't keep looking, even if they're having a good time and you also want to laugh and smile. You can't keep looking, though the kids are cute, and then sweet, and then pretty. You can only say hello and take a passing glance at an outfit, a tight shirt, a painfully short skirt. Meet the young lady's gaze in the mirror and you're going to see she's been staring. Why?

The reaction in your pants—you breathe calmly. It had better go down by the time you get to your destination, open the door, open the trunk. You think about the route. Can you take the extra turn, go slowly down the lane? Traffic on Nanjing East—perfect. Road conditions, work in progress—great, try to focus. By the time you arrive you've done it, you've deflated, you've settled back into your separate spaces.

Sven and Yumi were arguing. I felt instantly agitated. Whatever their little lovers' quarrel was about, I was ready to be on Yumi's defense. That was the hardest thing for me—when I knew the answer to a question they had, or when I was convinced that with just a single word I could help them understand each other. Still, I had to remain silent. It wasn't my place to act as counselor between them.

"I don't think it's a good idea, Sven," Yumi was saying. "What about your university acceptance? They could rescind it. What if you got a criminal record? Or, God forbid, jail time?"

"I'm not going to jail," Sven said. "I've got diplomatic immunity."

Sven's father was the Russian ambassador to China. His mother, an incredibly tall Swedish woman, worked at an art gallery downtown. Yumi and Sven often went to openings there where they drank too much free wine and called me after hours to pick them up and take them home.

"Ōbaka," Yumi said quietly to herself. "Anata wa hontōni watashi o aishite inaiyone?" She knew full well that Sven didn't understand. I wanted to tell her, I wanted to scream: *No, Yumi, he doesn't love you!*

"You're risking everything," she said more loudly. "What about this summer? What about us?"

"You know what my dad always says about cutting me off after I'm in college," Sven said. "Yumi, this way we can make it work. This way I can fly out to see you on school breaks. California to Boston. I can fly you out to Cali sometimes too."

I knew it was over. Yumi was soft, like her mother. Their men got away with everything.

"When is it?"

"This weekend. A couple of people dropped out of the race, and Eric told me about it just yesterday. I can take a spot. It's entry-level. If I place in the top two, there's the prize money, but also I can go on to future races. It's a whole thing. Imagine what I can make all summer."

"And you're driving your own car?"

"No, they provide the cars."

"But how will you be able to drive someone else's car?"

"I can drive a Mustang, same make."

I listened to them from the front seat. My heart was beating wildly in my chest. Not only because I felt a sense of outrage on behalf of Yumi, who was not getting her way. But also because I felt that old stirring, the desire to race, blossoming in me again. It was addiction, I suppose, how some people feel about gambling.

I dropped them off at Yumi's house and looked at the clock. I still had half an hour left before I had to pick up Kiko from her piano lesson. I called my friend Li on an encrypted line. I hadn't talked to him in almost five years.

"So how's the driver's life?" he asked me.

"It's slow," I said.

"I bet. You got yourself one of those Buicks?"

"Mercedes."

"Not bad. I'd like to see you do a burnout on one of those babies."

"You still managing?"

Li acted as the go-between for the drivers and the car companies.

"You bet I am. There's a race this weekend. You want in? Amateur, wild card, a couple drivers dropped out last minute, afraid of the press. I've been poking around, looking for a backup. But, you know, I never would have thought about asking you."

"Yeah, because I told you . . ."

"That you'd never race again."

"But I'm interested. What's the course?"

"You know I can't say until the day of the race."

"Right. Rules are the same, then? Prize money?"

"Rules are a little different. Things have changed since your last race, my friend. Cops are fewer since more autodrivers came onto the scene, but CCTVs are everywhere. Facial recognition is amazing. You've got to cover your entire face now. We'll provide the suits."

"So, better tech. The prize money?"

"The same, five hundred thousand, on top of the fifty."

Racing always reminded me of the arcade games from my childhood, my friends crowding behind me because I was about to beat the high score, my previous high score. The arcade wasn't really an arcade so much as a collection of three old games that had been thrown away and left to rot in the back corner of the shanty. We kids put a broken tin roof over the games and ran electricity through an extra-long extension cord we plugged in at Chen's house. His mom would unplug it when she came home after work, screaming at us about wasting electricity and hitting us over the head with her rags.

I sometimes thought about life as a video game. Shanghai was the location, and I was slowly leveling up. I started out with the night taxi, figuring out how to drive, learning where everything was in this city. Then I got onto the delivery scooter, and every successful delivery within the time limit was a gold coin, a ping, an advance. Then, weaving in and out of the city traffic, getting the girls to school, to all their activities. The races, the big money, the thrill of doing something illegal. The next level, though?

What was the next level for me? A life with Estelle—surrounded by tubs and bottles of gels and creams?

There was only going forward. I'd heard from my friends recently that old man Shi had passed away in his empty house. It took two days for his body to be found. Construction on a new shopping mall had begun the next day. The shanty was gone now.

The night of the race, I drank coffee all evening to keep my energy up. I hadn't slept well in months, but I knew that once I started driving my adrenaline would take over. I tried not to think of my heart. It was going to last as long as it was going to last. My palpitations had started to come back of late. The only thing that cured them was to keep my heart beating fast, so fast that it wouldn't dare skip a beat. Driving at night, accelerating, that was the only thing that fixed things up. I pulled a hat low over my eyes and left my apartment, taking a winding route down into the subway, walking out at the densely crowded People's Square station, and changing into another set of clothes in the public bathroom. When I exited the station, I was hit by a wall of humidity so thick I had to take a few breaths before moving. The sky had become a dark purple gray that could mean only one thing: an imminent downpour, heat lightning, flooded sewers, the works. I got into a small jitney on the back of a scooter and told the driver to step on it. We stopped in front of a warehouse on the North Bund. Inside, it was filled with shipping containers.

After a few handshakes I put on all my clothes and gear, got into the Ferrari, and turned her on. I sank into her seat and got acquainted with the machinery: adjusted the seat back and tweaked the rearview mirrors, felt the tension in her pedals, absorbed the weight of the wheel. She was beautiful—matte black, sleek, gorgeous. In camouflage, dark against the night. The other drivers were already in their cars, also black: a Porsche, a Lamborghini, and the Mustang. I saw the slight figure of a woman inside the Porsche, her delicate gloved fingers on the wheel. We were all fitted with intercom earbuds by our handlers. "In case you need to communicate," Li said. "Cops, whatever." Then, just before go time, Li bent down to my open window and said one thing: "Sanjia Port." The wide warehouse door slid open.

I laughed. Sven would have no idea where that was. Just north of the airport, near a string of second-rate beach resorts, sand that had been reclaimed from the ocean. He'd spend a minute plugging the place into his GPS. I knew I'd head south along the river, and then take the spiraling road up to the Nanpu Bridge to pass across Pudong. I was already on my way.

I kept to the water, the river dark and smooth and luckily at low tide, the angry clouds above reflecting off the glass and metal office compounds on my right. The sky was a blur of motion; the buildings had become melting pillars of aluminum. I heard the roar of the Lambo just behind me, and the Porsche, the woman, was slightly ahead. Sven was behind us all. We passed the Russian consulate general, and we all made our way to the Garden Bridge.

The Garden Bridge was three lanes wide, two heading south and one heading north. I was tailing the woman, and we got onto the bridge in the two south lanes. I was feeling good. The Lambo was edging forward in the north-facing lane, but an autodriver was coming straight on into its path. One of them would have to move aside. The autodriver was edging left and right, unsure what to do in the high-speed, narrow situation. Eventually its brakes turned on, stopping it before we passed. There was just enough room for the Lambo to squeeze through behind us and the auto. But I heard a screech of metal and saw the Lambo spinning out and crashing into the side of the bridge. "Fuck, shit," we heard over the intercom. I looked in my rearview mirror to watch it happen. And that's when I saw Yumi.

She was standing on the pedestrian walkway on the opposite side of the wreck. I was confused. Had Sven told her to wait there, asked her to come out and support him? Or maybe she had come out on her own, waiting on the bridge for a glimpse of him, for a glimpse of the Mustang? What was she thinking? Was she OK? I had the urge to turn around, drive back onto the bridge, whip off my mask—even to open the door and pull her into the car. Maybe to take her home.

I wavered. Would I be doing it out of subservience to the family, my own goodwill, my affection for Yumi, something else? And then reason kicked in. How could Yumi even know the destination, much less our route? No. It couldn't be her. I tore my eyes away from the mirror. It was just a girl, any girl. I resisted the urge to glance back at the bridge, growing farther and farther away by the second. Every flicker of the eye, every breath, every look back or to the side or around was energy that took you out of the race. The Porsche was pulling farther ahead. Sven was far behind. Maybe he'd slowed down on the bridge, thinking he'd seen her, too, thinking he'd make up the time later. He didn't know that you never got to make up the time later.

I pulled onto the wide avenue of the Bund. The Porsche tried to cut me off on the left and I moved right. She pulled away suddenly, and I saw that I was in line with a lion statue, one of many guarding the buildings along the road. I passed through the narrow opening between the lion and the curb, slowing down.

Who did the woman think I was? Who was she? I would never know. She might be attractive. She might be old. She might be a private driver, like me. She could even be Estelle. What did I know about Estelle, anyway? We led our own lives, mostly, meeting on the weekends or in the evenings. Tonight, though, we drivers were all sexy, superhuman, in our masks and suits and cars.

I followed her past the imposing buildings of the Peninsula, the Roosevelt. Then a cop on motorcycle pulled out of the alley between the Fairmont and the Peace Hotel and banked right, following the Porsche. Change of plan—I pulled away from the water to head inland, onto Nanjing East, usually blocked off for pedestrians only. In my rearview mirror, the Huangpu receded, and I saw a flash of lightning in the reflection. Still, the rain held off.

I sped down the walkway, shifting gears. Past the shops, the neon signs, the lights, as the skyline of Pudong and the water receded in my rearview mirror. A few people were walking in pairs, pointing at me as I flashed by. A trio of young men, all in chef's hats and white outfits, started cheering. A homeless man pulled out a phone to take photos. Old-fashioned red trolley cars were parked in the middle of the street. I weaved through them, for fun. At the end of the pedestrian walkway, I exited onto the Bund's web of backstreets. No sign of the Porsche, or of Sven.

Beyond the facade of the historic buildings are streets not snapped to a grid, streets crisscrossing like God threw a heap of soy-fried noodles onto the floor and mapped out Shanghai in their image. Behind the perfect veneer of the Bund, its banks and hotels, are the winding alleyways rich with cheap restaurants. The city opens its mouth, yawning with a steaming savory night breath.

I pulled back onto the Bund and saw that something was different. Several race cars had joined us, though they were not black. They were yellow, red, and pink.

"What is this?" I asked into the intercom.

"It's a joke," said the woman's voice, low and mean. "They want to be us."

People had been waiting for another race for a long time. There had been, ever since we began, copycats, self-started races, put on by underground organizations, nothing with the complicated level of corporate sponsorship that we had. They were easily broken up, easily fined, detained, these people who didn't know the right kind of masks to wear, didn't know how to stay off the roads with multiple CCTVs. They did it for fun. Because they could. They liked the big boulevards with the bright lights and pedestrian traffic: Nanjing Lu, Wukang Lu, the Bund. We were bumping up against one such amateur race now.

A Maserati pulled up to my left and rolled down the window. "Jia you!" he shouted. I revved the engine and pulled away, the Porsche nowhere in sight. Another Ferrari pulled up on my right. The man pulled off his hat and screamed over the engines: "Who are you, man? Just tell me, between the two of us!" I waved him away. They were interfering; I was going to lose. "Fuck them, right!" he yelled, as I pulled ahead. "I got your back!"

A street race requires, above all, familiarity with the streets. So the best drivers would be delivery guys, private drivers, cab drivers. Young, rich guys with collector's cars who drove pretty girls along crowded roads to restaurants in Xintiandi—these were not the competition.

I swerved by a few autodrivers. In my rearview mirror, Sven was catching up.

. . .

I HEARD THE BLAST OF A SIREN; there were police cars behind us, but they sounded far away. I was almost at the Nanpu Bridge. It would soon be over. And just like that, I switched into a feeling of clarity. Everything around me became sharper, brighter. It was as if time were slowing down and I could see everything with extreme focus.

I pulled into the left lane and then crossed over the double yellow line. I was now facing the oncoming traffic. At night the autodrivers were fast, speeding along the Bund. I went straight down the middle of the road. The cars veered off automatically to make room for me. I felt like a knife cutting through a leek, splitting it in half lengthwise as it flowered open. Like choreography.

Then I heard Sven's voice on the intercom: "You've got to help, my car is going crazy!" He was flashing his lights at me from his lane. I watched from my rearview as the Mustang swerved left and right.

As the cars spread away from me, I imagined a world without Sven. Yumi without Sven. Without Yumi rubbing Sven's hand under her thumb in the back seat of the van, without Yumi's upcoming trip to Russia over the summer, the flights to California come fall. An eventual marriage. The hot and cold. She didn't deserve that. I didn't want to help him; I wanted to go for the money prize. But I also did not want him to be the one caught by the cops, to be known the world over as a masked driver, revealed.

I slowed down. I reversed back to his car, rolled down my window. "What's wrong, kid?"

And without a word, Sven laughed and accelerated past me.

That little sneak. I went after him. My heart was in my teeth. No, it was beating in my eyes. I was so angry I could barely feel my hands on the wheel. I was so angry I was having an almost out-of-body experience. Instead of seeing him directly ahead of me, hearing his laughter on the intercom, I was seeing myself now from a distance. Like I was sitting once more in the old arcade, the wheel dismembered from the car, the street flashing between the driver's view and bird's-eye view.

I was taking Yumi to school on my first day of work. No, I was hitting delivery targets on my old scooter. No, I was thirteen years old again, learning how to drive. No, I was ten and beating my own high score. I could hear my friends cheering me on, screaming. I would do anything for the win. Old man Shi would be relaxing in his hammock, cigarette dangling from his lips, eyes closed as if in sleep, but when I came near, he'd say, "You're number one, kid."

I approached the Nanpu Bridge at 240 kilometers an hour. The thunder was loud and close now, its growl penetrating past the roar of the engine. The rain would come down at any moment, as fast and as dark as the close of a curtain, the show's final act. It would hide us; it would protect us. I pulled the wheel sharply to the left, my car skidding with the effort, as I climbed up to where Sven was. I bumped his car, hard, and took us faster up the spiral of the road. Higher and higher, twisting up in a tight coil to the entrance of the bridge. In this state I felt I was spinning up forever, into the sky, into the clouds, ready to break. I closed my eyes for one second. Then another two. Every one of my movements was slow and precise. I was weightless, easy, one with the car, the street, the city.

Flash

August 2035

The summers were getting hotter and hotter in Shanghai—well, they were getting hotter everywhere. It was nearly impossible to go out midday; the girls spent long hours at the club, underwater and poolside. Tonight, another heat storm was brewing. What was it in the air? Static, atmosphere, humidity? Whatever it was, the night was heavy, full of it.

Eko and Leo lay in bed. Outside the window, thunder groaned close and then far. Lightning cracked its whip. They'd opened all the curtains and turned off the lights to watch the show outside. Cold air was blasting out from the vents, directly onto Eko's body. She was wearing nothing but underwear, the blanket tangled between her legs. She couldn't get cool.

"The spiders are really going to be flying tonight," she said.

Years ago, during another heat storm just like this one, the girls had all run into their room, their bed, screaming and insisting on protection from the thunder. Leo loved nights like that, everyone crowded in, the girls loud and dramatic and clinging on to him tight. He laughed and opened all the curtains, and they counted the seconds between the lightning and the thunder. Leo could make anything fun. His confidence was infinite, magnetic.

Leo found a documentary about lightning as energy being zapped into the earth, and how spiders use that energy, diffusing back into the air, as tail winds, to fly, even across oceans. The girls watched the screen intently as the lightning struck around them. At one point it flashed so close to the windows that the building shook in response. A tree just outside their building, a tall palm, had been seared, sawed into a steaming black stalk.

"Lightning never strikes the same place twice," Eko said, stroking the girls' hair, in an attempt at reassurance.

Yoko stared outside, her face pressed up against the glass, despite Eko's entreaties to step away. Yumi was telling Kiko how everyone eats spiders when they sleep. Kiko responded that she was going to tape up her mouth every night, so spiders could never get in.

Tonight, though, Eko heard nothing from the girls' rooms. No pitter-patter of footsteps. They were no longer afraid. She placed a hand gingerly on Leo's chest, then hopped it up onto the tip of his nose.

"What are you doing?" he asked.

"It's a spider. Trying to fly into your mouth," she said. "He's energized by the lightning."

Leo put his tablet down and gave her a glance. The glance said: *There you go, being you again.* Still, it was not a bad glance, but rather a loving one. She had taken her chance. He turned toward her, quickly, sneakily tweaking her left nipple with his fingers, and using the pad of his thumb to flatten a bead of sweat dripping from her neck to her chest. A clap of lightning illuminated the room.

In that moment, Eko saw him, muscular, erect, moving to get onto his hands and knees. On his face the focused grin she had seen so many times, over so many years, that always meant the same, simple, reliable thing.

At forty-five, she was fit and attractive. He did not say it freely, and so she sometimes asked and he answered—but in any case she knew, and sometimes she found him staring at her from across the room. He was handsome too. He had kept his hair, his wide shoulders, his fine shape.

Her heart felt hot, was racing. Another bead of sweat dripped down her face. He licked it away. His hand was pulling off her underwear, gauging her readiness. She felt charged. A curl of thunder, far away.

His head traveled down, his tongue exploring. Eko closed her eyes. She listened to the rain that had begun to rush outside. She ventured a look to the window: water beat down against it in gusty waves. There would be another flood. She would have to check if school tomorrow was virtual. She would have to remind the driver to change to the mud tires. She wondered if all the windows in the house were closed. But Eko decided to ignore that train of thought. She shut off her mind.

He entered, and somehow there was a burst of pain. But before she could gasp, his lips were on hers. She tasted herself. Leo kissed like it was the last kiss on earth. He'd always kissed like that, heavy, wet. No matter what—the rising heat, the summer storms—there would always be this.

Ponies on the Mountain in the City on the Sea

May 2034

On weekends Yumi practiced her survival skills. On the family property a half hour outside Shanghai center, Dad made her and Yoko and Kiko chop wood, light fires, construct rudimentary weapons, and hunt small game. With Mom they studied plants and farming and how to bake bread in the wood-fired oven.

Yumi was good at farming. Yoko was good at trapping. Kiko was good at making clothes. Well, she wasn't *good*. She just made really cool designs. Kiko and Mom could spend all day sewing while the others were out on the land or in the woods. They made beautiful stuff—pants of green patchwork embroidered with vines crawling up the legs, shirts of leather and fur.

The house was surrounded by the forest of a small park, on a mountain and near a lake. After Dad bought the plot of land, they spent six months building the house, planning a garden.

Everyone had to play their part. That was what he said all the time. They had to build the house together—that was the important thing, the entire point. So they spent their weekends for the better part of a year chopping, sanding, planting, hammering alongside the construction crew. They broke land after the Lunar New Year and were ready to move in by the fall.

Yumi hated those weekends. She wanted to go to parties with her friends. She wanted to spend time by herself. She was a teenager now, and life happened on the weekends. Yoko turned down most of her party invitations, but she never cared so much about friends and things like that anyway. Kiko, still a kid, was happy on the farm.

Mom and Dad fought a lot when they came out to the farm. Mom didn't like it; after all, it was *his* pet project, they were *his* paranoias. Dad just dragged everyone along for the ride, like always.

In protest, Mom did as little as possible. She helped cook and clean, but anything related to survival that she did not like—trapping, camping, building fires—she stayed away from. Some weekends she didn't even come. Those weekends were spent with Dad, eating grilled cheese sandwiches for every meal. He wanted to make a game, a project, out of everything. *Let's farm! Let's go for a ride! Let's practice hunting with our bows and arrows!* It was exhausting. And when they came back to the house, he took his shower and retreated to his corner—near the fire—with a big book. Yumi was left to do all the cleaning, make sure the girls were warm and dry and had a snack. Yumi got the starter going and made a hot loaf of bread. Yumi fixed the satellite connection and put on a movie for Kiko. Yumi much preferred it when Mom came along, but not when her parents fought all day. That was the worst.

This weekend, Yumi was packing her bags. She was going to get away from the fighting. Under her folded clothes and lighter and knife and water filter, she placed the small black SIG Sauer. Dad had purchased two of them on the black market, through a friend who had a connection to the factory where parts were made in Guangzhou. The girls weren't allowed to touch them, though Dad had taught Yumi how to shoot when she turned fifteen.

"Where are you going?" Yoko was standing in the doorway, watching her older sister.

"I'm taking Hayami for a ride," Yumi said.

"Why are you packing so much?"

Yumi stared at Yoko. Yoko stared back; then she was looking at the folded-up tent in her sister's hands. The sound of a plate crashing against the floor rang from downstairs.

"How long are you going to be away?" Yoko asked.

"I don't know. However long it takes."

"For what?"

"For them to stop fighting," Yumi said. She spoke without adding *idiot* at the end, but it was there.

"They're not fighting about you," Yoko said.

"So what?"

"So you leaving won't fix their problem."

"Still, maybe they'll stop," Yumi tried. "When they see I'm gone."

"That's not logical. I don't get your reasoning."

"You don't have to. Just don't tell them anything."

"I'm coming with you," Yoko said.

"I thought you didn't get my reasoning," Yumi shot back.

"I have my own reasons."

"Yeah? And they are?"

"I'd rather be out in the woods than trapped at home, listening to that all weekend."

"OK." Yumi didn't know what better to say.

"See? That's logical."

"Whatever. I'm leaving in ten minutes."

"Where are you guys going?" Kiko was standing in the doorway, holding her cat, Doris. Doris was a ragdoll they'd got from a breeder on Kiko's birthday four years before. She lived on the farm, due to Yoko's cat allergies.

"Baby, we're gonna take the ponies out for a ride."

"I want to come," Kiko said.

"Kiks, you can't ride Lucy well enough yet," Yumi said.

"I can so! I had her out all day last weekend with Daddy. I'm good with her now. She listens now."

"Kiks, it's better if you stay at home," Yumi said, in her voice that meant the conversation was over.

"I don't want to stay home. I want to go with you guys."

"No, Baby. You can't," Yoko said.

"Why? And don't call me Baby and think you can just tell me what I can and cannot do."

"Just—you can't, Kiks. We'll be back later," Yumi said.

"I hate you! I hate both of you!" Kiko ran out of the room and down the stairs.

Another plate crashed in the kitchen. Yumi and Yoko paused, listening to the sounds below. They would not end anytime soon. Mom would make a simple dinner and leave it on the table, Dad trailing her all the while, talking, talking, angry. And then they would disappear into their room. There would be shouting and screaming and Dad's loud voice booming through the house. He could go on all day. Then the entire weekend would be ruined—silent, tense. Dad brooding in his corner, taking Py out for long rides. Mom would be better, would be nice to them, but pretend nice, pretend happy, her lips always ready to tremble. Yumi hated that tremble.

"Two minutes. I'm leaving through the hatch."

"I'll be quick."

YOKO RAN TO THE CLOSET and stuffed socks, underwear, and a raincoat into a bag.

The girls had one big room. The luxury of separate spaces wasn't realistic in a postapocalyptic world, Dad said. And anyway, it was better for bonding. Since they were all so busy during the week, and so different. The girls' room was the entire second floor of the house. Three beds in three corners, and a large teepee in the fourth. Books, toys, dresses, and makeup everywhere, despite their father's insistence on survival minimalism.

Under Yumi's bed was a hatch that led to a slide, which passed through the house's thick walls and down into the family's underground bunker. At the bottom of the slide was a door with a combination code: 252525. *Yumi*, *Yoko*, *Yukiko*. The door opened into a passageway that extended to the far corner of the property.

The idea was that if something happened and the house was invaded, they could grab their horses and run away—or they could stay underground, periodically emerging to harvest vegetables. There was a camera system attached to the sprinkler system.

A robot with a night-vision camera was capable of digging up roots and picking vegetables in the dark. In the stables were packs of food, water, and camping gear hidden under the riding supplies, the grooming equipment.

"I'm ready," Yoko said. She'd put on jeans, boots, and a hat, and had a backpack in her hand.

Yumi nodded and slowly, soundlessly, pushed her bed away from its spot. She folded the pink rug aside and located the loose floorboard. She unlatched the bolt and pulled the hatch open—just like they practiced on the last Saturday of every month.

"Dad is going to be pissed."

"I don't care," Yumi said. And she slipped into the hole.

Yoko balanced on the ledge just inside the slide and shut the hatch above her head. Then she pushed off and slid through the wall, down into the underground tunnel. Yumi was ahead, turning on one of the flashlights they kept in a pile at the bottom of the slide.

"Let's go," she said, working the combination lock. The door popped open and they walked through the rest of the tunnel until they got to the ladder and climbed up, up, up. The hatch let out onto an empty stall in the stables, beneath a pile of hay, and Yumi cleared it away while climbing up and out. Then she started laughing. Yoko climbed out and saw what was so funny—Kiko in the stable, already dressed in her riding gear. Lucy was wearing her saddle.

"Took you guys long enough," Kiko said.

"OK, Baby. A for effort. You can come."

Yumi and Yoko saddled up and the three of them rode out toward the forest, keeping the stables right in the line of sight between them and the house.

"Keep up, Baby, or you can go back home," Yumi said. They disappeared into the line of trees.

The forest was like a vacuum. As soon as they entered, they were surrounded by cool silence and darkness. And they each felt, to their varying degrees, relief at leaving home and the fear of moving forward.

But leaving they were. The ponies were excited. The girls never went out without their father and Py, who was now left alone with the old workhorse in the stables. Even Hayami, Raven, and Lucy knew that today was special. Yumi's Hayami took the lead particularly well. She was a chestnut mare who was getting too small for her rider's tall frame, but who had acquired all her rider's oversize conceit. Raven, so dark she was nearly purple, was Yoko's pony. Kiko's Lucy was white with gray spots. Lucy was the old girl, coddled and nicknamed Rainbow Baby. Kiko put Lucy's coarse hair into many tiny braids that she then adorned with rainbow-colored beads.

The two younger girls were on 12.2 ponies. Yumi was on her 14.2, but she was ready for a full-size, and Dad sometimes let her onto Py. They weren't allowed to go into the forest on their own. Dad forbade it. When they did go, with him, they had to practice their navigation. Or foraging—on the days their mother went with them, riding with Dad on Py's broad back, her slight body curved up against his. It was the one thing on the farm that Mom was interested in: collecting plants, berries, roots, mushrooms. In the kitchen were stacks of Japanese and Chinese and French books on the art of foraging. For the farmhouse, she designed intricate embroideries of the edible plants in their forest and hung them on the kitchen walls. Or she glued small magnets to the backs and arranged them on the fridge, the dishwasher.

"I want to go over the mountain," Yumi said.

"They're not going to look for us there," Yoko said.

"That's not our property," Kiko said.

"So?" Yumi kicked Hayami and led her deeper into the forest. The path was lined with bamboo on either side, the leaves whispering to one another as the girls moved forward. The path was paved, and for a while the only sound was that of the horses' shoes clomping against stone.

The girls had ridden the path numerous times. With their father, they went up into the forest, onto the mountain, around the park. *Beyond the park is a pair of small hotels. Pass those and get to the stream. Follow the water, and stay away from strangers. From there, find the small boat docked on the Huangpu River.* That was the plan—that was their meeting point. In case they needed to leave the city, the country, in case they were separated in the chaos of catastrophe. Once on the Huangpu, they could pick up their big sailboat parked up north, then make their way to the ocean, out to the East China Sea, to the small island in the middle of the Pacific.

The truth was that their father had bought a majority share in a hotel. Their house, their farm, their stable, their chicken coop were all built on its grounds, and during the week the hotel staff attended to the family's animals, watered and fertilized the crops, brushed and washed the horses.

The hotel grounds comprised the south side of the low mountain. Another private residence sat at its very top. The girls stayed away from the north face, the one for the public, with hiking trails filled by city folk like themselves, getting away for the weekends. On very hot days, the girls walked over to the hotel, where all the staff knew them, where they were served free mocktails at the bar, and where they spent hours swimming in the pool. When their father complained about Yumi spending too much time at the hotel, she would reply, "If you don't want us to use a hotel, then don't buy us a hotel."

By the time Yumi was fifteen, she was used to being watched at the pool, by the young men who cooked, cleaned, and served her virgin cocktails. Yumi put on her bikinis, made a show of slathering sunblock all over her very pale body. She helped her sisters with their application. Yoko read books in the shade. Kiko preened like her oldest sister, wearing sunglasses and sipping drinks, and she never said a word to Mom or Dad when Yumi went to the bathroom for fifteen, twenty minutes at a time, disappearing with a hotel staffer or a stableboy.

In the pool, Yumi floated, staring up at the sky. The floating was what had made her fall in love with swimming, the feeling of being held, submerged, voices muted. In physics she'd learned about the weight of water. She was surprised to discover that such a thin thing, accumulated, could become so heavy. She calculated that the pool at the hotel was likely thirty tons of water. An elephant weighed five tons. She imagined six elephants, stacked on top of one another, filling the pool. She was swimming through elephants. She was floating on the backs of elephants.

Kiko was in thrall to Yumi. She was also a little bit scared of her. Yumi could be anything at the flip of a switch—demure and polite, charming and funny, hideously cruel—sometimes all in the span of an hour.

Yoko, who for too many years had borne the brunt of Yumi's wrath, now kept a distance from her older sister, when she could. But there were times, when Yumi was being nice, confessional, that she found herself drawn back in, her heart and hopes opening up, only to be inevitably crushed.

Yumi led them up the mountain, along the path that eventually hit the fence, where a sign read: *Private Property, Keep Out*. When they got there, she unlatched the gate and held it open as the other girls went through. They waited for her to close it, and she took her place out front once again. There was no more paved path, no more wall of bamboo to the left and right. They were alone now, on the real mountain.

"Let's go to the house on the top," Kiko said. She was obsessed with that house. As they drove up toward the farm each weekend, Kiko pointed it out: "The house!" Or maybe: "I'm going to live there someday. You can visit me if you're nice to me." Or, once, "I think it's a haunted house."

"But people probably live there," Yoko said. "We can't just barge in."

"No one lives there," Yumi said. "It's empty."

"How do you know?"

"I went up there once."

"With whom?"

"By myself. Why do you care?"

"Yeah, right."

"We can go. I know the way."

"I want to go!" Kiko shouted, bouncing up and down on Lucy. Lucy was an old girl, and she was used to Baby Kiko's antics, the unexpected bursts of laughter, shrieks, cries, kicks to the belly. Lucy tolerated being ridden so, as she walked smoothly, unperturbed, through and toward the end of her life.

"We'll play at the house, and if we want, we can set up camp in there," Yumi said.

"That's breaking and entering," Yoko said. But she was talking to herself, again.

"I think the house will be amazing," Kiko started. And she went on, for a long while, about all the things she imagined would be inside: a pond full of frogs in the main entryway; a spiraling stone staircase fit for a princess (or three!); chandeliers coated with dust and cobwebs; a family of cats and a family of dogs; rooms full of grand clothes, hats as wide as ceiling fans, walls lined with shoes; a pool painted emerald green on the bottom, now filled with ducks and fish and ferns; and—oh—the basement. She didn't even want to say. She couldn't bring herself to imagine it. No one would ever make her go down there. There were unspeakable things.

Despite themselves, Yumi and Yoko smiled, then laughed along. It felt like the time before—before Yumi had gone off to middle school and grown up, grown out of them. When they would all three get in their mother's Jacuzzi bathtub and play and slip and make bubble-foam bikinis that covered their flat childnesses, their nothings.

"How long are we going to stay out here?" Yoko asked. She looked up at the darkening sky.

"Do you like the farm? Do you want to keep coming here every weekend?" Yumi asked.

"I don't know. It's not so bad," Yoko said.

"Come on. It's the worst. No one likes it except Dad. Mom hates it. I hate it. Kiks, do you hate it?"

"Yeah, I hate it," said Kiko dutifully.

"No, you don't," Yoko said. "You like it here. You like the animals. You like making all those clothes with Mom."

"No, I hate it. You have a hearing problem?"

"Yoko has more than a hearing problem," Yumi said.

"You want to come every weekend, Baby," Yoko continued. "You have your bag packed and ready every Friday. You're the one who still wants board game night on Saturdays."

"Well, that was before," Kiko said.

"Before what?"

"Before I said so just now."

"You mean before Yumi said so. You're a follower. And a brat. And worst of all, you're a liar."

"I am not."

"You are. And I can't stand it."

"I can't stand your face."

"My face looks just like your face, idiot. I hate your stupid tap dancing. It sucks."

"OK. Shut up, Yoko," Yumi said. "I don't know how long we'll stay out here. We'll go back when we get bored, or if it rains or something. But we have to get our point across. We shouldn't have to be here if we don't want to be."

"*You* don't like the farm. This is stupid. I'm going back," Yoko said.

Yoko turned Raven around and started down the trail. But once she was out of sight of her sisters, she got off and hitched Raven to a tree. The sun had set and the way back was less clear now than it had been when they left. She was confident of her navigational skills. But in the dark?

Yoko took out a few carrots from her saddlebag and fed them to Raven. She rested her head against her pony's warm neck and felt the silky hair. Raven was more a sister to her than both her real sisters, combined. She spent more time hating them, envying them, judging them, fighting them, than she did enjoying her time with them. But her mind, above and beyond anything else, was rational, logical. Her chances of getting lost were not low. And she would be alone. With her sisters, at least, she would have safety in numbers.

"We have to go back, Ravey," she said into the horse's neck. "We don't want to, but we must." And she untied the rope from the tree and hopped on, steering her straight back.

YUMI AND KIKO SAID NOTHING as Yoko reappeared. Their silence held reproach and gratitude, relief and fear. They all felt it and understood one another, without a word exchanged. They rode until they were tired and their horses were slowing down. They let the ponies drink from a small stream and found a clearing to make a fire.

Yumi felt, in the quiet, the presence of Eko—she imagined her mother sanctioning this rebellion. At other times, Yumi experienced a certainty that their mother had died and left them. It was a recurring dream, a nightmare. Yumi looked just like her mother, almost an exact replica. They had the same thick, long hair. The same straight nose, the same black eyes. The same delicate lips. They were the color of chalk, a white that looked as if it might blow away like powder. The only difference was that Eko freckled in the summer, a trait that sometimes made mother look even younger than daughter. At any other time, Yumi had the funny sensation of looking in a mirror when she looked at her mom.

Maybe it was because she looked so like her mother that she felt she understood all her pain, all her frustration, all her stifled arguments with Dad, as if they were her own. Why did she tolerate it? And there were, too, words addressed by her father to Yumi, as well. *Yumi, you need to speak up. Yumi, you need to be nicer. Yumi, you need to put all your efforts into whatever you choose to do.*

Don't bother me. That was all she wanted. *Stay away.* She liked the feeling of expansive freedom when Dad was away on work trips. Otherwise, there he was, taking up space, sucking in the light like a large black hole. *Where are you going, Yumi? Out where? With whom? Who is driving? Take the driver. When will you be back?* As if peppering her with questions was some kind of show of love. It was fake. It was worthless. She had always been alone, had always taken care of herself.

Now, Yumi felt her sisters looking to her, waiting for her to lead them. She resented the burden of being the oldest. She was supposed to be smarter, kinder, better, more generous, more caring. But she wasn't. She was not smarter, kinder, better. She was not even by leaps and bounds the prettiest. She hated being da jie jie. She'd always hated it. She wished they'd never been born. She had an urge now to say to them, *Go away*, the way she did so often—two, three times a day, when they were together at the farm. But where would they go? The night circled in around them. The birds quit their twilight songs, and the wind and the trees took up the refrain.

Yumi felt like she was far away, in another world, in another body. Yoko knew they were close to home; they were, after all, still on their mountain. Kiko couldn't help thinking of the haunted house. Would they still get to go? Now her sisters were in a bad mood. Could she go on her own? She and Lucy? How badly did she want to see it? Would it even be fun there without them? Kiko imagined herself, alone, moving through the empty, abandoned rooms. They took on a sinister, threatening tinge. The unspeakable things had come upstairs and were lurking about.

"Let's eat something," Yumi said. They all got to work, silently, gathering kindling, setting up the circle. The routine nature of the task put them at ease. Yoko joined her sisters by the fire. Kiko had packed ingredients for s'mores. The two younger sisters took marshmallows from the bag and stuck them on sticks, then held them above the fire.

Yumi watched Kiko roasting her marshmallow. It was becoming black. Yumi could nearly taste the ash just by looking at it, the thin, charred skin of it, the gooey, sticky near-liquid sweetness encased within the bitterness. She had the urge to make Baby give her a bite. Instead, she got up and walked to the edge of the clearing.

The ponies, tied to their tree, were hoofing the ground. For them, too, it was the first trip unaccompanied by Py. They felt happy, if just a little unmoored. Kiko ate her charred marshmallow and moved to Lucy to stroke her soft neck, feeling the warmth through the beaded plaits of hair. She let Lucy lick the sticky sugar off her fingers.

Yumi thought about the swim team. They'd kept her on junior varsity, to be kind, most likely. But there was no future for her in competition. She was eventually going to have to join the recreational team. Fine. She'd have more time for her friends, for her schoolwork. But she mourned it already, the loss of her thing, the thing that was hers and hers alone. Yoko had math and Kiko had dance. How long would they be able to hold on to their respective things? Yumi loved swimming, but she was not very good at it. In meets, she came in last. She didn't have the strength. But water was where she belonged, testing the limits of her lungs—the propulsion upon first kicking away from the wall, moving through water like a bullet, a missile launched from a submarine. Sometimes Yumi felt she liked it better in the water than on land, her body pushing against the weight of water, but also feeling weightless.

Yumi suddenly had an idea. They could go back to the hotel instead of the house, book a room for the night, go for a dip in the pool. She and Kiko. If Yoko wanted to stay in the woods, she was more than welcome to.

They were hungry. She hadn't thought about food, only escape. Yumi held the hunger in her stomach, wrapped herself around its emptiness, treasuring it, loving it. Today it was a small hunger, a baby, a baby bird. Her sisters were roasting three, four marshmallows at a time now on their sticks. She stared, benevolent, the sacrificial older sister. *Let the little ones eat*, she told herself.

But before she knew it, she had made her way around the fire, to Kiko's side. Yumi's hand was in the bag of marshmallows. They were filling Yumi's mouth. The baby bird was being fed—was being fed too fast.

"Hey! Save some for us!" Yoko exclaimed. The voice felt distant, although nearly just at her ear. Yumi stood up and walked into the forest. Just far enough; she could still hear the crackling of the fire. "She's going to throw up," Yumi heard someone say, just before she was rendered thoughtless, the familiar burn rising to her throat.

Eko tried the hotel first. The girls were not there. Eko had never had to call the police in all her years in China. She racked her brain for the number. Was it 110? 112? In Japan, it was 110. In France, 17. 120? 911? Would she have to wait twenty-four hours? Forty-eight? She fumbled with her phone and tried 110. She got it right. A policeman was asking her, "What is the problem, ma'am?"

"My daughters, they're missing."

"OK. When was the last time you saw them?"

"This morning. No. This afternoon—after lunch. Around two o'clock."

He took their names, their ages, their physical features, their last-known location, the description of their ponies.

"If they've taken the ponies, it's not likely they're going into the city. My guess is they're heading into nature, maybe up the mountain. What else did they take with them?"

Eko told him about the camping pack. A tent, a packet of snacks.

"Are they capable outdoors?"

"Very."

"It's a good thing there are three of them together."

"They're very good at fighting."

"Like, kung fu?"

"Jujitsu."

There was a pause. "So do you want a search team sent out? Or . . ."

"Yes, I want a search team! Dogs. Whatever you have. If it requires money, we can pay additional, no limit. A helicopter. Yes—why not a helicopter? Can you get us a helicopter? There's no time to waste!"

"We'll get on the case right away," he replied. "We'll dispatch a team to your home to get more information. Please stay where you are."

Eko hung up. Leo came in and said, "One of the guns is gone."

. . .

How she would hate him—never forgive him—if anything happened to the girls. For he had gone on and on in the way he was prone to, the way she had let him, always, through the years. A lecture, a talk, a lesson, while she tried to pin down and silence her anger, to listen, to understand. To resist the feeling of futility and failure. She would never be enough, she would always be a work in progress. She, usually too tired to put up a fight, had by that evening had enough. No one but her would cook the dinner. No one would even think about cooking dinner until it was too late. And it was nearly five o'clock, the sun low in the sky between the trees that stood erect and proud outside the window behind her storming husband. She stood, silent and proud, like them. The sun would soon go down on this argument. And because of what? Because she had not wrapped the wet swimsuits properly and half the clothes in the hamper were now damp, drying on the balcony. That was indicative of a long-standing pattern, apparently. Her casual and sloppy manner, her inability to live a good life.

Eko had tried to remain calm. Through his accusations, through the inevitable generalizations about the flaws in her character, through the exhausting enumeration and evaluation of her efforts at improvement over the years.

But she had mentioned dinner. And then she had mentioned it again. She knew it irked him. What he wanted was not a signal to cut the argument short, even though it had been going on for the better part of four hours, but an acknowledgment of his correctness, a dialogue about the probability of conquering this personality flaw and therefore of securing happiness, about establishing a three-step program of accountability.

Eko did not give it to him, however. Instead, she said quietly, "If you don't let me get started on dinner, I'm going to go insane."

Of course, that escalated the pitch and tenor of his anger, his disappointment, his demand. And so she opened the cabinet, took out the porcelain plates one by one, and smashed them onto the ground. They were so satisfyingly fragile.

At the mention of the gun, Eko jumped into action. She was packing her things. She was getting ready to leave. Leo hovered over her, placed himself in the doorway.

"Don't leave this house. If you leave now, that's the end. I won't stand for it. I won't forgive you."

Eko turned from her packing, which was difficult; she could feel the pull of it, the pull of her daughters, calling her away. It was irresistible.

"You have asked too much of me," she said. "It is enough. It is enough. It is too much." And she pushed past him as she walked out the door.

Eko, entering the forest, was thinking of the time she'd lost Yumi, when her daughter was almost two. They'd gone to the mall, were walking around the grocery store in the basement. One moment she was reaching for a pack of frozen pizzas, Yumi standing next to her. The next, Yumi was gone, nowhere to be seen from the frozen section.

She ran up and down the nearest aisles, and then she went to the cashier. "Send out a message, please," she asked. Her Chinese was not good, but she could get that much across.

"Yumi Yang, Yumi Yang. Please come to the checkout counter. Your mother is looking for you."

She showed the clerk several photos of Yumi and described what she was wearing—a dress adorned with bumblebees and blueberry bushes. Her hair was pulled back into two pigtails. She had bangs that sat low over her eyes.

Eko nearly cried when describing her daughter. It might have been that she was heavily pregnant and hormonal. She thought of losing her first on the eve of birthing her second. It would be the saddest of happy times. What was that? Tragedy? Irony? She couldn't find the word for it. She'd lived between two languages, and now a few years in China. Her vocabularies were all mediocre, blending into one another, replacing one another. Yumi, on the other hand, spoke Chinese fluently. It was her language of choice—with ayi, with Daddy, with her nursery school friends.

Eko put her phone away and told the clerk, "Keep her here if she comes. I'm going to look for her as well."

"Yes," he replied. "And I'll alert the mall, in case she left the grocery."

"The CCTV!" another cashier cried out. And then the three of them were shuffling into a side room—a closet, really—filled with screens.

Eko scanned each one quickly. The bumblebees, the blueberry bushes. The chocolate-and-sweets aisle, the cereal aisle, the ice cream aisle—the places Yumi liked best. Oh! There was the little red triangle of the children's shopping-cart flag, alert on its pole. Yumi was standing in the fresh seafood aisle, staring at an enormous grouper. Eko was in the seafood section before she knew it. So she had taken the fastest route, so she had memorized the twists and turns and layout of the store even better than she'd realized. So she had been living this life for so long.

Yumi was still right where she'd been on the cameras. Her cart was filled with candy and chocolate. She had visited her favorite aisles first.

Eko ran at her and folded her into an embrace. "My little one. Where did you go? Why did you run off like that? Mommy didn't know where you were. Please don't ever do that again."

"Mommy, I kept saying I wanted to go pick some chocolates."

"Did you, my love? I didn't hear you. I'm sorry."

"You didn't hear me, Mommy."

"Oh, sweets, I'll listen. Let's go home now, though." Eko bought all the chocolates in Yumi's cart.

Back at home, while Yumi happily played with her nanny, Eko thought about what she'd been doing, thinking, that she hadn't heard Yumi's repeated requests for chocolate. She had been letting her mind wander, thinking about getting a job. She had been questioning whether things would be different if she had found work instead of being just a mother. Whether *she* would be different. Whether her relationship with Leo would be different. Her relationship with herself. She had been thinking, when reaching for those pizzas, of how she would have been better off as a career woman—independent, strong, and capable.

AND NOW, AGAIN. Were they really gone? Were they lost, attacked, kidnapped? Eko felt the tragedy roiling in her gut. And yet she moved quickly, propelled forward into the dark of the forest. Nothing mattered—not even the thought that her marriage would collapse—that old, familiar fear. Her girls were missing. They were missing!

Eko screamed into the darkness: "Yumi! Yoko! Kiko!" How many times had she called out for her girls like that—just like that, in that order, from oldest to youngest? She thought of them as babies, those lovely days filled with happy memories of Leo holding them, throwing them into the air like dolls. But the girls were in the forest. They were in danger. She knew it. She knew them like she knew herself.

AT HOME, the rooms were dark except for a corner in the living room. Leo sat in his armchair, trying to read a book on a battle during the First World War. He was agitated. He couldn't focus.

Eko had left. And now he was sitting at home, on principle. She had not wanted to sit with him, to wait out the girls' coming home. She'd wanted to call the police. No. He'd been confident—they had enough survival skills. "Even Kiko?" Eko had asked. Yes, even Baby. Maybe she was the savviest of them all.

Even the gun wasn't something to worry about, not really, although Eko clearly didn't agree. As she packed her bag, he followed her around the room—telling her in a firm and then angry voice that he would not join her in her expedition. She was doing the wrong thing, coddling them. She always coddled them.

"Those are my girls," she said, turning to him, her eyes burning. But he matched it. "They're your girls? They aren't mine too?" He told her then that she must not leave the house; but Eko threw her bag over her shoulder and ran out the door.

Leo was alone now. It was the thing he hated most. Leo wrestled with himself, sitting beside the lone lamp. They were all gone. And Eko—Eko was going to make a mess of it. Had she even taken a horse? If so, had she remembered her helmet? He had been thrown off a horse once, riding in France. His back still hurt on rainy days.

The girls would have taken their helmets, he was sure. But now, with the question in his mind, he would have to head to the stables. Just to check. If he didn't check, he would think about it all night, wouldn't sleep a wink. Damn! He was going to have to go, wasn't he? He knew the trails better than anyone else. He had the best navigating abilities in the family. Eko didn't know her left from her right. He collected his things. He walked out the door, but halfway to the stables he was running.

They were all out on the mountain now. The girls were packing up the fire, close to the top. Their mother was making her way up the path, on foot. And Leo was getting set up on Py. He was rushing. He would find them; he would find them before she would.

"I THINK IT'LL BE BETTER if we go back to the hotel," Yumi was telling her sisters.

"They'll find us at the hotel," Yoko said.

"Yeah, but it'll be comfortable. There will be snacks."

"You just threw up your snacks. Seems like you didn't want them."

Yumi looked at her sister with what Yoko called, without affection, the "death stare." "Kiko, get your things packed," she said.

"No, Kiko," Yoko said. "We're going to finish up here and then continue up the mountain. We're going to the empty house."

"Oh my God, you're such a loser," Yumi said.

"That's the best you can do?" Yoko asked. "You don't make a promise to Baby and then just change your mind."

"Since when are you so excited about the house?"

"I'm not. But if I say I'm going to do something, I'm going to do it."

"It doesn't matter," Kiko said. She was standing next to Lucy, weaving her braids together. "I don't care."

"Yes, you do, Kiko," Yoko said. "Don't lie. Don't lie! I hate it when you lie, both of you. You're such dirty liars!"

"It's not like this was set in stone, Yoko. Chill out," Yumi said. "I mean, I know you have a hard time with 'transitions,' or whatever Ms. Evans calls it. But if we say it's not a big deal, just go with it."

"What?" Yoko asked. "Ms. Evans?"

"Yeah, everyone knows you're, like, underdeveloped. I heard Ms. Evans talking to Mom about it the other day when she was picking me up from school." Yumi was cool and collected now. She was enjoying her infliction of pain. She didn't wait for her sister to reply. "You know, your mental condition."

Yoko watched her sister, hating her, and said, "How could someone be born so evil?"

"Just come with us to the hotel."

"No. I'm going to the house."

"Move your ass and get on Raven. You know you're going to follow us anyway. Let's just skip past this bullshit and go."

"I'm going to tell Mom and Dad what you do at the hotel."

"No, you won't."

"Yes. I'll tell them who you go off with. I remember each and every one of their names. I read their name tags. I'll get them all fired too."

"I'll seriously kill you."

"No, you won't."

They looked at each other. Yumi felt it. The hate, the strength of it. But she would not back down. She would take it to the end.

"I'm not interested in listening to some autistic freak like you." Yumi narrowed her eyes. There, she had said it.

"I'm not . . ." Yoko was breathing hard.

"Come on. Everyone knows it but just keeps their mouths shut—I don't know, to be nice or whatever. But you're a freak."

Kiko said, "It's OK. You're not so bad, Yoko."

Yumi shot Kiko a glance, and it shut her up. Kiko returned to playing with Lucy's hair.

"You're just jealous, anyway," Yumi said. "No boy in his right mind would like you."

Yoko was staring at her sister. It wasn't true. Last month, apparently, Doug Freeland had told his friends at a laser tag party that he had a secret crush on her.

"Doug Freeland likes me," said Yoko.

"Oh yeah? Doug? He kissed me on the bus after a swim meet last week."

"I don't believe you."

"He had to take the rubber bands off his braces before we made out. I mean, ask him yourself. I don't want him stalking me anymore anyway; you can have him. His breath stinks up close."

Yoko, who rarely thought about boys, had heard about Doug's crush on her through Ximena and Yasmine. She'd been hiding out in the bathroom during lunch and overheard the two girls talking at the sink. "He thinks she's beautiful," Ximena said, laughing. When the girls left the bathroom, Yoko had emerged from the stall and looked at herself in the mirror, as if for the first time. A boy thought she was beautiful.

Their mother repeated constantly that Yoko was beautiful. All of them. She said it nearly every day, like a habit. As if it were the only thing that mattered. And everyone who met the sisters—the first thing they commented on was the girls' beauty. Was it such a statistically improbable thing for three girls to be beautiful together? Yoko had heard the word so many times throughout her life that it had started to lose its meaning. But a boy—that was something new. And now, Yumi was taking that away from her.

"You're a slut," Yoko said.

"Yeah, well, better a slut than a retard."

"I'm not retarded. I'm gifted," Yoko said. She paused but then barreled on. "Unlike you. You're bad at everything you do."

Yoko saw that the words had hit their mark. She steeled herself for the counterattack but felt a dawning realization that her sister—even at words—was not as adept, not as original, not as cutting as she herself could be. She had landed a decisive blow. Everything else would be denouement.

"I'd rather be mediocre than retarded."

"You keep repeating yourself. It's boring."

"You'll never have normal things. You'll never have a boyfriend, never have a life. No one's ever going to love you."

"Me and Dad are smart. Mom and Kiko are talented. What are you? You're nothing."

Yoko felt the invisible string between her and her older sister pulling taut. It drew her closer, against her will, to Yumi, closer to the pain. Why? The string between herself and Kiko had always been looser, with slack. Yoko felt the heat—the heat of anger and sadness and even a little love, burning through the connection between them. If only there had been more space, between them, around them. Yoko wanted nothing more than to cut the string, to release herself. But how?

"Retard."

"Don't call me that."

"Retard. Retard, retard, retard."

Yumi turned around, as if to finish the conversation, as if it were not worth having anymore. Yoko reached for her sister's bag and fished out the gun she'd seen her packing earlier. She pointed it at Yumi's back.

"Call me a retard one more time."

To the left of Yumi was Kiko; to the right, Lucy. Yoko aimed just slightly away from Yumi, between her and the old pony.

"You wouldn't dare," Yumi said, turning only partially back to look at her sister, as though she couldn't care less about the gun. "Put it down."

Yoko kept the gun raised. She wanted to scare Yumi. To put an end to all the cruel words, all the hatred. Even when they were little, Yumi's idea of a good time had been chasing down and tickling Yoko until Yoko was red with tears, breathless and desperate for air. Her attentions, her love, had always been laced with pain.

"You can't even fire a gun. Worthless," Yumi said. Then she screamed, "Do it or don't do it—just don't stand there like some idiot!"

Yoko closed her eyes and fired. When she opened them again, after the force that pulsed through her body had replaced all sound with a high-pitched whine, she saw Baby running to Lucy, who had crumpled to the ground.

The sound came back. Kiko screamed. "Help! Help! My pony! My Lucy! What did you do? Yoko, you shot Lucy! I hate you! I hate you!"

Kiko's small hands were placed over Lucy's neck. They were drenched in blood. The girls all knew their first aid. Kiko was pulling off her pants, to tie the legs around Lucy's neck. Yoko watched her little sister. She dropped the gun. Yumi stood in place, in shock.

A shuffle in the bushes brought the older girls back to life. Yumi and Yoko made eye contact, and Yumi edged closer. Standing nearly side by side, they looked, terrified, at the rustling leaves. Their father emerged into the clearing.

So he had arrived first. He took it all in: Lucy on the ground, no longer breathing, the old girl gone; Kiko, in her underwear, splayed over the pony's neck; Yoko and Yumi, the SIG Sauer on the ground between them.

"Girls," was all that would come out of his mouth. It was a statement, a question, a reprobation, a plea. "Girls."

"Daddy!" Kiko was sobbing. She was a bloody mess. Yumi and Yoko said nothing.

"Come on, girls, let's go back home," he said.

"I'm not leaving Lucy!" Kiko said.

"I'm not going home," Yumi said.

Leo took a step toward the girls, but Yumi bent down to grab the pistol and held it out in front of her, aimed at his chest.

"OK. OK. Calm down, Yumi," he said. Of all the scenarios he'd run through in his head, he had never practiced this one; he had never imagined this one. Where was Eko?

"You guys leave!" Yumi shouted. "You go to the damned farm. I'm not going. I'm not going with you! I hate you. I hate you all. I hate this place."

"Yumi, let's talk about it," Leo said. Kiko had stopped crying. In Yumi's hand, the gun was shaking.

"Talk? All you ever do is talk! You don't care what I say. You never listen. All you care about is the world coming to an end. You wouldn't even care if I shot myself in the head." Yumi lifted the gun to her neck, pointing it up into her chin.

"Yumi. Put the gun down," Leo said, his hands extending out in front of him. Then louder, angrier: "Put the gun down!"

"Who do you even think you are?" Yumi said.

"Yumi Yang!" he bellowed.

They were interrupted by a scream. Yoko's hands were over her ears, her eyes were closed, and she was releasing scream after scream after scream: long, shrill sounds punctuated only by gasping breath.

WAS HE GOING TO LEAVE them forever? Yoko had been watching Yumi point the gun at Dad, imagining life without him. No father. No father. No ally. No father. No one who would understand her.

He was the only person she'd ever told about the string—the string that holds the entire world together. They joked about it. They called it "string theory," or sometimes "our string theory," which Yoko liked best.

When she told him about it, she was desperate. She'd been holding those strings together in her mind for nearly ten years. Walking along the same routes, trying to make sure the strings attached to her and her family didn't get too tangled up, too crossed—otherwise she'd have to untangle them one by one in her mind. She had to let the strings layer atop one another nicely, and sometimes below, and occasionally weave them together so they wouldn't collapse. In some places, the layers of string were so thick that she felt she might be able to walk across the mass of them. Hers, her sisters', her parents'. Her home, the bathroom, the kitchen. Back and forth, to school. Back and forth, to the farm. She was exhausted.

When she told him about the strings, he told her that he, too, had thought about strings like that in his youth! He had been even more strict, rigorous. The string could never be crossed by a person, or a dog or a kid on the street. Sometimes he'd have to walk back to untangle the string from the ankles of a pedestrian.

When he told her that, the string that connected her and him grew tighter, thicker, unbreakable. Yet it was invisible. No one else could see it. Yoko made him swear on his life never to tell anyone, not even Mom.

Over the past few years, Dad had worked with her on letting go of the string. If she did nothing, the world would not collapse. He didn't deny the string. He didn't tell her to relax. He just explained that the string could handle itself. She had to try to trust the string. It existed before her, and it would exist after her.

Yoko had been loosening up over the years. Though there were still moments when she thought the string would drive her crazy. Like when Kiko had one of her dance recitals, and they had to sit in the audience with so many people shifting in their seats and getting up to take photos. And that wasn't the worst part.

The worst was Kiko tapping her feet in all kinds of complicated rhythms, spinning, jumping, along with a crowd of other dancers, tangling themselves all up in their strings.

Watching Yumi pointing the gun at Dad, Yoko could see the trajectory of the unshot bullet. She could see that it would go straight for his chest, that the bullet would pull along its own string, a string that would unravel so many others, that would make Dad and his string go slack all at once, and so would pull Yoko herself into a kind of whiplash for God knows how long. And the tragic irony was that she herself had unraveled that string. She had shot the gun first. Lucy was lying on her side, in a pool of blood. Yoko had done that; she had set this in motion.

For Yoko it was too much to handle. The burden of the strings, and the collapse of the entire system. It felt like the inside of her head was burning up.

WHEN EKO REACHED THE CLEARING, Yumi was shaking, the gun dancing in her fist. She was shaking so hard, she could barely hold it in her hand. Yoko was curled into a ball on the ground.

"I want you to go away," Yumi was saying to her father. "Just go away and leave us alone."

"OK, I'll go," he said.

"Go," she said. "Now!"

He backed away, inching out of the clearing, his hands up above his head. As if he were a criminal, as if he were guilty. Eko watched as Leo receded, until he was nearly invisible through the thicket of trees.

. . .

THE GIRLS NEVER WENT to the farm again. Their father promised a new set of ponies. He said they didn't have to do all that survival stuff again if they didn't want to. But they refused. They didn't even want the ponies. He could no longer make them go. The girls, like their mother, felt their own authority rise, from the trip that had brought all the systems crashing down.

The end days were coming, but they no longer cared. Let them come, they said. What was the worst that could happen?

Baby Kiko locked herself in her room for three days, taking meals on a tray left outside the door and leaving the empty plates for the housekeeper to pick up. She was in mourning, her mother said. Let her be. After three days Kiko came out of her room. She never spoke of Lucy again.

The farmhouse grew over; for a time it became full of moss and mold. The ponies went to work at the hotel, where they would be used for kids' rides for the next ten years. Later, they all thought of Lucy's death as an accident. Lucy jumped, hadn't she? It was understandable that Yoko unintentionally pulled the trigger. And, of course, Yumi didn't really want to kill Dad. Who could even say—even think—those words?

The Sledgehammer

July 2032

"We all know how architects can be."

Leo's colleague Bibi coughed out the word "Divas," and the boardroom chuckled. *This is going well*, Leo thought.

Leo continued, gesturing to the presentation tablets in front of everyone, "We are a firm, as you know, built on structural engineering as an art form equal to architecture and design. Built to last, to outlast, and to do no damage. This house will become a private residence but also a model for what luxury living should be, self-sufficient and self-sustaining. Steel pillars coated in concrete, covered with intumescent paint. Shear walls, bracing frames. We're going to be reinforcing this structure up and down, with no expense spared. Here: inconspicuous, nearly invisible solar panels. Here, in the kitchen: a sophisticated compost system. Here: a state-of-the-art water recycler, imported from Singapore.

We will build a panic room in the basement. Everything resistant to water damage, flooding, warming, fire, energy crisis, attack. We're talking fortress here.

"Gentlemen, when Shanghai is a pile of rubble and ash three thousand years from now, this house will still be standing. Hell, I want to move my own family in!" He was only half joking.

"You have had some challenges of late, we know." Leo was referring to the high-rise that had recently gone up in flames, putting all its residents in mortal danger. Luckily no one had died. But the mayor was under pressure. "Our firm does it all, from top to bottom, inside and out: from the engineering to the design to the plumbing. With construction and design working hand in hand, there is no room for miscommunication or miscalculation."

Leo nodded and Bibi turned on a projection of the historic building they were proposing to renovate: the mansion built in 1933 that was now a multiunit residence. The projection highlighted all the areas that would first need to be demolished. "You'll see here and here where new supports will have to be installed. And on this side of the building, we'll add an elevator. So often, families want their elders to live with them but are discouraged by stairs or slippery stone flooring. We will also build out the room off the kitchen into its own apartment. For a childcare team, or for grandparents to live comfortably alongside their families.

"Most certainly, the plumbing and electricity will have to be completely redone. We'll try to retain the original flooring as much as possible, though it will have to be uprooted. The tiling on the floor can perhaps be reused on a door or in a new bathroom."

Leo pointed to the first and second floors. "What you can't see here, in this display, is the black mold that has taken hold behind the kitchen on the first floor, through to the second. This entire section needs to be gutted and cleaned. And no one needs a kitchen in the hallway anymore. A true chef's kitchen will be on the ground floor. The staircase can be preserved, but most of the wooden elements are beginning to rot. They'll need to be replaced.

"Gentlemen, this building is in bad shape. It can be restored to its former glory and even beyond, but that will require care and talent, something we have far and away above the competition. Quality materials, authentic period décor—you don't want this place to feel cheap or throwaway. Imagine it as it was. Jazz clubs and dancing girls; Shanghailanders and gangsters. Timber from the United States. Stained glass shipped from Italy. We want to do things right. To honor our past and to write it anew."

Leo looked at the men across the table, and he switched into Shanghainese. "Listen, I know this city like the back of my hand. I grew up here, and I love this place, its buildings, everything good and bad and beautiful and ugly. Well . . . maybe not ugly," he said. They laughed. He had a reputation. Good.

"I grew up three streets away from Yuyuan Lu. I walked past this building on my way to school. Yes, we're here to invest, to make money. Who isn't? But I promise you: no one waiting outside this room will care about this building, this neighborhood, more than I."

Leo switched back into Mandarin to close his presentation. "Thank you, gentlemen, for your time and for the opportunity to bid on this special project. Just to note, we're also happy to reinvest a small portion of the bid into relocation costs for the current residents. We also propose offering them school permits for their children. The kids are unlikely to attend, but if they do, they'll take only a few spots. A small price to pay."

Leo packed up his documents. Then he shook every one of the committee members' hands.

"How do you think it went?" he asked Bibi in the hallway.

"I think they liked it, Leo. I liked the local touch at the end, heh. They kept the proposal, did you see? This isn't a done deal. I think we have a chance."

On their way out, Leo and Bibi passed the Moon and Stars Group and nodded tersely to the competition. Leo had heard that the Hong Kong group's proposal consisted of a hotel and museum combo. Another team, he knew, was proposing turning the mansion into an exclusive four-unit luxury apartment building with a swimming pool.

Leo had a lunch commitment back at their waterfront office, with its 360-degree views of Shanghai from the eighty-eighth floor. He was supposed to deliver a virtual lecture, followed by a Q and A, on the topic of resilience. But he had an extra hour or so. And he wanted to spend that time moving through the city rather than staring down at it from on high, as he did most of his days. An urban planner's model of Shanghai—everything became minute with enough distance.

"I want to take another quick look at the house before going back to the office," he told Bibi, who passed along the message to their driver once the car pulled up. Leo got into the back and Bibi took a seat up front.

Leo reviewed the presentation in his mind as they made their way to the city center. He thought of his upcoming lecture. His life was one presentation after the next these days. But this house, this renovation, was something special.

He hadn't told anyone except his wife, not even Bibi, but hc had a personal connection to the building. His heart had leaped when he learned that the government was taking bids to renovate it. It was where his mother had grown up, where she'd lived for nearly a decade, between the ages of ten and twenty, with her parents and five siblings.

When he'd told Eko about it, about his plan to bid on the development, she had been supportive, even enthusiastic. But then again, there was hardly anything she didn't want him to buy.

Now, when he drove around Shanghai, he saw value. He knew what each neighborhood, each street was worth, how it could be developed, if it hadn't been already.

As they made their way to the house on Yuyuan Lu, Leo realized that they would soon be passing through the former French Concession, and by the French school's new campus, a recently renovated former estate that now housed two large schoolhouse buildings, a gymnasium, and a lepidopterarium. He asked the driver to slow down, then to stop the car at the curb for a moment. They parked up against the school's iron fence, laced with ivy. Leo stared into the property.

Eko wanted to transfer the girls to this school—to let them enjoy life, study French, to avoid the Chinese and American education rat races. Why else, she asked, did they hold French passports?

Leo was holding on to an idea that had disappeared long ago, perhaps. A dream of meritocracy, of a China that had blinked suddenly in and out of existence. When everyone, for a brief moment, had been equally poor, with the country just beginning its ascent into wealth.

A lepidopterarium! Did kids really need to study butterflies? As a student, he himself had ascended from one school to the next, moving up from district to city level, on the basis of high test scores. His time had been unique, fleeting. Everyone had nothing, but he'd hardly known it, hadn't felt the crush of poverty until the accident, when he was left with truly nothing, becoming an orphan. Living without his parents had calcified an awareness of lack for him that remained, forever, in his gut.

His daughters—to let them go to this school would mean bringing them up as French, with French friends, French culture all around. French holidays: he hadn't celebrated them since his time in Paris. Leo looked in at the school and thought of the long summer vacations taken with Eko throughout Europe. He thought of the weekends, when the stores and groceries were closed or closed early. How quiet the city and the entire country became at certain hours, for stretches of months, even. One's country of residence dictated one's experience of time over a year, over a week. The ebbs and flows of energy and rest.

Leo kept up with a few friends who'd returned from Paris, all Chinese who had studied and worked abroad, like him. But mostly, nowadays, he saw old local classmates from high school, middle school, even primary. Shanghainese who had stayed. When they met, they spoke in their native dialect. It was Eko who remained connected to the French community in the city.

How easily, it seemed to him, Eko made new friends. One picked up here, another there. Meetings at the patisserie, café, bistro. It had been the same for him, maybe, abroad—finding a fellow Chinese and clinging to him, becoming friends by default, comrades, fellows.

And what of it—if his girls were to grow up in this little French enclave? What, really, was at stake? If it meant so much to Eko . . .

She had insisted on giving birth to the last two of their daughters back in Paris. To be with her mother, she'd said. But also, to be in a French maternity hospital, a place where she could understand what the hell the doctors and nurses were saying about her *vagin*. "Water birth, water birth," she'd said, insisted, as if it were some sort of religion. After Yumi, he'd planned to let her do what she wanted. But then, following the horror of Yoko's birth, the blood and the scare of losing Eko, they did Kiko's in the operating room. In fact, he was surprised, after Yoko, that Eko was even willing to try again.

"It's not that France is better," she'd said, diplomatically. He knew, though, how the French really felt about their country. That it was the apex of civilization. This was the fundamental mythology of Frenchness. And not only the French bought into it. Wasn't this part of the reason he'd married her? Part of her appeal to him, surely, so many years ago? Her fluency, her comfort in a world where he would always be a visitor; her ability—her destiny—to be both Asian and European? Who could understand the workings of the heart, the rules of attraction, so different for every person? She was his, and therefore he knew that his children would never be Shanghainese. These thoughts, as he looked at the school gates, felt mostly rational, but underneath was a cloudy current of sadness.

Leo had studied structural engineering in graduate school, in Paris. It made sense to pursue something practical, and something related to real estate development, given his investments. Sometimes he wondered, however, if he'd made the right decision. The career he'd chosen had panned out, but the work he did—buildings, walls, sketches, numbers, pillars, counterweights—could feel barren of human connection. Yes, there was plenty of scope to think about safety, survival, resilience, about how humans live and move and see light and feel stone. But that was all sensory: the trappings of life, the scaffolding of a family.

How interesting, important, dynamic it would be to work in politics, by contrast, or to be, like Baby Kiko, a performer, an explorer of the human soul. A medical doctor, even, a surgeon working within the body, touching skin and muscle and bone all day long. Buildings were like the clothes people wore and the things they bought, necessary but too often wasteful, weighing down the planet in a thick, toxic shield of concrete.

He signaled to the driver, and they moved on.

WHEN YOU TEAR SOMETHING DOWN, you're presented with an opportunity to build anew: better, stronger, more magnificent, more perfect. Leo had worked with a lot of architects and designers over the years. He did not like to waste his time on people who concerned themselves with replicas. Renovation, restoration, was an art, and should be reflected as such in its execution.

Leo had a great respect for history. But a building was a living thing, an aging object, and, if it was important, a documented work of history. So why couldn't it, shouldn't it, evolve over time? The house on Yuyuan Lu had originally been a family home. Then, after the war, it had been partitioned into many units to accommodate multiple families. Now, decades later, Leo was going to bring it back to its original glory.

So much happened to a house that had been squeezed full of residents, filled to its brim with squalid life. Forty people and three toilets, two kitchens. He had grown up hearing from the older generation, "You'll never understand. You'll never understand." But he understood—on a structural level—that things needed to be used as intended. Otherwise they would not last. That was called abuse.

Leo, too, had grown up in a tiny apartment with his family, had slept next to his desk and all their clothes and belongings and food. They had been together, every day and every night, in that one room, until the accident. For years after, he'd been scared to sleep alone, even to be left in a room by himself. That feeling stuck until Paris. Somehow, after leaving Shanghai for the first time, he'd never felt afraid.

Leo got out of the car and took a good look at the house. It was a wide structure, too heavy, with dark brick and a thick cover of ivy reaching the tiny second-floor windows. He saw, too, at the same time, the house that it could be, that he and his partners had envisioned: large, sun-filled walls of glass, the stone that would brighten up the building. He walked around to the side entrance. From there he could see the backyard, lush and overgrown, with laundry on clotheslines hanging among the trees. He would relandscape it, bring it back to a stately greenness. He imagined a pond with fat koi and even the terraced pools at Shangri La, which he'd visited with the girls in Hawaii just last summer. He had never seen a more fragrant house, an act of imagination and grandeur, an appropriation of culture, an obsessive attempt at owning it. It was commendable. The mansion on Yuyuan Lu, too, could really be something.

When his mother had first moved in, her family had been assigned the entire second floor. For her and her parents and her five siblings. By the end of her time there, their space had been trimmed down to two narrow rooms. His aunt, a spinster, was the last to remain, until she finally moved away, years ago.

He imagined his mother as a child. There had been one photo, sepia-toned with a blush added to the cheeks. That image, and the photo from his parents' wedding day—the two faces staring out without humor—those were all the images he had left of his mother, long gone. The other memories he had of her were vague, fuzzy, nothing definitive.

But he knew little girls, their joys and sorrows, their charm and beauty. His own were the same age that his mother had been when she first moved in, when she played and fought and sang and danced and cried together with her siblings. When the garden was a verdant green, when the fountain spouted clean water. She would have hidden from her brothers and sisters, maybe behind that tree, her face peeping out from the thick trunk, heart beating in anticipation—would they find her? They always would—and then the shrill cry of joy, defeat, resolution, running, running across the grass, up the back staircase, weaving through the hallway kitchen, filled with smoke and bodies, up the stairs, two by two, to her room, under her bed, shared with an older sister. The wait, the approaching footsteps, then a small face appearing at ground level. It was over, the hunt. And she had lost. Again, and again . . .

In the mornings, after becoming a young lady, waiting in line for the cramped bathroom, a ruby-red hair clip in her hand . . .

Summer nights, old men on their low wooden stools in the lane, cigarette butts blinking along the length of the narrow street, the pitter-patter of pebbles on Go board, a black stone, a white stone missing here and there, replaced with a lopsided chunk of brick, of granite . . .

Leo knew nothing. It was all conjecture. He no longer had a connection to this place, no more claim to it than the next developer, the next bid. But still, he felt—and he knew the feeling to be irrational, ungrounded—that on some level, this house belonged to him.

A WOMAN LEANED OUT from her balcony and began hanging laundry on her line. Leo looked up when a drop of water landed on the back of his hand. The woman—white curls against a blue, cloudless sky—scowled down at him.

"Measuring and sizing us up and making your plans, eh? All before we've even seen a cent for relocation!" She shook a blouse violently in the air and a spray of droplets rained down on Leo. He shook his head and brushed off his shoulders, laughing. Was this his mother's childhood?

"Ma'am, did you happen to know the Huang family? They lived here a long time ago."

"Huang, Wang, Tang, Yang. There are so many who've lived here."

"There were six kids. They were originally from an aristocratic family down in Suzhou."

"Oh, *those* Huangs." The woman finished adjusting a shirt on the line. "They in some kind of trouble or something?"

"No, why?"

"Because I remember the mother was always gambling. I ran around with those kids."

"So you've always lived here?"

"You think I would have come here by choice? Yes! I grew up here and stayed when my parents passed. My son works in Germany, you know? In Europe. He wants to buy us a new place or bring us over there. But we've been waiting for the relocation allowance. We knew they would take this place sooner or later. You know, it used to be beautiful."

"And what were the kids like—the Huang kids?"

"You one of those developers or what?"

"I am."

"Don't tell me they're getting a cut too. The Huangs, they moved out years ago! They don't need the relocation money. Never did. Snobs, really, that never changed."

"Seems you don't need the relocation money either," Leo said.

"I may not need it, but I sure as hell deserve it for living here, like this, all my life. I've been waiting. I had friends in old houses who were bought out twenty years ago already! I never gave up hope. I kept suffering."

"Could you show me your home? It would help."

Why would he ask that? It wouldn't help. But still, this woman might have been a friend of his mother's. If he could see her life, her home, then maybe . . .

"Help what?" she asked.

"With planning. With presenting a bigger offer for resettlement," he said. Knowing that this was the only answer she would be happy with.

"Fine. Come on up. I'll meet you at the top of the landing."

Leo had toured the site before. He had glimpsed the partitioned rooms; the doors had been left open to anyone who cared to look inside. He knew his way around. He went in and headed up the stairs.

The woman stood waiting for him. She was tiny, around his mother's age, if she were alive. Leo smiled at her watching him.

"You're taller than you seem," she said, once he reached the landing. "Come on." She moved past the cooking range in the hall. It was covered in thick, black layers of grease, textured, solid. The gas line ran exposed down the hall. Numerous extension cords and power lines—white, gray, black—tangled, snaked inside room after room. In the blueprints Leo had presented to the city council, the second floor would be transformed into a large family room with an extended balcony branching out over the backyard. The third and fourth floors would house the bedrooms. In the garden would be a freestanding room and bath, for an office suite, or another set of grandparents, or a children's playhouse.

"This is our place," the woman said, stepping into a small room. It was the size of Eko's closet. One side was filled to the ceiling with cardboard boxes.

"You'll have much more space in your new apartment," Leo said.

"Yes, but I'm used to living in the city center," she said. "I'm a city girl. Always have been. If I'm leaving this location, you'd better be offering a sweet deal."

"It's ultimately up to the government," Leo replied, and it was. "I'll put in a recommendation, but I'd only be in charge of the renovation."

"You guys are all in cahoots. I'm old enough to know how it works." She looked around and sat down on her bed. "My husband passed last year. This is the only home I've ever known."

"I'm sorry for your loss. Your son grew up here too?"

"Yup. With us in this very room. Until he was sent to boarding school. There was no longer any space. Whenever he came back to China, he always stayed in a hotel."

Leo wanted to hear more about his mother's family. But he did not want to reveal himself as the son. He wanted the unfiltered truth. What did she mean—that they had been snobs?

"What was it like growing up here?" he tried.

"Here? You know, it was what it was. No space, no money. I didn't get to go to college. I came back after my stint on Chongming Island. What is there to say? It was a hard time." She waved him off. "What are you doing, some kind of oral history project? Leave me alone. I've already started packing."

"Packing? There hasn't even been a deal made."

"I have a source."

"It's at least three months till you'd have to leave."

"You never know. You type of guys have been lurking around lately. I know it's coming. Leave me in peace now."

Leo lingered in the doorway. It struck him, looking at the old woman sitting alone on her single bed, in her single room, that he hadn't felt what she must feel—he hadn't felt loneliness—in years.

LEO WALKED DOWN THE STAIRS and stood at the bottom. Something felt off in the space. He circled the foyer. Why would the stonework be perfectly aligned except for the uneven bottom stair? He looked at it for a long time. His mind worked like that, without agenda. If he simmered on a problem for long enough, sometimes just stared at the page, an idea would come to him out of the ether.

The house was exquisitely built. No corner had been cut, no cost saved. It must have been a very wealthy family that had lived here a century ago. They did things well back then. Not like now—prefabricated, cookie-cutter things piercing the sky, made to last just a couple of decades. Leo stared at the smooth wall, which was made of stone, and cool to the touch. An idea came to him. He felt the wall again. Yes, he was sure he was right. It was incredible, really, that no one had noticed what they'd done. For so many years? For a century?

Leo left the house and went back to the car. It would help him win the bid if he was right. The driver was leaning against the car, smoking a cigarette, while Bibi sat in the front seat, in the air-conditioning. Bibi rolled down his window. "Good to go, Leo?"

Leo spoke to the driver. "Pop the trunk."

The driver popped the trunk and opened it wide. "What do you need?" He took a drag on his cigarette. Leo hated the stench but said nothing.

"The sledgehammer," Leo said, pointing to a handle poking out from the bottom of a stack of tools.

Bibi got out of the car and watched as the driver unearthed the hammer. "We haven't won the bid yet," he said, unnecessarily.

"But we will," Leo replied. He took the hammer from the driver and walked back into the house. Bibi trailed him at a respectful distance.

Leo knew that he was right. He felt it in his bones. Something was there. He also knew that if he didn't act on his hunch, he would always regret it. Over the years, Leo had gotten much better at making decisions, quick decisions. He'd gotten better at knowing himself and what his future self would expect from him. He aimed for the wall adjacent to the stairs and struck it with the sledgehammer.

The impact shocked him up his arms and into his spine. He shook his head and rolled his shoulders. He hadn't done this in a long time, and it felt good.

"What are you doing?!" A few residents had quickly gathered behind him. He struck again. "Stop it! Who do you think you are?"

Leo ignored them and struck again. He broke through. "There's something behind here," he said. The layer of rocks began to crumble to the floor. Behind it was a broken wall of plaster. Leo had cut through a wooden door as well, splinters clinging to the chunks of plaster on the ground.

The small crowd behind him silenced momentarily, before they began again: *It's a door! It's a passage. There's something behind the wall! No, it's a secret passageway. It must be a room. Do you think there's someone buried behind there? Don't tell me this has been there the whole time!*

Bibi handed Leo a flashlight that he'd brought from the car, and Leo peered into the dark. A steep stone stairway led underground. But it ran in the opposite direction from the existing basement of the building. Leo took off his coat and hung it on the banister. He rolled up his sleeves.

Leo looked back at the crowd of residents, by and large old, bespectacled, and crooked, and said, "Stay here. It might be dangerous." Then he climbed into the hole.

. . .

He squeezed his way down an uneven and narrow flight of stairs, the stale air enveloping him. Looking back, he could see several faces blocking the hole, straining to catch a glimpse.

The door had been carefully boarded up, the only sign of its existence the slightly uneven alignment between wall and floor. How many times, over the years, had it been painted over? Leo could guess when and why it had been hidden away. To prevent confiscation.

He hit the bottom of the staircase and looked around. The walls were made of layered stone, sealed with plaster. As opposed to the clutter of the tiny apartments upstairs, this was a well-organized array of solid wooden trunks and furniture. And surprisingly spacious. He ran his light over the space slowly: 250 by 150 by 240 centimeters cubed, was his guess.

He could hear scrambling from above. They would want to join him at any moment. He walked to a line of trunks along the nearest wall. They were belted shut with iron. There was no way he could open them himself with just a flashlight and the Swiss Army knife in his pocket.

Leo stepped toward a dresser of ornate black lacquer and tugged on one of the drawer pulls. It was stuck. He shifted his weight and pulled harder. With a cracking sound, it came out, unhappily, from its shell. He pointed the flashlight into the drawer and saw a small bed of jade—tokens, beads, bracelets, amulets. He held a piece up to the light. A bat, small enough to fit on a lady's ring, or on a chain.

He heard Bibi's voice calling down. "Everything OK? Should I come down?"

"I'm fine, Bibi! Give me a moment. There's a small space here. I'll be up in a sec." If he lingered too long, he might be accused of plundering these treasures. If he let the residents down, what would even remain? "Bibi," he yelled. "Call city development right away. Tell them to get here as soon as possible."

Leo would hand everything over—and this find, its publicity, would surely secure his chance of winning the bid. He pulled open another drawer and saw dozens of thin bars of gold. He rubbed a piece on his shirt and bit into it: solid. Without thinking too much, he slid the bar into his pocket. He also plucked out the small jade bat. He could make it into a necklace for Eko.

"Leo, they're wanting to come down!" Bibi shouted.

"Don't let them!" Leo said. "It's not safe. There's mold. It's slippery." The lies came out of his mouth quickly, easily. He braced one foot against the wall and with a grunt pulled open the largest dresser drawer.

What had he expected? He felt a surge of disappointment when he saw that the drawer was filled with paper, with art and scrolls. He dared not touch them—such old paper was fragile, and his hands were dirty.

He kept at it. Another drawer held a crowd of hair combs and pins. Flowers and birds and butterflies. Had these been passed down from generation to generation? His daughters would love them. Would they end up in a museum?

The dresser contained a collection of female treasures. Maybe even an original dowry. Leo thought of the family that must have lived here. The lady who had so loved her jewels, her pins, that she did all this to hide them away before they could be stolen.

That lady could almost have been his own grandmother, who herself had said goodbye to great wealth. Of course, that had been before this house was requisitioned, before it was partitioned—before his mother's family was moved out of their estate and into the second floor.

What was in those trunks? Maybe more treasure, documents. Leo wanted a few more hours with the hole. He had been searching for something. For what? For clues, for a piece of history more important than gold. A sign. His mother. He was looking, urgently, like he did when he had lost something. A sock in the morning before heading into the office, his phone before stepping into the elevator.

Why? Because he'd been doing so his whole life, looking for the reasons he was who he was, looking for his own history, his lineage, his past, which could determine his future and everything that could be. His parents had left nothing behind. They'd saved nothing. What was there to save? They'd been killed much too soon to even leave him many memories.

To whom did these objects belong? Maybe it would all come to light. A descendant of a descendant of a descendant. Whoever it was, it would not be Leo. He knew, suddenly, definitely, that he would not be living here. He would renovate, but not with Eko and the girls in mind. The secret room would become, most likely, given its size and location, a wine cellar.

Leo knocked on the trunks to pass the time while waiting for the officials to arrive. With each knock, the clipped, curt sound of wood in an airless room, he felt more and more removed from this cellar, this building, his mother, his family. Finally, he sat atop one of the trunks and closed his eyes. He felt as though he were a nameless king, buried among treasure deep within a pyramid, a long-forgotten grave.

小心, Little Heart

June 2028

Kiko woke up in the morning and her heart was broken with sadness. She'd learned in Chinese class just recently that sadness was "broken" and "heart" put together. Being nice was "good" and "heart" put together. Being careful was "small" and "heart" put together.

Kiko was brokenhearted because she missed ayi. She was also brokenhearted because she hated going to school and never wanted to go again. Why did she have to? She liked being home with Mama. She wanted the weekend to last forever. But suddenly she remembered that it *was* the weekend, and this weekend was the princess day, and then she felt happy—"open" and "heart" put together.

Why, she'd asked in school, were there so many hearts? And if a heart was open, wouldn't it also be broken? "The heart is important," Miss Gao told her. Which didn't really answer her question. She hated when grown-ups did that.

Kiko was sad again. She cried, let loose a long, undulating wail. For the past year it had been Wu ayi—young, sweet, and indulgent—who always got her dressed in the morning. Now Mama just handed her clothes and made her put them on herself. And Mama didn't care if the socks were on backward or forward. When she had cried for a few minutes and no one had come to get her, Kiko got herself out of bed and opened the door.

They were already turning the living room into a castle! A woman was busy inflating balloons—so many of them! They covered the floor. Pink and purple and white and orange, all Kiko's favorite colors. She ran into the middle of them and began to throw them into the air.

Her mother came out from the kitchen, wearing her baking apron. "Happy princess day, my little princess."

"Mama! Are you baking a cake?" Kiko's face crumpled into a small wavering thing. She tried hard not to cry, but she was feeling it—her broken heart—again. "You started baking a cake without me," she wailed.

"Oh, Yukikochan. I was waiting for you to get up and come to the kitchen. Come on. I've only just got out all the ingredients. We'll have some cereal while we bake."

Kiko wiped her eyes with her sleeve and made her way to the kitchen. She stepped up onto her ladder and stared at the flour, eggs, baking powder, sugar, butter, pink frosting, and chocolate chips, all in little bowls on the kitchen island.

"Mama, I want to mix!" Kiko said, grabbing a bowl.

They got to work. Kiko half helped her mother with the cake and half supervised the balloon woman, who was slowly setting up the castle using a complicated set of wires and sticks. The nice lady occasionally threw a balloon or two over to Kiko when she peeked in.

KIKO'S PARENTS HAD decided this year on a princess day instead of a birthday party. Kiko had had birthday parties, apparently, all her life. A Hello Kitty party when she turned four, a unicorn party when she turned three, a bunny party when she turned two, and a rainbow-themed party when she turned one. "Because you were our rainbow baby," her mom said. She called Kiko that a lot. Kiko was the rainbow baby because her third sister, the one she never met, had left Mama's belly and flown into the sky.

Kiko had seen photos from all these parties, though she remembered very little. This year, her sisters hadn't had birthday parties either. Yumi, in December, had chosen to celebrate with travel. Their family flew to Paris for a weekend and ate and walked and ate until they were tired and full to bursting. It was like any other vacation, except Daddy made them sit in the small seats, not the big ones, on the airplane. Yoko, in November, wanted to go with Daddy to the planetarium. Kiko didn't go with them. She had ballet.

Daddy and Mama talked about it a lot, the birthday plans. Daddy said the girls had too much stuff. Parties sent the wrong message. Kiko knew that Mama wanted the parties. She said she would reduce the number of things she bought for the girls. But Daddy said Absolutely Not and told her that she needed to Get a Grip on Her Spending.

Anyway, when June came around and her parents asked what she wanted for her birthday, Kiko was ready with an answer. She wanted a princess day! Her best friend, Courtney, had had her birthday party just one month prior. It had been princess-themed. They all got princess water bottles to take home. Kiko's was Snow White.

After the cake was in the oven, Mama washed their hands in the sink and then pulled out a ring from her pocket. It had a pale pink stone set in a circle of shiny white stones, the kind Mama had on her wedding ring. The ring was a lovely, sparkly flower.

"Is this—?"

"Shhh," said her mother. "Yes, it's a princess ring, only for the most special of little princesses. But you can't tell anyone I got it for you. It's a secret, magic princess ring."

"Thank you, Mama!" Kiko squealed. She put it on her pointer finger. "I'll wear it every single day of my life."

"Oh, sweetheart. Mama loves you so much. Happy non-birthday birthday!"

"I love you so much too," Kiko said. "Now I have to go check on my balloon castle!"

THE BALLOON CASTLE was nearly finished. The woman was twisting the pink balloons on top of the tower into a point. Kiko went inside the castle and looked up and around. Pink and purple and orange. A true balloon castle, just for her. There was a window, even, to look out of.

"Mama! I want to wear my princess dress," Kiko shouted. "Where is my princess dress?"

"In your closet, dear."

"I want to wear it!"

"Go put it on."

"I need help."

"Give it a try yourself first."

Kiko walked into her room. But she was not happy again, not openhearted. If ayi were here, she would help Kiko put on her dress, brush her hair, and make two braids that would loop into each other at the back. Ayi used to call it Kiko's hair crown. Kiko made a mess of the dress and called for her mother.

When Eko came into the room, Kiko was sitting on her bed with the sleeves of the dress pulled half onto her arms.

"Mama, I miss ayi." Kiko began to tear up.

"Oh, I know. I do too, Kikochan." Eko helped Kiko get dressed, and then she brushed her hair and did the braids just like ayi used to.

"See, Mama, I told you that I needed help."

"You were right, Baby."

Her mother let her choose between the blue crown and the pink crown. Kiko chose the pink. "Mama, you can wear the blue crown today," she said.

"Oh, I don't need to. You're the princess today."

"Mama, please. You can be the princess mama."

"You mean the queen?"

"The queen, yes."

"OK." Eko pulled the crown onto her head.

"Mama, you're so beautiful."

"Not as beautiful as you, sweetheart."

"That's true. But you look very nice."

"Let's go get the cake ready."

. . .

When they had finished frosting the cake and were eating breakfast at the counter, Daddy and Yoko and Yumi came home from their Saturday soccer practice.

"Yumi, Yoko! Look at my castle!" Kiko shouted when they walked in the door. Daddy came to look, too, and then went into the kitchen to talk to Mama.

"It's not a present, it's an experience," Kiko heard her mother say. Kiko opened the kitchen door and saw that her father was about to say something in response. His face was scrunchy.

"Daddy! You have to be the prince!" Kiko said. He kept talking to Mama. Too many things. Incomprehensible. The value of money. Spoiled rotten. Kiko started pushing him out to the living room. "Daddy, pick me up!"

Leo picked her up, but he was frowning. Kiko pressed his forehead between his eyebrows until it was all smoothed out.

"Daddy, don't be bad. It's my not-birthday party." Kiko gave him a big hug. "Let's go fight the wicked witch!"

He smiled. "Who is the wicked witch? Your mother?"

"No!" Kiko brought her mouth to her father's ear. "It's Yumi."

Daddy lowered his voice to match Kiko's. "And how do we fight this wicked witch?"

"We have to cover her bed in toilet paper!"

"Why?"

"So she can't fall asleep. Then she will be so exhausted that she won't be able to function properly."

"Who taught you that phrase?"

"I heard Mama say it."

"Oh."

"Let's go!" Kiko shouted, kicking her heels into Daddy's stomach, like her riding instructor taught her, to make a pony move faster.

"You get started. I'll come join you soon." He dropped her abruptly, gave her butt a pat, and went back toward the kitchen.

Kiko didn't feel like toilet-papering her sister's bed alone, so she went to sit in her castle. She got her toy tigers and sat them in a circle around her. She told them all kinds of secrets.

"When I was little, I used to be scared of bats. Tigers can't really jump up and down on their tails, sorry. I told Mama and Daddy I don't like school, but actually I really like it. And I love Courtney. OK, I have to tell the truth: I'm still a little afraid of bats."

The tigers went on to have a tea party and to sing "Ring Around the Rosie." But it was too difficult to make them all move around in a circle at once, so she gave up and stepped out of her castle.

Yoko was watching her from the sofa.

"Do you want to play?" asked Kiko.

Yoko nodded and came near the castle. She walked around it several times, staring at it.

"It's the tiger castle. I am the princess of tigers," Kiko said. "ROAR!"

Yoko asked, "Can I take it apart?"

"No! You cannot!" Kiko pushed Yoko away from the structure.

Yoko walked away, but then their parents came out of the kitchen. Mama was holding the cake. She directed everyone into the dining room.

"Listen up, girls," Daddy said. "This year we're not doing presents, as you know. For Kiko's gift, instead, we'll each say aloud one thing that we will give her this year—something that doesn't cost money." Kiko kept her eyes on the cake. She knew that inside it was loaded with chocolates. "I'll go first. I'm going to give Kiko math lessons every weekend! OK. Eko, you want to go next?"

"Sure. I am going to give Kiko lots of love."

"Seriously?" Yumi said. "That's too easy."

"Well, what are you going to give your sister?" Eko asked.

"I will go watch Kiko at her ballet lessons five times."

"Yay!" Kiko always wanted Yumi to accompany her to ballet. She loved showing off her sister to her teachers, and she loved showing off her skills to Yumi. "How about six times?"

"OK. Six times," Yumi said.

"Yoko?" their father asked.

"I don't know."

"It can be anything."

"I don't know." Yoko buried her face in her hands.

"That's fine. You just think about it. Wow! Kiko, you're getting love and math lessons and Yumi at ballet for your birthday. How great is that?"

"And I get to be a princess!" Kiko added.

"Of course."

"You can be my prince."

"Sure."

"Kiko, a princess has to marry her prince. Daddy's already married," Yumi said.

"Well, he can marry me too."

"It doesn't work that way," Yoko said.

"Yes, it does!" Kiko was feeling broken again, like she might cry again.

"It's OK. We can make it happen," Daddy said. "Should we have some cake now? Just a tiny piece for me, please."

"No, Daddy! You have to have a big piece. I made this cake!"

"All right. A big piece, then."

Eko lit the five candles. "Princess Kiko, make a wish."

Kiko closed her eyes and wished for: ayi to come home very soon; everyone—but especially herself—to have as much chocolate as they wanted, and not only on the weekends; a real pet baby tiger; and her mother and father to always be happy. Even though a happy open heart was actually broken, wasn't it? So happiness was sort of the same as sadness.

She blew out all the candles.

Hanami

February 2028

I left your grandfather in the cherry blossom season of 1993. On the last day of March."

"Okaasan, they don't need to hear this."

"Well, maybe I want to tell it."

"Tell it nicely, if you must."

"I'm always nice!"

"Maman. You are nice-looking. You are nice to talk to. You have nice stories, yes."

"Tell me, when was I ever anything but nice to you?"

"Truthfully?"

"Oh, never mind. Why don't you go on and busy yourself with whatever it is you have to do?" Daphne winked at her granddaughters, and they giggled. Eko rolled her eyes and walked up the stairs, calling back to her daughters: "I'll be in my studio in case your grand-mère starts with the horror stories."

"My dears, where was I before I was so rudely interrupted? Ah, yes. The last day of March 1993, just days before the peak of the bloom. The thing about hanami is that everyone is always so happy. Remember when we went last year? Happy, happy, happy. But in 1993, I was miserable. I had been, for a long time.

"You see? Your grandfather was the firstborn, and not only that, but a firstborn son. Those things mattered back then. Oh, I suppose they still do. But I'll give you an example. I remember there was one time he slapped me across the face because—and we were in the car with the whole family—Eko wanted to open the window and I wouldn't let her. In the middle of the winter! Firstborn of the firstborn. You see? I was treated this way. (Oh, but then, after I left, you should have seen how he begged me to come back, to bring your mother home.)

"That year, the blossoms were particularly full. I remember taking Eko on a walk along Tetsugaku no Michi, the Philosopher's Path. The petals were already covering the ground. Spring snow. (Your grandfather, by the way, when he was courting me, he used to say that I was the real-life version of Satoko. That's Mishima. You will read him when you're older. Then you will think of me. You will remember this day.)

"All the petals on the ground. Everyone with their film cameras. It wasn't like now. But actually, it was, wasn't it? Eyes covered by little windows. Nobody looking at things directly. I didn't own a camera. I didn't own anything in that house. I couldn't even eat a chocolate without it being offered to me by his mother, who was always there, always watching, criticizing, ratting on me.

"Eko was starting to know things too. She was even younger than you, Yukiko—but she saw the way they treated me. Like some housemaid. She'd started treating me the same, talking down to me. That was the worst part, I tell you. The beatings? I could take it. Every Japanese woman of my age—well, you don't know, and things have changed, a little. But my own daughter looking down on me! Do you know what she would have become? That's how I knew I was running out of time.

"The old house—your grandfather still lives there now. With his, what, fifth wife? So that tells you something, eh? That house was *unlivable.* Maybe it was tolerable in the summer, but in the winter, his mother took her spot at the kotatsu and shared with no one. Your grandfather loved the cold. Said it rejuvenated him. He was always siding with her, saying that I didn't need to be warm; that the kotatsu was only for old women and children.

"You see, I grew up in a danchi. Not that old kind of Kyoto home but a great big apartment block. People say now 'les taudis,' 'les quartiers pauvres,' you know—and, yes, we called those danchi 'rabbit hutches,' 'usagi goya,' but *avec amour.*

"My father was fifteen at the end of the war. He never was able to go to university to become a scholar, his dream. He worked, a little. Mostly he read books. He never, ever talked to our neighbors. He was always too good for them, for the danchi. But I loved it. I loved growing up there. All my friends, all our adventures. The grass, the fountains. No one watching us. So you can imagine going from that to the big house where I was always alone, with her. Always: not allowed to go out.

"And, you know, I loved to go out. I met your grandfather out. Yes, at the discotheque. Well, needless to say, he seemed all right when we met. And I was something too. Oh, back then I used to slick my hair back, line my eyes big with kohl—wings like daggers, silver glitter to my brows. Haha! You should have seen me then. Dresses up to here, shirts down to there. Girls, you must enjoy your beauty while you have it. Be sexy when you can!

"We went out to the clubs, the all-you-can-eats. We saw Pink Lady! Twice! I had this Pink Lady hat, a Pink Lady set of roller skates. I loved those. No? You don't know Pink Lady? I'll have to play you some. The Bee Gees? 'Stayin' Alive'? No? *Ah, ah, ah, ah, stayin' alive, stayin' alive*? Oh, girls, you are killing me.

"Back then, do you know what they called me? They called me Birdie. Badi. Because of my eyes, the wings. I didn't have the name Daphne; that I only started to use after I was working in France.

"But your grandfather. That wretched old man could dance, I'll tell you that. I remember it was '79, at a party at the Petal Club called Ladies One Night, and we had to go, we always went, me and all my girlfriends from the danchi. Me—Badi—in heels that were like samurai weapons. Oh, we were dangerous. 'I'm So Glad That I'm a Woman.' 'Lady Marmalade.' 'Le Freak.' 'Hot Stuff.' Yes, that's what was playing when your grandfather and I met. I was free dancing, and the lights were going, and there he was with his friends in the opposite corner of the dance floor. He had a mustache back then. A joke of a mustache. We danced toward one another and then around each other, like animals gearing up for battle.

"You know, girls, a man is never as he seems at the discotheque. Remember that. He only reveals himself at home.

"So, yes. Hanami.

"I had been thinking of leaving for some time. That day, there along the path with Eko, I knew that the flowers would continue to bloom and then fade, as they do. And then bloom again, and fade again. Would that be my life, forever? I didn't need a camera for the trees. Nothing was ever going to change. But the main thing that mattered, that needed saving, was Eko. Your mother.

"The very next day I went to apply for a visa to France. Do you know how hard it was to get a visa back then? I needed everything to be the utmost of secrets. I squirreled away the little food allowance your grandfather gave me (cheap, he was always cheap, which is why, even though I never had anything, I always knew what it meant to spend when necessary), and we ate potatoes and roots for a few weeks, so I'd have some spending money once we left. The man processing my visa, he asked for my letter of permission to take Eko out of the country. He almost denied my application. I won't go into how I ended up with those visas. Another story, for another day. When you are older.

"We left before the final flowers opened. Eko and I dressed for a trip to the market. I had only my basket, lined with all the cash I could find, which your grandfather had kept hidden in the bedroom.

"When we finally landed in Paris, I changed the cash to francs, and we walked around all afternoon. I was surprised to see cherry trees there as well, and in bloom. We took up at the first hotel I could find. That night, alone with your mother, and free at last, I felt so light and fresh, unburdened by a weight that had been pressing down on me for so long.

"The trees, they need to shed their flowers. To them, I realized, that extraneous beauty is dead weight, like a brittle set of fingernails, or too-long hair. When the flowers fall, the trees can reach their gnarled, naked fingers through the air, breathe in the sun and the rain. I was only just entering the warmest season of my life.

"Ahh. Ladies, Grand-mère needs a drink and *une petite sieste.* Shall we take a little break from story time?"

"Yes, Grandma," Yumi and Yoko said. Kiko had fallen asleep. It was just after lunchtime, and she still sometimes took a nap.

Daphne pulled her shawl over her shoulders and raised herself out of the hard chair, her hands grasping the blond skeleton of wood that wrapped itself in a contorted weave around a single thin cushion. "I don't know why your mother buys such ugly, uncomfortable things," she said before she walked up the stairs, to the guest bedroom.

Yoko looked at Yumi and asked, "Is that true? Is that what happened to Ma?"

"I don't know. She said to take what Grandma says with a grain of salt, remember?"

"Oh, right."

The girls, nine and seven, put on their shoes and went out to play in the backyard, where they were constructing a fort from old sheets, hung from the shoulders of patio chairs.

Torpor

December 2026

You spend your mornings meditating. In your meditations, you see gardens—the gardens of your childhood. The gardens of Kyoto, karesansui gardens, the sand and stone carefully arranged into stillness, silence.

The gardens are married, in your meditations, to other gardens you've visited in your life. Gardens in Paris, in Sicily, in Suzhou and Guizhou. The gravel of a stone garden flows down from one rice terrace to the next, moving like water; the sound of rocks pouring onto rocks, eternally.

The gardens are teeming with life. The flower, the bonsai, the bumblebee. Such solace. You breathe in and out. No one can touch your garden. In your meditations, you are always alone.

Hedges from the Jardin du Luxembourg rise among scholar's rocks from the Humble Administrator's Garden. A hummingbird, as small as your cupped palm—no, smaller, a baby hummingbird—hovers in and out of the stone's holes. A large koi in a nearby pond swims lazily back and forth, grotesque mouth gaping in the murky green water. He is watching you.

You open your eyes to find yourself on the patio of your home. The sun is out; the maid is dusting the cupboards just inside. You go to the kitchen to fix yourself a cup of mugicha with ice.

The image of the koi haunts you. What did he want from you? Who invited him into your garden? You realize, with fear and disgust, that he wanted to eat the tiny hummingbird. He wanted you to feed it to him.

You sit down at your desk to collect your colors. The orange silk thread calls out to you. The koi wants to come to life, wants to be created. No. Instead you pull out an emerald green, a grass green, a royal blue. Black and gray for feathers. White for the soft belly. A small onyx bead for an eye.

You used to have to sketch out your creations beforehand, and then draw your sketches onto fabric. But now you simply thread your needle and go. You can see your design from start to finish, envision the process. Like a painter who begins a portrait with the underlash of an eye rather than the perfect oval of a face.

Years of needle and thread have weakened your eyesight. After an hour of stitchwork, you take a break and open your nature encyclopedia:

> The hummingbird lives between three to five years.
> The hummingbird remembers every flower and every bird feeder it's ever visited.
> The hummingbird goes into a hibernation-like state of inactivity called "torpor" when it is fatigued or starved.

> A baby hummingbird is the size of a penny and
> cannot fly.
> Hummingbirds do not mate for life.

You will finish your work before lunch, because after noon you will go to pick up your youngest daughter from her half day at nursery. Then your middle daughter from her special education class; she's not ready for regular school. But before that, as they nap, you will meditate once more. Before the patter of four little feet becomes the patter of six. And then, at seven, the splashing of bathwater onto cool tile; at eight, the cries and protests of bedtime; at nine, "Daddy!" when he comes home and wakes everyone up just as they're dozing off to their last story.

And, finally, the silence after nine thirty. He in his study and you back at your desk. All the lights on, as you affix the glimmering onyx onto the bird's lovely face.

You will retreat back into your garden just before bed, before the terse "good night," your garden that changes and grows with every visit. The Japanese garden. The Chinese garden. The wild and overseeded British garden. All the gardens of your life—their flora and fauna, their incongruent roots tangling together under the soil. Sunshine. Breath. Wind. Fragrance. A chipmunk nibbling on a chestnut. A butterfly emerging, wet and heavy, from its cracked cocoon.

The Girl of My Heart

February 2020

Doroteia was nearly fourteen months old when her parents told me they were going back to Portugal. I had only twenty days left with her.

I was in shock, even though this wasn't the first time I'd parted ways with a family. Things usually end abruptly, and you are never quite prepared. One day, you're chasing after each other in the park or buying vegetables together at the market for lunch; the next, you're out alone on the street with your suitcase and, if you're lucky, a red envelope of severance. You'll probably never see your kid again. Teia's mother was looking everywhere but directly into my face as she spoke. "Ayi, can I have a word?" was how she'd begun. It was how she always called me when she wanted to point out an area in need of improvement or to put in a request. I said nothing and held back my tears as she explained the details, her husband sitting silently by her side. It was because of the virus that had recently erupted all over China. Teia needed to go out and play, needed to start nursery school, and staying in Shanghai was too dangerous. They'd already explored the option of bringing me along to Portugal, sponsoring a work visa for me, but it had not proved possible.

I was upset, of course—angry at the short notice, angry at the secrecy with which they had planned everything, angry at them for leaving, for taking away Teia. But I was holding the babe, and she was nuzzling against my neck, saying "Ai Ai," calling me. I touched her perfect little cheek and said, "Yes, yes, Ai is here."

"It's not going to be easy for Teia," her mom said. And a moment later, "It's not going to be easy for any of us."

Was she thinking of herself, who slept in till noon and had never once in Teia's life changed a diaper? Was she thinking of her husband, who played with the baby for just ten minutes after work each day, before I took Teia for her bath? Or was she thinking of me, who had spent nearly every moment with Teia since she was three weeks old? I had hoped that I might stay on with them until my retirement in several years' time, that I might see a sibling for Teia, or at least see her grow into a child.

"This is settled?" I asked.

"Yes, it's settled. We've bought our plane tickets, and we'll leave on February tenth."

I excused myself, handing Teia over to her mother, and went into my room, closing the door. My room was also Teia's room; I slept on a kid-size mattress on the floor, just beside her crib. One day the mattress would belong to Teia, when she transitioned into a toddler bed. All this time, I thought to myself, they'd been preparing for this day, the day I'd no longer be with them. I lay down on my bed, pushed my face into the pillow, and let myself cry. I took care not to let them hear me—I knew just how barely soundproof the rooms of the apartment were—and let the news settle in slowly until it became real. I pulled a small blanket out of Teia's crib and inhaled her scent. It was partly her scent and partly my scent. Our scents had mixed. I looked at the blanket with its little pink lambs, and I swear it was the first time I thought, in Teia's home, *Would they miss this if it disappeared?*

The reality of my situation hit me. I would need to find a new job in twenty days, and a new place to live. But how would I do that when I couldn't leave the apartment and when employers likely weren't conducting interviews? Everyone was scared of the virus. Teia's parents wouldn't even let me step out into the hallway to throw away the trash. Who would be looking for a nanny to come into their home now?

Then came my concerns about money. Would they pay me through the rest of the month? And how about my bonus that was due at the Lunar New Year? I bolstered myself, looking into my phone's camera to check that my eyes weren't puffy, and went back out to negotiate.

Teia's mom was holding her. When I emerged from the bedroom, Teia reached out to me, and I took her, resting her on my left hip, my arm around her belly. Only twenty more days. I would not get to see her run, to hear her first sentences, to see how naughty she would become at the age of two. These thoughts made me want to cry all over again. Teia stuck her finger up my nose, and I reflexively said, "Nose, nose."

Teia's mom sat down on the couch and gestured for me to sit too. I put Teia on my lap, facing sideways, so they could see her as well.

"My husband knows a forum where foreigners post nanny recommendations, and he will add your information. We will help you find a job as soon as possible." Teia's father nodded when his wife translated what she'd said into English for him. He was Portuguese, and he'd met her four years ago here in Shanghai.

"Thank you," I said. "But I can't imagine it'll be easy to find work during this time."

"It'll be a glowing recommendation," she said.

I nodded, thinking. What else could I do? I decided to bring it up. I had to speak up for myself. "And what are your thoughts about my final salary?"

They would prorate my bonus and pay me through the end of the month. "And if you can't find another job in the next twenty days, you can stay in our place through the end of our lease, though it will be empty—"

Teia's father interrupted, and they spoke among themselves. I could make out only a few of the words they said, including "ayi," "day," "Teia," and "go." Before that moment, I had been proud of myself, thinking that I'd learned so many English words over the past year working for this foreign family. But I realized, sitting there with Teia on my lap, wondering about my future and what my employers were planning for me, that I'd picked up mostly useless words from the electronic vocabulary toys that I put in front of Teia to distract her while changing her diaper: "birdie," "banana," "sun," "moon."

I looked around at the apartment—the small two-bedroom, one-bathroom apartment on the ground floor, the windows getting little light and the floors damp with mold in the summer. I had been happy in this cramped and dingy space, even though

I'd had to wear my outdoor shoes inside because Teia's father, European, didn't like taking his off.

But what would this place be without Teia? How could I stay here on my own without her? How could I live, at all, without her? I remembered with relief a group that I had a membership of my own in, where I could post my services. My thoughts seesawed wildly between the tragic and the practical.

It was time for Teia's nap, though. I took her into our room, holding her tighter than was necessary. Suddenly I regretted the times I'd felt tired, bored, cranky in the middle of a long day. If only I'd known that those days were numbered. I pushed back Teia's dark curls that were just starting to grow out and frame her face. I took in her eyes, heavy with sleep, lashes thick and long. Her heart-shaped mouth and thin lips, the pointy chin. She was the most beautiful little girl I'd ever seen. But was that true or only my bias as her nanny? I stared down at her and rocked her in my arms, stepping over my bed as I walked the figure-eight pattern I repeated while putting her to sleep. I didn't really need to rock her anymore, but I couldn't bear to put her down just yet, not today.

When Teia was tiny, she'd been an ugly little thing. Barely a month old, with a wide mouth that took up half her face, wrinkly eyes, and hair like a balding middle-aged man's, receding from the forehead in a deep arc. As a nanny, you always hope for a cute baby to care for, a lovely child with a good personality and deep sleeping skills. Teia had neither of these.

That girl had a temper from the beginning. If you took away her favorite toy—a stuffed dog the size of my palm—she screamed at the top of her lungs. If she finished all the milk in her bottle, she screamed at the top of her lungs. If she was given an extra bottle right away, she screamed at the top of her lungs: you were too late, you'd lost your chance to make things right! And what a scream. She'd stare right at you with those big, brown, wrinkly eyes, as if to say, *I understand everything. I blame you entirely, and I will never forgive you.*

Teia was sleeping soundly now in my arms. How many tantrums I'd endured with this one! How many thrown bottles and thrown toys and thrown clothes. "Wait, just you wait, till she turns two," I'd always say to her mother. "We're really in for it with her."

But I would never see Teia turn two, never see her become a feisty brat, never get the chance to discipline her, or to spoil her, or to answer her curious questions about the world. I put her down in her crib. She slept best there, and she'd be grumpy all afternoon without a good midday nap. I couldn't help myself, however: I stroked her forehead, running my hands through her soft curls. She stirred, and I slowly moved away.

I'D TAKEN CARE OF a few babies before Teia, all girls. They were fine, and the families were nice enough—some more demanding than others, some more complicated. But what I felt for those previous babies paled compared to what I felt for Teia. Even my feelings for my own son, raised by his grandparents back in the village and now at marriage age himself, seemed muted in comparison. Maybe it was because I'd been with Teia from the very early days of her life. Or maybe it was because her mother had chosen not to breastfeed, and so I'd fed Teia almost every meal, formula night and day. Maybe it was the work I'd put in dealing with all her tantrums. Whatever it was, Teia was something different to me, something special.

I had only become a nanny seven years earlier, after the accident. I'll always remember it clearly. It was the day of my son's high school entrance exam. There had been a big snowstorm in Dongbei, and I was at work, doing double duty for my friend at the dried-sausage-cutting station. She was interviewing at another factory, across town. My mind was wandering. Should I switch factories, as well? I was getting older, and standing all day, looking down at the assembly line of sausages, was taking its toll on my neck. Should I ask for a few days' leave to go back home and tend to my son, Xiling? To cook him his favorite spicy rice cakes, wish him luck on his exams? It was those spicy rice cakes I was thinking of when I brought the knife down clean through the last joint of the fourth finger on my left hand. The blood gushed out immediately, but it took me a while to realize what was happening, to register the pain. Already the girls to my left and right were jumping into action. They'd all seen something similar before—a finger, a fingernail, a chunk of flesh, the greater part of a hand.

So I got to go home early, in the end. My son failed his entrance exam. And I started to look for a new job. It took a good three weeks for my hand to heal over. I tended to it myself at home with cotton gauze and alcohol wipes and iodine and fresh snow. It hurt like hell. I can still sometimes feel the pain, still sometimes feel the finger's missing length wriggling around.

During my time off from the factory, an acquaintance of a friend of my cousin's suggested I consider working as a nanny in Shanghai. I could make a good living, double what I was making at the factory. And if I lived in, I could save money on meals and rent as well. I thought about going back to the factory, filling sausages the width of my lost finger, the ground pork crimson and pulpy as my open wound was for nearly two weeks straight. The fever that had raged through my entire body for several days as I fought off infection. Never again did I want to go back there.

I called my husband to tell him that I was considering moving to Shanghai to find work as a nanny. At that time, he was in Ningbo, working on a construction site for a shopping mall. He scoffed. "You really think you can take care of kids with your finger like that?" I had sent him photos and videos every day of my hand's recovery. "Shanghainese won't like us northerners looking after their kids. And with your disfigured hand? Good luck with that!" My husband's doubts made me want to succeed even more. His cruelty to me in the first years of our marriage, plus his constant philandering, had left scars that would never heal. It was when he brought up Xiling that I made up my mind. "You never even raised our own kid. What makes you think you can raise other people's?" I hung up and booked my ticket to Shanghai.

I *had* raised our boy until he was one, before giving him over to my in-laws when I left to find work in the toy factory, then the sausage factory. My husband had a point, though. What did I know back then, what did I remember now? I was only twenty-six when Xiling was born and had little interest in being a mother. All I'd wanted was to find work, make money, and get away from my husband. Even before I left, I'd had help from my own parents in taking care of my son. But if women all over the world could raise kids, could it really be so hard?

The acquaintance gave me the contact information of an agent, and I came to Shanghai on the slow train, a journey of four days. I paid for a three-day course on childcare, got my certification, and passed a health check at the community clinic. With those documents I landed my first job, taking care of a five-month-old girl until she was two. It was much easier, and much better, than working in the factory. The pay was good too. After the first girl, another baby for about a year; then another, a toddler. And then I came to Teia.

Two nights before Teia's departure and I was still looking for a job. Her parents were busy packing the last of their belongings into boxes for the shipping company, and Teia was jumpy and wired, sensing a big change coming, confused as to why pieces of furniture were disappearing one by one. I was anxious as well; I needed a job, and I needed the money to keep coming in. Not only because I planned to pay for the construction of my son's house, where he would live one day with his future wife, but also because we were having a family crisis back in my hometown. My younger sister's husband and daughter had been arrested for running an investment-fraud scheme, and we were all pooling money together for a red packet for the local police, a gift that would secure visitation rights. I really couldn't afford to have a long stretch of time between jobs.

After posting to various nanny groups online, contacting an agency that would take the entirety of my first month's salary, and doing several video interviews with prospective families, I'd almost found someone willing to hire me. Local Shanghainese, an extended family, which I did not prefer—grandparents were a nuisance, always home and often opinionated, or otherwise wanting to chitchat. In the end, though, they'd decided against hiring me. The agent tried to put it nicely, but the family simply didn't want a nanny from Dongbei. Shanghainese were like that, thinking they were better than everyone else.

I was scrambling. Sending messages whenever I had spare time, spending all night on my phone, forwarding my resume. I was asking my friends to ask their friends. Meanwhile, Teia's parents were done with me. They didn't ask me to cook or clean anymore. They didn't want me to help them pack. I did not complain, because it also gave me more time with Teia and more time to find my next job.

Just when I was about to book a bed at the domestic-worker hostel—a top bunk in an eight-person room with a shared bathroom in the hall and free board if I was willing to help cook the two daily meals in the canteen—I got a message from an acquaintance of Teia's mother. She and her husband were switching out their daytime nanny for someone live-in, to lower the risk of contracting the virus. We scheduled a video call for that night, after Teia went to sleep.

I crouched in the corner of the small kitchen, waiting. At eight o'clock sharp they called, their handsome faces squeezed close up into the screen. They looked like kind people. They'd never had a live-in before. They accepted the terms of my salary right away, even though I took a risk and asked for two hundred more a month than I received at Teia's. We were all desperate people in a strange, desperate time. They asked me only two things. One was: Would I mind not leaving their apartment for a while, until the virus situation calmed down? I was fine with that; I had nowhere I was planning to go. And I was surprised when they also asked me if I had any requirements for them, like room or bed size, or a TV. I had never been asked that question in all my working years. Why would I be making demands like that? I told them, truthfully, that I only required a place to sleep. Then I said, "There's just this one thing," and I showed them over the phone my damaged finger. They asked about it, how the injury came to be, the father translating my Chinese into another language for his wife. He asked me if there was anything I couldn't do because of the missing finger. And I said no, it didn't affect my work or life at all. And with that it was settled. The father would come to pick me up the very same afternoon of Teia's departure.

Teia knew something was special about that last day, but she didn't understand what it was. She was crawling all over the empty apartment, slapping the suitcases and squealing with joy. Something new, babies always like something new. Probably she thought she was going to a restaurant or on a daytime outing with just her parents, which she sometimes—not often, but occasionally—did. I kept an eye on her as she surveyed the vast new play spaces in the apartment. Finally the truck arrived and her parents brought the last of their luggage to the street.

"Goodbye, my Teia," I said, as we stood in the doorway, holding the door open for her parents. "I'm going to miss you so much, so much." Teia thought we were saying goodbye to her father, who holed himself up every morning in his bedroom to work. She kept waving at him and saying, "Bye-bye, Dada." I kissed her cheeks, which were silky-soft, more yellow than pink. She had her mother's Chinese coloring, rather than her father's. I touched her hands and her little feet, rubbing them in my hands and nibbling on her toes the way she liked, the bursts of laughter warming my heart but also filling it with fearful sorrow. No longer would I hear that cackling laughter, that naughty giggle. My Teia! I hugged her so tight that she pushed me away, but I held her head firmly in my hand and I kissed her cheek again and again, again and again. My own cheeks were damp with tears; I could not hold them back.

When it was time to give Teia to her parents, I wanted to take photos, but at the same time I didn't want to let her go for the one moment it would take me to grab my phone from our room. I hugged Teia and gave her a last kiss on the cheek. Teia's mother gave me a pat on the back, saying she was so sorry it had to be this way, that I had been the best nanny they ever could have hoped for. I was embarrassed. I wiped away the tears and turned my face.

But then she had taken her daughter, and I turned back to see them leaving. It all happened so fast. Teia was watching me over her mother's shoulder as they walked away, saying "Ai? Ai?" I broke down, the tears streaming across my face, my mouth pulling itself into a sorrowful frown. I saw Teia's eyes locked on mine and crumpling up in preparation for one of her legendary tantrums. Oh, how I wanted to run to her, to wrap her up in my arms and comfort her in the way just I knew how. Her mother would soon be at a loss, frazzled and frustrated. She would pat Teia's back awkwardly and look around for someone to help. In my mind I was already out the door and in the car with Teia, helping her complete the difficult journey, her first. But I could not budge from the doorway, because I was still holding the door open, the door that would close and lock automatically, and I did not have a key.

THE NEW FAMILY WAS PICTURE-PERFECT. The mother was young and pretty, Japanese; the father handsome and rich, a local. Their apartment was spacious and modern and bright, decorated in different shades of gray.

I was given my own room, with floor-to-ceiling windows overlooking the skyscrapers of downtown Shanghai from the thirtieth floor—a far cry from the small room I shared with Teia in the ground-floor flat in the Pudong outskirts of the city. In my new place, I had a queen-size bed with such soft sheets whose washing instructions I couldn't understand because the tags were written in Japanese.

My first night there, I felt so lonely I could cry. The baby girl, Yumi, slept through the night in her own spacious room, and in any case her father insisted on taking care of the occasional wake-ups. With nothing to do, I sat at the edge of my expansive bed, looking out at the constellation of lights that made up my adopted city. It was what one always imagines when one thinks of Shanghai from the countryside. I thought of Teia, sleeping alone for the first time in her life. She would think that I'd abandoned her. *Where is Ai Ai?* Would her mother know what to do, how to prepare the bottle of milk Teia always expected at five in the morning?

Thoughts like these kept me up till the early hours. Worry for Teia, mostly, with flashes of anger at her parents, then understanding toward them, and finally resignation at the realities of my line of work.

I told myself, as I shed the last tears of my first night at the new place, that I would soon find myself just as attached to Yumi, who was nearly the same age as Teia, as deliciously plump as a southern squash, and, I could already tell, much more gentle natured.

. . .

More than six years passed in the employ of Yumi's household. At first, her pretty Japanese mother and I would butt heads on child-rearing ideas. Living in a new home always requires a time of adjustment. I was also not used to sharing work with a hands-on mother. But I was not young when I first entered Yumi's house. Full-time childcare had begun to take its toll on my body, and eventually I grew to enjoy my partnership with Yumi's mother. She watched the children as I cleaned and cooked, and in her spare time she pursued her hobby—a passion for hand embroidery that slowly grew into a small online business.

Over those six years, she gave birth to two more children, both girls, both as mild-mannered and pretty as Yumi and she. Each time a new baby came along, we moved into a larger place. From the gray high-rise where I first came into their employ, we moved into a fifth-story apartment in an old building a few blocks away, overlooking a neighborhood park. And from there, into a gigantic seven-bedroom villa with two floors and a large fenced-in garden in the back. The children's father clearly did very well for himself, and he worked long hours, though I was never quite sure exactly what he did. In the last house, each child had her own room on the first floor, while the parents slept upstairs in a suite and kept two offices for their separate work. His had a tall drawing table against the window, always covered in blueprints and rulers and pages full of numbers. Along the opposite wall were large computer monitors. The cracks in the keyboards always needed dusting because of his habit of snacking on sunflower seeds. Hers was an embroidery room, with shelves and shelves of rainbow-colored thread, silk pincushions stuck with endless needles, and intricate embroideries of trees and flowers displayed on the walls. The loose and discarded materials required constant reorganizing. I had my own bedroom, of course, a small one on the ground floor, separated from the children's area and just off the kitchen. When I showed my friends and family pictures of each new house, they were always impressed. I had to admit, it was nice living. Though it was difficult to clean such big spaces.

The spring before the youngest, Yukiko, was to go into preschool, Yumi's mother informed me that the family would be taking a summer trip to Lisbon. Then she said, "If you want, you can get in touch with Teia and see her. I don't know if you're still in contact . . ." Yumi's mother had never forgotten. That was so like her. Every now and again, in the first year I worked for them, she'd ask about Teia, and occasionally I pinged Teia's mother for updates. But those updates had grown sparser as the years passed.

For a while, after I first arrived, I would take breaks while Yumi slept and watch old Teia videos on my phone. I did not share them with Yumi's mother unless asked, because I know that truly one's charge is never that interesting to others. Over the years, I thought of Teia sometimes, especially as Yumi grew and changed in the same ways Teia would—walking, running, attending school, trying ballet. But I became busier with Yumi, then Yoko, and then Yukiko, and gradually I'd come to bond with Yumi. It was much easier to connect with her sisters, as their mother was busier, less attached to her second and third, and starting to see her embroidery business pick up. I like to think, too, that she'd grown to trust me more and more.

The lead-up to the trip was busy and exciting. The family traveled abroad often, at least twice a year since travel resumed, and they always took me with them. At that point, I'd joined them in Thailand, Korea, Germany, Singapore, Italy, and the United States. And for one month every summer, I accompanied the girls and their mother to Kyoto and to the French countryside. I really saw the world with them. Two days out from our flight, the girls' suitcases were all packed, Yumi's mother was checking that every corner of the house was clean, and Yumi's father was working late to prepare for a week out of the office. It was only then that I received a reply from Teia's mother:

> *Hello auntie! My, it's been such a long time. How are you? Definitely, we'd love to see you—where will you be visiting and staying? Sorry for the late reply, I don't check WeChat that much anymore.*

I saw the message as it came through, and I waited, hoping she'd send a photo or video of her daughter as well. I wondered how Teia had grown, how her features might have expanded or contracted into girlhood. But no such photo appeared.

I replied with a smiley emoji. And then I sent all our details—the dates, the fancy hotel in Lisbon where we'd reserved two suites, even our flight number. Teia's mother replied: *Perhaps afternoon tea on the sixth?*

I rushed into the kitchen, where Yumi's mom was bent over the garbage can, checking for stains and sniffing out a faint odor. "Yumi Mama?" I said, and she popped up, with a slightly distracted expression that meant she was thinking, or that she was unhappy.

"Yes? By the way, we may need to wash this when you have some spare time," she said, pointing into the empty pail.

"Sure thing," I said. Yumi's mom always expressed her demands in this way—as optional and flexible—but I knew she expected prompt action. I picked up the can and brought it out to the patio, where I began to fill it from the outdoor faucet.

"So I've heard back from Teia's mother," I shouted back into the house.

"Wonderful! Are they still in Portugal?"

"Yes, and they're wondering if tea on the sixth is possible."

Yumi's mother paused to think, likely considering the family's detailed itinerary, which she carefully planned before every trip. I finished rinsing the pail and returned inside. She looked at me and nodded. "That's perfect, actually. Early enough into our trip that it will let us consult the locals for suggestions. You'll have to insist they come to our hotel for tea. We can do it all together."

I was both relieved and dismayed by this response. It would be nice to have the family there as a buffer for any awkwardness, and yet I did not know how much time I'd have with Teia—if it would be enough. I could already see Yumi's mother dominating the conversation with her gently persistent stream of questions about local restaurants, museums suitable for children, and off-the-beaten-path attractions.

"Sure, thank you," I said, and went back to my room to make the plans.

Portugal was the most beautiful place I'd ever been. Italy came closest—but from where we were in Lisbon, everywhere we turned we could see the ocean.

So many places there were in the world. If only I'd known earlier, I would have started my career as a nanny for foreigners much younger. I hadn't even left Dongbei for the first time until the age of forty.

The first couple of days in Lisbon, we rode a trolley tour and visited a beach. Everywhere was seafood and meat—cured hams—and no green vegetables in sight. Yoko, five years old and most attached to me, got so blocked up that I had to hold her hand and rub her belly for an hour while she sat on the toilet. Yumi, preferring only her mother in infancy, continued to prefer her. Yukiko, the most outgoing and fearless among them—and in that way, the most like Teia—had always been happy to venture forth on her own.

And so we walked along the cobblestone streets of Lisbon, up and down hills that gave me calf cramps in the middle of the night, in our pairs: Yumi and her mother, Yoko and me, and Yukiko and her father, who indulged his littlest, his last, and often wore her atop his shoulders.

I thought about the end of my career, my working life, my comfortable and, you could even say, luxurious time with the Yang family. The little girls I'd raised. Had I loved them? I had, especially Yoko. Had I loved them as much as I'd loved Teia? Over ice cream the flavor of pistachio nuts and as pale green as a budding ginkgo tree, I imagined Teia tasting for the first time this savory ice cream in her new country. It cut a sharp pain in my heart not to have been there, here. No, I'd loved Teia like none other. Doroteia, who had been so tiny I could hold her for hours on end in one arm. Maybe for a nanny there was always only one—like a true love. Naturally, I loved my own son, now grown and married. But it was different with him; in a way, Xiling was never truly mine. His own son, turning one in a few months, I'd met only once, briefly—but I'd been working then, too, bringing the girls and their parents to Dongbei for a ski trip during the winter holidays.

The sixth arrived. The girls were less jet-lagged and cranky, and I took particular care in the afternoon to brush my hair into a nice bun and put on a dress. Over the years, Yumi's mother had given me some pieces she didn't wear, and I'd brought along one of those, a long dress, for the occasion. I checked my reflection on our way out. Older, a bit thinner, but not too different from six years ago. Would Teia recognize me? Would she remember at all? In my rational mind, I knew she wouldn't. Babies don't remember anything before the age of two or three. But still I was nervous, was anxious to meet her expectations, if she had any.

Yoko insisted on holding my hand the entire elevator ride and walk into the restaurant. I was flustered because we were already twenty minutes late to a meeting in our own hotel. But taking three children anywhere, even downstairs, took time, and Yumi's mom had taken a longer bath than anyone expected.

The restaurant was only half-full, and I spotted Teia and her parents right away, almost directly in the center of the large, open room. Oh, Teia—she was a big girl now. I'd known it, but I'd not been prepared. Her face had grown long like her father's, her jaw protruding a bit, her wide mouth more masculine with the years. I guess I'd expected her to look like a larger version of her baby self, which was now only vaguely present.

Yumi had retained her baby face, with thick, long hair that everyone commented on. The possibility hadn't entered my mind that Teia wouldn't be as beautiful as Yumi, Yoko, and Yukiko. I guess because I hadn't loved them as much, and love always makes someone more beautiful. Still, she was the girl of my heart. Memories flooded my mind—feeding her in the first weeks of her life, playing with her on the lush grounds of a university near her parents' place.

Her parents had aged. Her father was fatter than he'd been when she was born, and her mother looked worn out. Likely she didn't have help raising her daughter. I knew she'd quit her job in fashion design once they moved to Portugal.

I, on the other hand, was flanked by beauty. In a way, it made me feel somewhat victorious: *Look at the beautiful family who hired me, and look at the beautiful girls I raised, and look at their high-quality clothes and the fancy hotel we stay at and how long they've kept me around.* As if all this would make Teia's parents regret their decision of six years ago, to leave China during the virus, to let me go so abruptly, so devastatingly. Hadn't the virus spread everywhere else, anyway? Their leaving had been, ultimately, in vain. And yet they'd had Teia, and so, even with all this beauty on my side, I still managed to end up with the loss.

I could not help myself. I let go of Yoko's hand as soon as she was seated, and I walked around to the other side of the table. I cupped my hand against Teia's face and embraced her. She didn't move, and so I ended up hugging her sideways while she looked at the Yangs one by one. Words poured out of my mouth: "Teia, you've become so big! Oh, Nanny remembers you as a little baby. Do you remember nanny? 'Ai Ai'? You used to call me 'Ai Ai'! Oh, how I've missed you. Are you well and healthy? Do you like Portugal?"

Teia continued to stare at the Yangs. Her mother interrupted me, pulling me out of my embrace with Teia. "Auntie, I'm sorry to say, but Teia doesn't speak Chinese. It's tough here—no one but me to speak with her, and ever since school started, it's been Portuguese nonstop."

"She forgot . . . everything?" Six years ago, I would take Teia to the grocery store every day and point out all the fruits and vegetables. By the time she left, she'd known so many words: "pingguo," "xiangjiao," "qiezi."

Yumi said something to Teia in English, and the two seven-year-olds began a conversation, showing off their dolls to each other. I sat back down in my seat and watched them speaking a language I could not understand. Yoko slipped her hand into mine, and I gave it a squeeze.

The parents were also chatting together in English. I heard "ayi . . . ayi" several times at the start of their conversation, but the pace of it was so fast. At first, my heart jumped because I wondered if they were comparing my monthly salary. If so, Yumi's parents would know that I'd lied a little bit about what Teia's family paid me, hoping to increase my rate, all those many years ago. I watched their faces—the smooth, pretty faces on my left, and the fat, tired faces across from me. They were not concerned. I realized, finally, why they were referring to me over and over. The only thing these two families had in common was me.

Teia and Yumi played together peacefully nearly the entire time, as I nibbled on some sweet fancy cakes and breads that were the colors of baby blankets and hats and shoes. But suddenly there was a commotion, as Teia screamed "No!" and sharply slapped Yumi on the head. The two girls had switched dolls, and Yumi had begun undressing Teia's baby, in order to give her a bath in the breadbasket.

Everyone was silent for the briefest of moments, and then everything erupted into action. Yumi began to sob, and her mother rushed over to hug her and to check for any bruises. I also went to Yumi, taking with me some clean napkins from the next table over, so I could wipe her tears and runny nose. Yumi was quick to cry; she had been coddled so as a baby. Teia looked sulkily at us and quietly pulled her doll from the breadbasket. So she had become as naughty and unruly as I'd expected! My heart raced. Her mother began to scold her, in a language I assumed was Portuguese, but with a little bit of Chinese mixed in. "What a bad girl!" I heard. And then, "How many times do I need to repeat myself?" Teia folded her arms across her chest and looked around the table. Her eyes met mine. I had to say something. Maybe she did understand some Chinese after all.

"Teia, it's not right to hit another child. You have to use your words to express your frustration. You have to say what you feel." I explained this patiently, but she looked away from me, an act of rebellion. I almost laughed, almost smiled. Her mother, however, stared at me in disbelief. "Ayi," she said, "in Portugal, we don't discipline or comment on other people's children. Thank you." And after a pause, she added, "I already told you Teia doesn't understand Chinese." She turned her attention back to Teia, and spoke to her now only in Portuguese, without a single word of Chinese mixed in. I looked away, back to Yumi, who was calming down. Yumi's mother had been watching us, too, but set about fixing Yumi's skirt and smoothing her hair. I burned inside—I felt angry, embarrassed—and yet I did not know what I could do. I returned to the other side of the table and attended to Yukiko.

It was approaching time for Teia's family to leave, anyway. And little Kiko was starting to get cranky for her midday nap. They stood up, and Teia was made to apologize to Yumi. Yumi was made to accept the apology. But we all parted soon after that, and nothing really seemed resolved.

On the way back to our suites, as I carried a grouchy Yukiko in my arms, I thought about how you can only ever own a little baby. A baby, an innocent baby, is yours to love and cherish and mold up until about the age of three. Kiko, at that age, was on the cusp of childhood. After three, children move further and further away. Where were all these children going? What was their rush?

And when it came to disciplining children, there would always be conflicts between a nanny and a family. Everyone had so many strong ideas about discipline. Saying goodbye to Teia that afternoon, I'd felt suddenly cool, with none of the warm emotion that had been bubbling within me before and during the first days of the trip. There was no Teia for me anymore; that was clear.

IT WAS SHORTLY AFTER the trip to Portugal that I announced to the Yang family my decision to retire. I was turning fifty-five that year, and I had developed persistent back pain and an issue with raising my right arm above my head. My son had also begun requesting my help with his kid.

My last days with Yumi's family went quickly, and less emotionally than I'd expected. I'd been in a kind of funk ever since the trip to Lisbon, like I had no capacity to feel anything directly, like I was seeing things through a misty veil. I guess you could say I was a bit depressed. I had become nothing to Teia, and we could not even communicate. Whereas all this time she had meant so much—everything—to me. It really made me feel like all my efforts were meaningless. Who was I to the babies and children I'd loved over the years? The Yang girls—they'd one day move on and forget me. Even Yoko, whose mother would take my place next to her as she strained and cried, red-faced on the toilet. Little Kiko would not recall me at all, most likely. At best, I would be a vague memory to her, someone her family occasionally talked about in the future.

The day before my departure, Yumi's mother presented me with a thin blanket, soft and pure white, of the same high-quality Japanese make of all the things in their house. On it was an incredibly intricate embroidery: her three girls and me holding hands and dancing in a circle around a magnolia tree, its petals falling all about us. Yumi's long hair was blowing in the wind; Yoko's was in the French braid she liked me to make for her every morning. Yukiko's cheeks were flushed with energy. My own face was squinted into a smile that I recognized as mine. Oh, the lovely, sweet-hearted girls. This blanket was the most exquisite thing I'd ever seen. Tears welled up in my eyes, but I blinked them away. "Thank you," I said, "thank you." Yumi's mother explained, "The magnolia is the official flower of Shanghai." I had never known that.

I took their generous gifts; their heavy, bulging red-packet cash bonus; and the two carry-on suitcases that had come with me from house to house over the years. Finally, my work was done. My long, sleepless nights rocking babies and patting toddlers, steaming milk bottles and folding little squares of laundry. I was going home.

I could count on my hands the number of times I'd returned to my hometown. It was not that I disliked it, or my family. It was just that the more days I worked, the more money I made. The longest trip home I'd taken was two years earlier, when my son got married. I'd spent twenty days there. It was the second time I'd met my daughter-in-law; she seemed nice enough, if a little young, at twenty-two. But I had been around that age myself when I'd married.

After a lengthy but enjoyable train ride (the Yangs had purchased me a first-class sleeper ticket), I got off at Jilin and transferred to a four-hour bus that would take me to my village. The landscape changed slowly from urban to mountainous, and by the time we arrived, the roads were shaded by a thick canopy of tall trees on either side. The fresh mountain air rushed in through the open windows. How often I'd talked of my hometown and the wealth of nature we possessed. The city kids I'd raised over the years—they grew up on pavement and in cars and apartments and museums. A wave of sorrow washed over me; I remembered Yoko's face, perfectly round with just-as-round black eyes and blunt bangs that framed her wide brows. Maybe one day I'd visit her in Shanghai, or maybe they'd come to Dongbei again. It was much closer than Lisbon.

But would that be any better than seeing Teia? I was no more a part of the Yang family than the steaming pot I used to make Yoko's favorite vegetable buns, no more than the doormat that said *Welcome* in Japanese, upon which they all wiped their shoes on wet, muddy days. No matter how I felt, I was not the girls' mother, pretty with dainty hands that were used to make equally dainty embroidery designs—flowers abuzz with bees, blossoming cherry trees, items from nature that she re-created from her native Japan.

At the bus station I waited for my son and his wife to pick me up. Finally, I would get to know the woman Xiling had married, my daughter-in-law. Would she be like Teia's mom, lazy and carefree, messy and unmaternal? Or would she be like Yumi's mom, meticulous and busy, protective and loving? Which would I prefer? If I were to help out as much as possible, maybe someone like Teia's mom would be easier to work with. On the other hand, for the past six years I'd become a kind of neat freak, as careful a worker as Yumi's mother required.

The cool wind blew against my face, and I noticed that in the time since I'd visited, they'd put up lampposts along the road. I observed this because at five o'clock sharp, they all turned on at once. I was wondering what other changes I might be able to catch around my hometown, when my son's car came up the lighted path.

His wife was in the front seat, holding the baby, Ping Ping, on her lap. Yumi's mother never would have allowed that—she strictly followed the rules when it came to infant safety. When we traveled to Japan, we'd be flush with luggage, folding strollers, and car seats for the little ones.

Xiling rolled down the window and waved as they approached. He stopped right in front of me, then jumped out to put my luggage in the trunk and open the back door. "Ma," he said. "Get in. You must be hungry."

His wife, Lei Lei, turned to greet me, and she waved the baby's hand at me. "Nainai, hello!" she said in a high-pitched voice. It had been years since I'd been called anything other than "ayi," and the new role felt strange, like it belonged to someone else and I was just trying it on for size.

Without warning, Lei Lei handed me the baby and we zoomed off, the streetlamps disappearing as soon as we left the vicinity of the station and entered the country roads. If I had known she was planning to give me the baby, I would have sanitized my hands with the gel I had in my bag, now in the trunk. I kept my dirty hands out of reach of the baby's mouth.

My son explained that I'd be staying with them for a while since repairs on my house hadn't yet been completed. Over the years, the money I sent back had gone to the construction of two large homes next to each other—one that I would share with my younger sister, and the other for my son and his wife. Apparently they were repainting the walls of my home because of some water damage. I listened to him recount the details while Lei Lei talked over him, exclaiming how tired I must be and wondering aloud what a first-class ticket might be like without asking me to give her any description.

The overlapping, loud chatter in the car was familiar and comforting—the style of my youth—and I sat back to soak it in while bouncing the boy carefully on my knee.

He was extraordinarily fat. They must have been overfeeding him to get him this large. His cheeks drooped, and his eyelids were thick. He stared at me and repeated, "Ba ba ba ba." He looked more like his mother than my son. Maybe it was because of all I'd been through in the last few weeks, but I still felt drained of much emotion, and I watched the boy as if he were a baby on a television show. I wondered when I'd be able to wash my hands properly.

We arrived at the houses. I'd often seen them in photos; I'd followed along as Xiling and my sister selected materials and designed layouts, and then as they were being constructed. But I'd only laid eyes on them for the first time during Xiling's wedding festivities. The houses were striking: twin buildings of light gray brick, topped with spires that pointed up into the sky. They were connected by a glass walkway between their third floors. The walkway had been Xiling's idea, and indeed it looked spectacular. During the wedding, the buildings were dressed in bright red garlands, lanterns burning bright on each corner. Inside, the houses had been full of people—neighbors coming by to eat the free food we served for weeks before and after, to check out the houses and the quality of our furniture, and, of course, to congratulate Xiling and me.

Now, in the evening light, and without the dressings of ceremony or the buzz of people milling through, the houses looked bare and forlorn. My sister was away visiting her ex-husband and daughter, and she would return to our village next week. Farmland and low hills surrounded the houses as far as the eye could see, speckled with homes and granaries.

I was shown into a guest bedroom. A photo of my late husband, from our wedding over thirty years ago, hung on one wall. I was glad they'd chosen a photo from his youth. It was nicer to remember him like that—not later, after he'd become gray with smoke and drink, after I'd lost track of who he was, of how many years we'd been apart, of how many other women in the village he'd bedded. I unpacked my two bags quickly, taking care to drape the blanket from Yumi's mother over the bed, the girls dancing right in the center. I did not turn on the light, and when I came back from the shower, the white blanket seemed to be glowing in the dark.

Outside the window, the sun had set, and I could see the black-on-black silhouette of distant hills. My bedroom was at the south side of the house, and I knew that one of those hills was our family's burial mountain. In it already were my parents, my husband, my elder sister, and her two babies who had died early of complications. There, too, were three generations of our ancestors. I stood in that window, staring out until the night deepened and I lost sight of the mountains. My stomach suddenly grumbled at the scent of food, and I went out to prepare for dinner and to see about the baby.

Ping Ping was crawling around in the kitchen as Lei Lei was frying up our meal. Yumi's mom would never let me bring the girls into the kitchen while I was using hot oil. I took the baby to the living room, saw that his diaper was heavy, and laid him down where they'd set up a small changing area near the sofa.

I got down on the floor. My knees hurt slightly—I had some joint issues after so many years of lifting and carrying and rocking. I picked up a diaper out of the pile and opened it flat. Ping Ping lay down obediently, staring at me and playing with his ears. Unsnap, one, two, three. I put the soiled diaper away and chuckled, surprised, at what I saw. Not that I hadn't realized Ping Ping was a boy—but seeing that small penis dangling between his thick thighs was a bit of a shock. After more than a decade of wiping and washing baby girls, I'd almost forgotten what a little hot pepper looked like.

Well, it was not rocket science. I took a fresh wet wipe and began to clean him. Ping Ping gave a chuckle. It was the first time I'd seen the boy smile. I smiled back at him and tickled his cheek, and he giggled, making me laugh. At that very moment, he smiled wider, shivered, and proceeded to let loose a warm stream of piss right up into my face. A touch even got into my mouth! I was in shock, but I also couldn't help doubling over in laughter.

"Oh, you little monster!" I babbled into Ping Ping's cheek. After I'd dried myself off, I called my son in.

"You won't believe what your son's done!" I said, still chuckling. Xiling came over and smiled down at me and Ping Ping. He began to laugh with me.

At that moment, I had a feeling of déjà vu, as if I were reliving a past that had been long buried away. Yes! I had been changing my son's diaper (cloth back then), and my husband was standing over me, watching us, as my son delivered that same naughty squirt to my face, so many years ago.

I quickly put the diaper on Ping Ping and gathered the baby into my arms. He was plush as a cloud but lighter than Kiko, who was already in school yet still liked to be carried around like a newborn. Ping Ping pinched my nose and let out a victorious squeal.

"Oh, you naughty little boy!" I said, feeling a bit more like myself again. "You're going to pinch your grandma? Then Grandma's going to pinch you right back!"

I gave the boy's nose a neat pinch, and his face squirmed up; he seemed unsure whether to laugh or cry at the sensation. I pressed my cheek to his—it was plump, warm, soft—and made a clucking noise with my tongue to distract him. "Oh, my little thing. No need to cry! A pinch only means I love you. Do you know that? What do you know? Do you know that Nainai loves you?"

I smelled the thick flavors of my northeast region wafting in from the kitchen, so different from the light Japanese fare I'd learned to cook at Yumi's. I settled down to play with Ping Ping before dinner, pinching at his thick thighs and belly. I was not going to leave this place, not until they laid me down inside the family mountain. I said to my grandson: "You little thing. You little thing. My little, little thing."

Lane Life

March 2018

For three months already, Eko and Leo had been living in their new apartment on the second floor of a lane house in Shanghai. When they moved in, thick bamboo scaffolding ran along the entire length of the building opposite, hiding all its windows. The district was completing its refurbishing of historic structures. The scaffolding did not prevent Eko and Leo from opening their own windows, but it filled the alleyway almost completely with a dense grid of bamboo, blocking most of the light that might have come into their apartment and any view whatsoever. Eko and Leo complained to the management company, Lane Life, upon arrival, even before unboxing their clothes, insisting they had been misled prior to their move from Paris. How could they live in such a dark place? The contract was signed, however, and the apartment was otherwise comfortable.

Men, thin and tawny and wearing hard hats, climbed through the bamboo all day long. They came into view around nine in the morning, and they dispersed around five. Leo, therefore, never saw them, as he was always at work then. But Eko saw them, and almost right away, she did not like them.

At first, she tried to ignore the situation, going about her business at home—cleaning, cooking, and reading *What to Expect When You're Expecting*. She wasn't yet pregnant, but her husband had bought her the thick book when they arrived in Shanghai. Their sofa was pushed up against the window, and sitting there, she imagined the men just outside the glass watching her as she read, the occasional graphics of fetuses in wombs visible to all who cared to see.

At some point, the workers began taking their lunch on the scaffolding across from her window. They squatted in a row, facing her apartment, lunch boxes in one hand and chopsticks in the other. Did they really need to eat right there? Could they not sit on the ground? Had she become their midday entertainment? The gall of it! When Eko sat down to her own lunch, she felt the familiar itch of anxiety, with the men lined up like pigeons just outside. Enough was enough. Eko shut the long blackout curtains, bringing their apartment into a twilight that lasted from nine to five for the next three months.

One morning, however, Eko awoke to a noisy clatter, and when she emerged from the bedroom to look out the living room window, she saw that the scaffolding had already been half removed. Long tendrils of bamboo were waving perilously in the air. The workers were busy stomping this way and that, cutting wires and dismembering the frames. Her and Leo's window let in much more light than she'd ever imagined. Their apartment was transformed! Eko almost danced with joy at the brightness streaming in. And across the lane, but placed ever so slightly higher than their own, she saw a window she'd never seen before. It was a small, almost perfect square. Inside was a door hung heavy with layers of coats and clothes and bags.

In her newly bright apartment, Eko felt a sense of hope. Things were going to be different now. She made her red raspberry leaf tea and circled around the kitchen island, considered her ovaries. She willed her system to work, whatever it was that needed to work. Maybe what had been missing all along was a dose of sunlight, vitamin D. She stretched out on the sofa with the curtains pushed back and the windows wide open. Noise from the lane drifted in: an amplified announcement on repeat from the fruit shop downstairs, a basinful of water hitting the ground with a splash, the creaking hinges of the communal trash hut. A fat bee drifted lazily into the room. *Maybe today I'll tell him*, she thought.

Leo walked out of the bedroom, fully dressed. "Well, look at that," he said. And then he kissed her cheek, grabbed his bike helmet, and was gone.

Eko was not a woman with many secrets. But she had never told Leo about one thing: the abortion in college. When they'd first started dating, it hadn't made sense to reveal something so delicate. As they grew closer, Eko feared the story would push him away. And when they married, it felt as though too much time had already passed. The withholding of the experience had transformed it into a lie—or, maybe, into something of no consequence, an object gradually shrinking into a point in the distance. It was better just to move forward.

But if Eko couldn't become pregnant in a few more months' time, she would be officially diagnosed as infertile. There would be tests and ultrasounds, and maybe they would learn that something inside her was broken or damaged. Leo would be surprised, shocked, angry, repelled. He was not one to hide his feelings; the doctor would see all those emotions playing on her husband's face. There would be a silence. The doctor would tactfully move on. Leo and Eko would have a row about it that night, at home. No, it would start before they arrived at their door. It would start as soon as they were out of the doctor's office. It would start in the elevator.

Eko, who had dressed in jeans and a white shirt, who had admired her figure in the mirror while noting her outfit's chic simplicity, now paced the apartment. If she went outside, she'd have to figure out where to go. She couldn't loiter in a café. Caffeine made her too jittery, too prone to an attack. Heart beating fast, breath caught in her throat, tingling sensation moving from her fingertips to her shoulders. No. She didn't want to walk aimlessly about; she could get lost. She sat down on the couch. She opened a book. She pulled out her phone and ordered groceries for dinner.

That evening, as Eko stood in the open kitchen considering her vegetables and how pretty they looked, unchopped and wet with droplets, she sensed a movement in the corner of her eye. She turned to see a man standing in the window—the window through her window, the one that had been previously blocked by the scaffolding. He stood in the center of the square, wearing a white sleeveless undershirt. He looked to be about her age, in his late twenties, and he was alone. From the movement of his arms, it seemed like he was washing something. Eko realized he was also preparing to cook dinner.

Eko sneaked peeks at him while she cooked her simple creamy pasta. He was incredibly focused, though, and never once looked up into her apartment. Eko kept the TV on—it was adjacent to their living room window—just in case she needed to quickly avert her eyes.

Later, during dinner, Eko said to Leo, "It seems we have a neighbor across the street."

"Of course we do." His tone of voice said, *Your statement is obvious; your statement is stupid.* "There are neighbors surrounding us on every side here."

This had been a point of contention between them. Back in Paris, when it came time to choose an apartment from a short list provided by his engineering firm, Leo had eyed the thirty-fifth floor of a new high-rise, very close to the office. But Eko had a severe fear of heights and a mild fear of elevators, and so she argued for the second-floor walk-up in the Lane Life building. Leo grumbled about the lack of privacy, as well as the lack of a view, but in the end, he relented.

"He looks like a single young man. Look how tiny his place is. You can see it, just there." Eko pointed out the window and Leo glanced at the lighted room. Nobody was visible, but Eko saw Leo take in the clutter of jackets and bags hanging from the pegs on the door. A nearby shelf held pots and pans and small, colorful boxes. Eko had been looking into the apartment from different angles all evening, and from one, she had glimpsed a bunk bed pushed up against the wall. The room was a tiny, densely filled square.

. . .

Outside, in the lane and on the streets, Eko was bombarded with Chinese. She could read the basic characters, having studied kanji during a university semester abroad in Kyoto. The spoken language, however, sounded jarring and unfamiliar. She disliked the tonality of it, and though she had an elementary Chinese book she sometimes browsed, she could still only say "ni hao" and "xie xie." She said them often. *Ni hao. Ni hao. Xie xie. Xie xie.* But she didn't want to linger for conversation, and she couldn't.

Her neighbors spent their time tidying small, low balconies, upon which they sat watching the day go by. Or they stood in their doorways, hands or hips resting against the splintered frames. Most of them were old. One extremely small and withered man brought a folding chair out from his building every day and placed it on the street, where he sat cross-legged, reading a newspaper all morning long. It was possible, Eko thought, that he had been doing the same thing every morning for the past fifty years.

Eko knew what her neighbors were like. They were the same all over the world. In both Kyoto and Paris, grannies stared out of their lace-framed windows, descending stone stairs to gossip about their sightings. What might her neighbors in Shanghai be whispering to one another now?

Look, a new couple moved into that building.

I heard a flat there costs . . .

She's quite pretty. Do you know what they say about Japanese wives?

Her husband is never home.

Eko passed them on the street and did not venture a hello. On occasion, maybe, she would offer a timid smile to a child. *Best not to get too involved*, she thought.

Eko didn't like China. There, that was the truth. She knew Leo wouldn't want to hear it, that he would say to her, "Eko, it's only three years. You have to give it a chance before you reject it." Since they'd married, Leo had been flying from Paris to Shanghai more frequently. Things were picking up with his small company in China, and six months ago he had said that now was his chance to do something real. The company no longer managed itself through phone calls, through his COO, Bibi, or through virtual meetings; his presence was becoming a necessity. They'd agreed to give it three years. During this time, he would work remotely as a consultant with the firm in Paris, while also trying to grow his own company.

But just a few months in and Eko already yearned for Paris, where Leo could easily return to his full-time job. Even Kyoto might be better, where Eko had spent happy days during university. Leo called her a Japanese elitist. Even though she was legally French, and had spent most of her life in Paris, he never called her "française." What was she, then—a Japanese or French elitist? She asked him, and he said that without a doubt, she was culturally still Japanese.

The mismatch between what he thought and what she felt swirled in her. After a while, she would look at Leo, who would be transformed, almost into a stranger. What were his thoughts, what were his feelings about her? Did he see her more clearly than she saw herself? He made observations, analyses; he said he was, above all else, rigorous, objective, and fair. Was she, then, the one in error?

What was it that made her recoil so from this city? No, she did not like the people who pushed past her in the subway. She did not like the men glugging phlegm in their throats as they prepared to spit on the street. She did not like the apartment at the corner of their lane, where she would look with trepidation into the grated ground-floor window and see, invariably, crate upon crate of pigeons trapped in the dusty, dark room, never a human being in sight. They were imprisoned. They were miserable. And no one seemed to care.

EVERY NIGHT, the man across the street came home at six o'clock and cooked dinner. He had a wife, Eko learned, a short woman who seemed to be on a different schedule from her husband. She came home irregularly; she was often gone. On the occasions she was home, Eko avoided looking into the apartment.

One night when Leo was out on business, after Eko had enjoyed cooking dinner in the distant company of her neighbor, eaten alone at the dining table, turned off the lights in the living room, and crawled into bed, she heard screaming. Eko froze. A crime? In her lane? She listened: a woman was shouting in Chinese, loudly, for all to hear. She was crying. She was hysterical. The words were streaming out at an incredible pace, shrieked in anguish.

Eko went to the bedroom window and looked out, but the street was dark. There were no streetlamps. How would she even call the police? She did not know the number for the police, and even if she did call, she did not speak enough Chinese to say, "There is an attack happening on my street." She could not even communicate her address in spoken Chinese. She kept a note on her phone with her address and cross streets and presented it to taxi drivers.

She moved into the living room and saw immediately that the attack was not happening on the street. Eko saw in the square window that the screaming woman was the wife. Her husband was looking down at the floor. The window was wide open. They did not seem to care that the entire neighborhood could listen in on their fight. Eko dropped into a crouch and crawled under the windowsill, out of sight. The room was black, but she took no chances. She remained hidden.

Eko's heart was pounding. The wife was crying out the same phrase again and again. It was a question. Eko recognized the word for "Why." The wife was demanding an answer, pounding on something for emphasis at the end of each refrain. Oh, to be able to understand! Eko imagined the most obvious of interrogations. "Why did you do it, huh? Why did you do it, huh?" She pictured another woman. Had he just looked at this person, provoking his jealous and insecure wife? Or had he taken it too far? Perhaps not "Why did you do it?" but "Why did you do it again? Why do you keep doing this to me?"

Eko slowly raised her eyes above the sill and watched the woman tirelessly repeating herself. It seemed as if she would never stop. The man didn't look up. Eko felt he was ashamed; yes, he was guilty of something, a repeat offense. Maybe she was mistaken about the details, though. Maybe he had a gambling problem, and their hard-won money had ended up in the hands of a cunning card dealer.

Suddenly the woman pulled her hand back and brought it with force across the man's face. Eko stopped breathing. He did nothing in response. The wife repeated her question one more time, then broke down in sobs. The man caught her and sat her down—most likely on the bottom bunk, but Eko could not see that part of the room from where she watched, still crouched on the floor, and she did not dare to move. The man came to the window and shut it gently.

Eko waited a few more seconds before she unfolded her limbs and noiselessly crawled into her bedroom on all fours. Her right leg had fallen asleep. She closed her bedroom door, got into bed, and pulled up the covers. She lay there, watching the slap play out in her mind over and over.

One evening, while again cooking together but separately with her neighbor, Eko discovered she was out of eggs. She stood with her hands on her hips, thinking, the empty carton dangling from her fingers. She could go to the mall outside the lane, or just down to the fruit shop, where they sold sky-blue chicken eggs. But she hated having to stop in the middle of a task. Could she make her dinner without them? No, Leo wouldn't like it. He needed his curry rice topped with a thin, whipped omelet. She would have to go out. She sighed and threw the carton into the trash. Already she could hear Leo's voice in her head, asking why had she left an empty container in the fridge in the first place.

She turned to see what her neighbor was doing, to stall her departure. Surprisingly, he was looking right at her. She froze. He reached to his left and held up a single blue egg.

She nodded. Yes, that was her problem. He smiled and lifted a finger as if to say, *Wait.* He turned, opened the door behind him, and walked out. Eko stared at the window, filled now with only the closed door.

What floor did he live on? The second, like Eko, or the third? She felt the anxiety building within her. How long would it take him to arrive? The doorbell rang. She went to the intercom and turned on the video. It was him, holding the egg close to the camera. What to do, what to do? She couldn't leave him standing there, could she? But what would he think of her? What might he do in retaliation if she rejected him? He knew where she lived, after all. She did need the egg; she was actually in need of two. After this, there would be no way she could go to the shop or the grocery. Dinner would be ruined. Leo would be in a mood. The whole night, if not the whole next day, would be colored by his unhappiness, and she would have to tiptoe around him. No, better to take the egg. Just take the egg.

She buzzed the door open and listened to him walking up the two flights of stairs. She thought her knees would buckle with the fear. And yet—the egg. She focused her mind on that single blue egg. She could treat him like any other deliveryman: take the item, say thank you, and close the door. He knocked. It was a very gentle knock. *Open, close*, she said to herself, and she unbolted the door.

He stood in her doorway, holding the egg out. He was taller than she'd expected, but that might have been the shock of seeing him up close. "Xie xie," she said, taking the egg. Try as she might to avoid touching his skin, she felt, with terror, her index finger graze his palm. Her face was flushing, her hand on the doorknob trembling.

From the threshold, he looked around, eyeing everything in the apartment. If he'd been watching through his window, he would have seen it all before. But still he took his time. When he turned back to her, he smiled, pointed at himself, and said,

"Neo." His voice was slightly high-pitched for a man's. "Eko," she replied. There was nothing else to say. He waved goodbye and nodded, but very seriously, looking her right in the eyes. She stared back at him, as scared as if he were a wild animal. When he walked down the stairs, she closed the door and rushed into her bedroom.

Eko was hiding; she did not want him to see from his window the state he had put her in. She was paralyzed and electrified. She had the egg. She had opened the door. Eko lay on the bed, gathering her breath, the egg lying next to her. She was thinking about his gentle, almost girlish voice. His name so familiar and yet so foreign. Neo.

EKO WAS IN TORTURE over the next few days. She wouldn't look out the window. She couldn't leave the building, lest she run into Neo. She wouldn't go for a morning coffee with Leo. She drew the blackout curtains closed again.

Whenever Eko had to go near the door, she walked carefully around the place Neo had stood. When deliveries arrived, she made a wide arc around it, as if he were still there, unwilling to let her pass. He had wanted to give her an egg, that was all. And yet she couldn't bring herself to tell Leo. He would say she was disorganized, letting the eggs run out and keeping an empty carton in the fridge. He would say she was letting her anxiety take control again. He would say she was choosing the easy way out, allowing someone to help her out of her own mess. He would say she needed to regain power over her life. She didn't want to hear those words. She'd heard them so many times before.

The secret of Neo burned inside her. She sensed that a dangerous possibility had arrived in the form of her neighbor. But what could she do now? On the first day after the egg, she told herself that she would never see him again. But what of the window? She couldn't very well keep it closed forever, especially now that they finally had some light in their place. They wouldn't move apartments just because of an egg.

But by the end of the week, Eko began to calm down. She had not done anything wrong. She had taken an egg from a kind neighbor. In Paris, her mother had often sent her to this neighbor for a teaspoon of vanilla, to that one when they were out of milk. In her childhood, there had never been enough; the entire building shared.

In Paris, there was a feeling of closeness everywhere. Paris, a village compared to Shanghai, was a friendly place. Nowadays, she thought about it often. What was the pleasure of living in an enormous city, a place where twenty-five million others congregated merely to make money? Shanghai was a city of strangers. Maybe that was what had drawn her to this building: the description of a lane community, in a close-knit Shanghai neighborhood.

Before she and her mother moved into their beloved one-bedroom in the Fifteenth, Eko spent her childhood in a tiny apartment in the Twentieth. Everyone had a window onto the central courtyard. The elderly looked on all day as children ran around, as wives conversed and bartered goods. The courtyard felt sealed off from the world, and indeed it was. The building's stone walls rose around it like a fortress, bolstered by the heavy iron handrails that wrapped around the landings on each floor and the staircases between them. From the courtyard one could see each apartment's front door, many ajar, emitting the smells of cooking, which wafted from floor to floor. She had known everyone in the building. On warm nights people would come out onto the landings or walk down to the courtyard, exchanging pleasantries, sharing gossip. It had been an entire world.

THE NEXT TIME she ventured to look at Neo cooking, he caught her eye and smiled. She nodded. In a moment, he was at her door.

He began to come over almost every evening. As a private joke, he always brought an egg with him, presenting it to her through the intercom camera when he rang. He would help Eko prepare her food, and they would teach each other the names, in Chinese and in French, of vegetables and fruits: eggplant, tomato, baby bok choy. It was as if Eko had a sous chef and a language teacher all in one. He excelled at chopping and dicing and rinsing. She understood, one day, as he gestured cooking and sleeping, that he was trying to tell her that he worked the night shift as a chef in a restaurant. In her fridge, blue eggs gradually replaced all the white and brown.

She thought often of Paris as she cooked with Neo. He spoke no foreign language, and she no Chinese, but still they managed to make cassoulet, pommes dauphine, soupe à l'oignon. With someone to do half the work, Eko was happy to make even more elaborate dishes, some that she hadn't had since she was a child. The day after they made profiteroles together, Neo brought over one pork and chive dumpling, freshly pinched, wrapped, and coated with a thin, dusty layer of flour. "Chinese," he said, dropping its plump white form into a pot of boiling water. When it had risen to the surface, floating in its milky bath, he fished it out with a pair of chopsticks. He pinched it, burning, between two fingers, and blew on it gently. He brought it to Eko's lips, his eyes glued to her mouth, her teeth, the breaking skin and steam.

Neo was beautiful in an objective kind of way. Any woman would find him attractive, Eko decided. He was an excellent specimen of his gender. Really, he was much more beautiful than Leo. He was also taller and his presence always made the apartment feel suddenly very small and very full. She liked that feeling.

Eko knew what Neo was to her. He was a gift, someone to help her enjoy China and her short time there. He made her life easier. That wasn't something Leo would understand. For example, Leo knew everyone in China hired help. But when she'd mentioned the possibility of bringing someone in—just once, twice a month—for cleaning, of course she'd gotten an entire lecture about the matter, an analysis of her lazy nature, most likely stemming from a childhood of being indulged by her too-loving mother.

It was not the money, he said. It was the principle of the matter. Why should Eko skirt domestic work just because she didn't like it? Everyone had to do things they didn't like. That was called real life. And she didn't even work. But it *was* about the money, too, she knew. Over the years, even as their wealth grew, his thriftiness had blossomed, something she had not realized was in him at the beginning of their relationship and that she did not like at all.

Maybe she had abdicated the high ground by giving up her income. Would he still have refused help if she was also working? Would she have even needed to ask? But maybe he was right; it was not asking too much for her to keep house. She would do it for now, at least.

Neo seemed to enjoy food prep. He also washed and dried the dishes as they went. For two weeks, after the meal was in the oven, they did not know what to do with each other. They would taste some of the food, but they would not be dining together, as the meal was prepared for Leo. They would clean up, Eko pouring Neo a glass of wine, and start pointing at things, identifying them in Chinese and French. Too soon, Eko would receive a message from her husband letting her know he had begun the forty-minute commute home. When the text arrived, she signaled that it was time to go.

Eko was not stupid. She knew what might become inevitable with Neo, what she'd invited in when she decided to open the door. But Neo made no move in that direction, and so she waited, with a mixture of excitement and trepidation at the power she seemed to hold over him.

As the days went on, to fill the silences, Eko began to talk more and more. Without fear of judgment, she began to tell Neo things she had never told Leo, things she hadn't even realized she felt herself. One day she told him about her jobs in Paris. Her university degree had been in public relations, but the job she'd landed at a PR firm just after graduation had proved too competitive, too stressful, for her constitution. She had started to suffer panic attacks while getting dressed for work. At Leo's urging, she'd gone on to do a second degree in interior design, which he saw as one of her talents. ("Even your student apartment was so elegantly designed," Leo had said to her.) She had felt, then, his concern for her happiness, and she was moved by his accurate understanding of her true nature. Eko found she often preferred the company of objects and art to that of people, and in her new design job, she relished the pleasant feeling of serendipity when a room came together after much planning and arranging. Indecisive as she was, she could sometimes spend ten minutes moving a lamp two centimeters left, then right, on a dresser. But it was those small details of creating the perfect tableau and the quiet accomplishment of that work that she enjoyed most. She liked the silence of design, and how an interior, unlike an exterior, was a landscape of infinite choices—white walls that could take on leopard prints or splashes of color or modern monochrome, depending on the client's taste and hers. Lights could hang, drip, sit, stand, hover, float, or spotlight.

She'd been there for only six months before Leo wanted to move to Shanghai. Her firm was a small one, with no international office in China. When Eko left, she was given reassurances from her boss that they would have a place for her if and when she returned. And yet a part of her was happy to give up the job. Even though the work was more suitable, the office and her coworkers still gave her anxiety.

With no proficiency in Mandarin, her job prospects in Shanghai were slim to none. Leo and Eko planned, then, for her to simply focus on having and raising children. Neo helped in the kitchen as she talked, and she felt in his quiet presence a comfort.

She told him about Leo, a structural engineer, who had been successful in Paris after his PhD, and about their move to Shanghai. Leo was a natural at his job. There was nothing he disliked more than disorder and risk. Nothing he liked more than precision. They had gotten into more than a few fights over the years because Eko's housekeeping was not up to par with his standards. "I'm not your maid!" she shouted at him once, after he had shown her for the umpteenth time how to perfectly fold a blanket over and tuck it under the mattress. After that she never tried to fold the blankets well again. She did them *fine*, like a normal person would, but never the way Leo had shown her, even though she agreed it was nicer.

It would be safe to say that Eko had been in the process of falling slowly out of love with Leo for the past five years. She blamed it partly on their childlessness. Things had gone on in the same manner for far too long. They had said to themselves and others that they were waiting. But waiting for what? They had gotten bored, or maybe dissatisfied, with each other. Eko felt increasingly like a child herself, like Leo was always trying to train her. For life? For work? For motherhood? The constant feedback exhausted her.

Sometimes she had glimpses of the future, Leo with his strong brow sitting low over his round eyes. He was an angry-looking man, though handsome, with a square face that surprised when he smiled easily and went on talking excitedly for hours. He had an opinion about everything: science, politics, the future of Shanghai and of China; Eko's cooking, her clothing, her choice of books and friends. She imagined the older version of him: angrier, more striking, more excited. What she could see less clearly was her future self. Neo, watching, listening, smiled and nodded.

Finally, she told him about Philippe. Back in college, before Leo, there had been a single one-night stand—a young man with pale blue, glittering eyes, like diamonds. She had been in her first year, and she'd met, straightaway, the most gorgeous man she'd ever seen. It seemed to Eko that he only had to look at her, to keep his attention on her own brown eyes, to get her into his bed. The sex was forgettable; what was not were the eyes, floating above her, neon in the near dark.

That same night, he drove her back from his apartment to her dorm. In one year's time, he said, he would graduate from the business school. It was the only piece of information he'd given her other than his first name. In front of her building, he said, "Thank you," and that was it. She had wanted to grab him, to claim him, to laugh and smile seductively, to kiss him violently and passionately. But fear and uncertainty seized her, and it was all she could manage to say, "You're welcome," and step out onto the street. Over the weeks that followed, she waited to hear from him. If Philippe wanted to, he'd be able to find her. But she heard nothing.

Philippe had gotten her pregnant. Eko managed to find a doctor, and he had given her a discount on the procedure due to her age and situation. Eko had only one second thought—because of the blue eyes—but altogether she felt no remorse about it. Afterward, there had been a lot of pain, but everything went back to normal in a few months' time. Not long after that, she dated a classmate, David, though he'd always been more of a friend. And then she had met Leo—serious, dark, older, and handsome—who'd come to love her so quickly, and so thoroughly, with so much certainty. He made her feel like she was the most exquisite human being on earth. He wanted to know about Japan, about France, about her childhood, her thoughts on art and design. It was as though he was so hungry for her that he wanted to exist wholly inside her, body and mind. When had she fallen in love? She remembered saying it first and only later coming to feel it.

But soon, very soon thereafter. There was his beauty, yes. And his strength. It was undeniable. But also his curiosity; his ability to talk, and to listen, for hours; and the nature of his love, pure and laser focused, so she knew that once she had it, it would never leave. She was happy. She felt fulfilled. She stopped smoking and drinking. She was the very best version of herself she had ever been.

Eko had always presumed she was a font of fertility. Her current condition, then, was a kind of shock. If she didn't have babies, what would she do with her life? She watched Neo, so precise and quick with his hands, in contrast to the strong build of his shoulders and arms. She asked him how she should fill her days, which felt like so many when looked at in this new light, from this childless angle. There was no reply.

Leo would expect her to work. If there was no baby, Leo would wait the appropriate, delicate amount of time before bringing up the topic for discussion, but it would have to be had. Eko had already imagined the inevitable conversation. She acted it out for Neo: "What are you going to do now?" Leo would ask. "What's your plan?"

Eko had no plan for work. She had come to realize that she did not like workplaces. When she'd been at the design studio, it took a lot out of her to keep up with the flamboyant, materialistic crowd. They were all so fully formed, so knowledgeable, their tastes so developed. When and how had they become so sure-footed? Sometimes, when making decisions at work, she would try to channel her mother. What would Daphne say, what would Daphne wear, what would Daphne like? But it took work, that impersonation. Eko preferred staying at home. And here, in this foreign place, in a city she didn't know, her life at home made sense. She felt small, yes, but also safe. She had always known that she would be a good mother.

Nowadays, she thought frequently about adoption. She would love to adopt. A Chinese baby, maybe from the countryside, could work. "I wonder what you think of adoption," she'd ask Leo, casually, as if the idea had just popped into her head. In her mind, she played with and modulated the tone of voice when she asked the question. But already, she could sense that he would not like the idea.

In telling Neo about Philippe, Eko realized that she had kept the story to herself all these years not out of fear but out of defensiveness. She had *wanted* to keep it to herself. It was her jewel, her life's adventure. She could still see clearly those shining blue eyes. Neo could not understand what she said, but speaking the story aloud had verged on its ruin.

The moment when things shifted between Eko and Neo happened over coq au vin. They were standing side by side, chopping mushrooms. She was feeling the hum of energy of his being close to her. He was silent. Then he put down his knife and placed his hand over hers. She stopped but could not move. He held her hand—still gripping her thin knife—like that, under his, for what felt like a very long time. Finally, he pulled her toward him. His eyes were so scared, so unsure, when they met hers. His lips trembled. She was moved by his fear, and hers seemed to vanish because of his.

One evening the next week, she lay together with Neo, their heads at the bottom of her bed. From this perspective, her room seemed entirely different. She rested her hand on Neo's head, pulling her fingers through his coarse hair. Silence with him was comfortable. With Leo, she rarely spent a quiet moment. Eko and Neo had no shared language, and she liked that respite, that relief from having to communicate, prove, defend, plan.

She caught a glimpse of a curtain's movement in a tall window the next building over. Eko had never registered any windows from where she usually lay, and she did not know who lived there. She hardly thought about anyone in the lane now except for Neo, whose presence felt so large, seemed to fill her apartment, even from across the street. But this window was closer and now she realized that it looked directly into her bedroom. She pulled a shirt over her head and held up her phone, signaling to Neo that it was time to go. She and Neo had only ever communicated with these kinds of gestures and guesses.

From that day on, her anxiety returned. Had the onlooker been the fruit shop owner, or the man who stood on the street with a cart of plates and bowls for sale? Had it been the old woman with a large tumor growing on the right side of her stomach? Eko wanted to leave the house even less now. Who on the street had seen her? Who on the street had been talking?

The foreign girl. You'll never guess what I saw. In bed with Neo!

She likes local men.

If I had known, maybe I would've tried my luck!

She kept her curtains closed most days. In the evenings, Leo sometimes wanted to go for a drink, and Eko reluctantly accompanied him. As they walked through the lane, often holding hands, she felt as though she were walking through judgment—that beyond the dark windows and sheer curtains, her neighbors were watching, and knowing: *She is the one having the affair.*

Eko wondered, resentfully, how many Chinese affairs had begun and ended in this lane over the decades. How was hers any different? When she went out, she kept her eyes on the ground as much as possible. But when she did, by chance, meet the eyes of the fruit seller or the garbageman, she flashed a cold, righteous look: *Dare to judge me and see if I care!*

But then she would punch in the access code to her building and run up the stairs and, fumbling with shaking hands, drop her key at least once, twice. As soon as she was inside the door, she rushed to close all the windows and curtains that Leo had opened in the morning, and she collapsed onto the couch.

She and Leo still occasionally had their moments—when she felt like her younger self, like the college self that had long ago fallen in love with him. Being with Neo, the excitement of it, made her susceptible to happiness with Leo again. Sometimes, lying in bed, she would giggle about a word she'd learned, or about something Neo had done to her that afternoon. She'd turn her smile toward Leo, to dissipate its meaning. "What are you giggling about?" Leo would ask. "Nothing," she'd reply. But then she would playfully stroke his cheek, and her happiness would commute to him. And they'd move into their familiar positions.

LEO WAS ATTENDING A CONFERENCE all through the April holiday. He asked if Eko wanted to stay with him at the Park Hyatt; she would have access to the pool and the gym. But Eko declined, saying he knew how she felt about heights. In truth, she was looking forward to spending time with Neo, maybe even having him stay over at her place. They would keep the curtains closed for days on end.

But almost immediately after Leo left for the hotel, Eko looked into the window across from hers, and she saw Neo's wife walking through their apartment door. That would have been disappointing enough, but in her arms, she held something Eko had never imagined seeing in that tiny apartment across the street: a young child, a boy, the spitting image of his father. Eko was horrified. Where did the boy live? With his grandparents? Were Neo and his wife migrant workers? And how could Neo have had a child this whole time and not told her? But of course he hadn't: he told her almost nothing, could communicate to her almost nothing.

Neo's back was to the window, and he was raising the boy up and down and up and down. His wife was crowding near, to tickle the laughing child whenever he fell into his father's arms. All this time, Neo had had a child. Eko stood behind the door of her bedroom, peeking out to see if Neo would turn. She wanted to see his face. What was she waiting for? She was waiting to see the look of happiness.

But he never turned around. Eko felt her stomach lurch, and she sprinted to the bathroom and kneeled over the toilet. Nothing came out. She retched. The nausea wouldn't stop. It arrived in waves for the next two days. Finally, an idea came to her. She ran to the pharmacy and bought a test. She had to search for an image of one on her phone and show it to the attendants over the counter. Back home, door locked and curtains drawn, she discovered that she was pregnant.

Eko told no one for the next three days. During those days, Neo's son was with his parents, Leo was at the hotel, and Eko was crouched over the toilet. She was sick, and she was thinking.

They had been careful, so it was not likely. But even if the child was Neo's, Eko did not want to take his wife's place on the top bunk. She realized she did not love Neo, not to the degree that she should. If she had, wouldn't she have been willing to go with him anywhere, to share any bed in any small room, to slap him and self-destruct in front of their one square window?

At the end of the three days, Eko had decided that she would tell Leo, and that she would never tell Neo. Neo had a child. And as soon as she had made her decision, she felt she could not wait. They would have a baby and life would be as it should. She did not want to tell Leo when he returned home. She wanted to tell him in a place Neo had never been and probably never would be.

The Park Hyatt Living Room was on the eighty-seventh floor of the World Financial Center, in the business district of Lujiazui. Eko had been to the building twice. Once, months ago, at the start of their time in Shanghai—a dinner date with Leo—and again shortly after that, for afternoon tea. Leo liked to bring her to tall buildings, so that she could confront her fear of heights head-on. That was the only way to overcome it, he said. Outside the windows was a panoramic view of the city, with the other skyscrapers of Lujiazui rising around them. Eko knew very little about what was what. That first time she'd dined here, she had been very afraid—the high-speed elevator shook ever so slightly, and she'd had to close her eyes.

But this time, focused on keeping her nausea at bay, she barely registered the speeding elevator. When she stepped off and found herself again on solid flooring, her first impression was of the incredibly soothing interior. The wide, open room was dotted with low-slung chairs, cushioned in white and beige. The sky beyond was pale blue, as opaque as a mural or wallpaper. She walked over to a seat by the window and peered down at the city below. It was an unfrightening picture postcard. And yet her heart was beating fast. They had been trying for a baby, but would Leo be happy? A waitress came by and asked if she wanted some tea. She said yes and chose something relatively inexpensive from the menu. Then she texted Leo. *I'm at the hotel. Living Room. Can you stop by when you have a moment?*

Soon Leo was walking toward her, followed by the waitress with the tea. "What a surprise! You came here on your own?" Eko nodded as he sat. They both watched the young woman's hands as she poured the tea, then bowed slightly before leaving. Leo turned back to Eko. "Is everything OK?"

"I'm pregnant," Eko said. She had meant it to come out excited and happy, but instead she sounded fearful, timid.

Leo reached across the small table and took her hand. "Are you sure? How do you know?"

"Yes, Leo. I took three tests. I feel horrible. I missed my period."

Leo broke into a smile. "We're having a baby," he whispered, squeezing her hand. "How?"

Eko shrugged. "I guess we got lucky," she said. "But we may need to move into a building with an elevator before the baby comes. A high-rise." She gestured to the windows. "See? I'm not afraid anymore."

AFTER THE HOLIDAY, when Neo picked up an egg and presented it from his window, Eko shook her head. She was content. Leo's happiness and approval were catching. She closed all her curtains that evening so she could be alone with the baby, with herself. She reread her pregnancy book with a renewed sense of purpose.

Leo came with Eko to her first appointment with the obstetrician. In the ultrasound room, the technician put a cool gel on her flat abdomen. Silent, everyone looked at the small screen. A blob appeared, and Eko's mind quickly focused on the thing, studying its shape and movements. Suddenly, another one slipped onto the screen. She felt the world sliding away, as if those two blobs had grown magnified and she could see and hear nothing besides them. They filled her entire mind. In some background place, she registered the doctor's words, in inflected English: "dangerous," "careful," "twins," "cervix." Eko nodded vaguely at him.

"Eko, Eko!" the doctor was saying. "Congratulations. Do you have any immediate questions?" Leo was speechless, looking at her with joy.

"Yes," Eko said. "Doctor, can I travel?" She felt the urge to go away, to not be seen.

"What kind of travel are we talking? A nearby getaway, or a long-distance flight?" He tilted his head and considered for a moment before answering his own question. "Well, it's very likely you may be required to bed-rest during your last trimester. We generally don't recommend travel in your first, mostly because you won't be feeling great. Second trimester, let's see how the babies are doing. You may have a small window when travel is possible."

On their way home from the appointment, Eko and Leo saw a group of men standing near the ceramics cart on their street. Eko felt their eyes on her from down the block. One of them—the fruit seller—stepped forward as Leo and Eko approached and said, "Ni hao!"

The couple stopped in their tracks. Their door was only a few steps away. Dusk had faded, and the sky was darkening. The men were beginning to look like shadows. Could they tell? That she was pregnant?

"Ni hao," Leo said in return. Eko stood staring at the man, wordlessly begging him not to say anything about Neo.

"You like China?" asked the fruit man in English.

"Yes, I'm Chinese," said Leo.

"She like China too," the man said, pointing at Eko.

"Yes," Leo said.

"She like China!" The fruit man turned to announce this to his friends, adding, "Arigato!" They all started to laugh. Leo started to laugh too.

"What's so funny?" Eko asked.

"I don't know," Leo replied. "It's just funny." He waved to the men, smiling, and said, "It's a beautiful night, gentlemen."

It was that night, after the incident in the lane, that Eko made another decision. She did not like China; Leo did not know anything about her after so many years. She was going to leave him. It might take time, but she would do it.

Before the pregnancy became noticeable, she and Leo moved into a high-rise apartment with expansive views of the city, in the building where he'd originally wanted to live. "Yes, this is real Shanghai living," he said.

They hired a part-time nanny who would help Eko with the twins and the housework. One baby she could handle on her own. With two, even Leo conceded she would need help. Eko thought and thought. She could go to Paris, and she could never return.

The weeks passed. Leo and Eko brainstormed baby names. She insisted on Japanese, so they compromised—one Japanese and one Chinese. At three months, however, during a routine ultrasound, they discovered that one of the babies had passed. Or, the doctor told them, she or he had possibly been absorbed by the other. Eko mourned the loss quietly. But it simplified her plan. She waited. She would stay for two years, until after the difficult period of infancy. Then she would go back to Paris with her child, to figure out what to do.

Eko never considered reaching out to Neo, but she thought of him sometimes. Always, in her mind, he was standing in his window, wearing his undershirt, smiling, holding out that blue egg.

When Yumi was born, she was exceptionally beautiful. She had a thick, jet-black head of hair and skin like butter. Eko looked at her, and smelled her, and couldn't stop touching her. But at odd moments she thought, *Somewhere inside this girl is her twin.* Had the twin's eyes become one with Yumi's, or were they half-formed still, with a frozen view of the murky insides of her daughter's liver or spleen? When she looked at Yumi, she thought of them both.

Je Le Veux, I Do

July 2014

A man always walks down the aisle by himself. Eko had left two seats empty in the front. A pale pink rose lay on each of the chairs; he saw them now, from the corner of his eye. She was lovely like that, thoughtful, creative. Putting out seats for the dead. But the gesture also pained him, and it pained him not to know whether he should feel self-conscious about it, whether he should avoid looking into those two emptinesses, like black holes pulling him in.

What was there? Spirit, grief, memory, and that, too, edited and faded over time. What came after? The question had haunted him since he was young. Since the age of eight, when his father told him about death on that summer trip—on the balcony of their hotel overlooking the sea in Fujian, when for the last time in

Leo's life tears had fallen from his eyes. Everyone would die. Everyone would disappear from this world.

The chimes started to peal. The breeze was soft and the day had turned out, after a nearly certain prediction of rain, to be sunny and perfect. And then Eko was standing at the end of the aisle. She felt so far away. He smiled, partly at the absurdity of it all: her lovely face plastered with makeup; her dress, heavy and long; and her attendants fixing the train, setting it straight and flat for the journey. "The East Is Red" was beginning to play from the bell tower of a nearby hotel. It rang out over all the neighboring buildings along the river, over their own hotel's rooftop, over their ceremony. Eko paused, seemingly unsure what to do. They whispered something in her ear. Now she was standing still. Wait until the clock finishes its chiming, they would have said to her. *The East is red, the sun rises. From China arises Mao Zedong.*

Leo was thinking about his father. He had built up such an image of the man over the years, bolstered by the stories he'd heard from his uncles. There were only a few memories of his own now, and Leo played them over in his mind. The trip to the mountains when he was four, a long train ride filled with people smoking, he and his father standing for what felt like an eternity. The time his father bought him KFC in Beijing, at the first outpost to enter China. They hadn't known how to eat the fries. They picked at them with chopsticks. The sound of his father singing Suzhou opera on the balcony—the thin nasal melody streaming through the air—on Sunday mornings. Or were they Saturday evenings? Finally, the neighbors running down the lane, shouting Leo's name. His parents had been hit by a truck. They were at the hospital. Leo running—chest and arms, so skinny then, pumping; crossing the streets at a sprint, despite the cars and bikes rushing forward; shouting at the nurses and scrambling through the confusing, dimly lit corridors of the hospital. His mother and father both brain-dead.

Please, he'd thought when he heard the news. *Please, please. Even if it's just one. Even if he's paralyzed. Let him live.* They'd died that night.

Forever after, at critical moments like these, he'd felt their absence—and in particular, his father's—more deeply. Achieving the highest score on the citywide math test. Training for contests and winning top marks. Earning a place at university. The fellowship to Paris, the PhD. The papers. Eko.

And now, with him coming home to marry in Shanghai, crisscrossing the globe for the final of their series of ceremonies and celebrations, what would they think? What would they have said? Could they have ever conceived of a life like his, when their own were so constricted, so constrained, so ruled by the whims of this country's swinging policies?

Leo was raised by institutions, by teachers. In name by his uncles and his grandparents, whose homes he stayed at on the weekends and during holidays. Boarding school since the accident, since the age of eight. Everything he'd done, he'd done himself.

Far away, down the aisle, Eko looked unreal—a mannequin in a shop window, a miniature bride atop a cake, the image of what a wedding, a life, should look like.

He could feel it, he was beginning one of his moments of dissociation, when time seemed to slow, when he became as if ensconced in a bubble, a soft protective case that allowed him to take in all the details of the world around him, that allowed him to see things from a distance, with clarity and objectivity. It happened most often on two types of occasions: when he was solving a math problem or when he was getting into an argument.

The chiming had stopped, and the quartet took up their instruments. *Here comes the bride.* She was walking toward him now, and he was thinking about the day when he arrived in his car to pick her up from a friend's party in the French countryside. She ran to him, introduced him to her friends as her boyfriend. But they had not yet made love. They had not even kissed. He drove them to the city, to the river, and they sat there, watching the moon hanging low over the water like a plate, its silvery nervous reflection wavering, shivering, just as she was in the late summer night. Then, his arms around her shoulders, his face moving in to touch hers, her soft lips, her body folding into his.

In his moments of hovering above life, he could see everything as if it were a model that he could zoom out of and freeze, zoom into and inspect from various angles. It had happened that night, with Eko, the night of their first kiss. By the river, under the moon. Time had stood still, and he could see it all, the future ahead: their first time making love, their first arguments, their first apartment in Paris, and their baby, wrapped in her arms, given the name of Leo's mother or father.

He could even see her past. In Kyoto, an impetuous toddler. In Paris, a teenager with her legs dangling over the Seine, maybe a cigarette between her lips. Men and boys she'd loved before, French, Algerian. He wanted to be better than them all. Eko, the stranger—he would spend his entire life knowing her, traveling down into the past, into those stories, and into the future, together. He saw her old, thin, delicate, elegant. He saw himself. He saw the moon, a lake; he saw them sitting side by side. Leo had never experienced the bubble, the stoppage, with a girl before. That night by the river was the first time. He took it as a sign. So this was love, feeling time unfurl from a moment.

There had been other relationships, including the most overwhelming, his first. When he had just arrived in Paris and met Fei, the fellow in his program, from Beijing. But always there were the arguments, the missteps, the doubts. Was Fei the one, the right one? He knew, theoretically, that no one was perfect. But he could not help holding out for closer to perfection, the closest he could get.

Leo knew the probabilities of a successful marriage. That the chances for happiness were small. Still. What else could he do but try?

THE MONTH ON THE BEACH in Fujian recurs—staring out at the ocean, thinking about mortality, about the death of every living thing. On that trip, he had taken his first plane ride. The first few days he spent imagining how he'd tell his classmates about the experience—about the plane, the flight attendants, taking off, the clouds in the sky. No one in his school had ever flown on a plane before.

Leo had been the first at a lot of things. The trip to Beijing. The soldiers in the streets. And then the chicken, the Pepsi-Cola, the fries.

After returning to the city, Leo's father had taken them to a company cooperative, and somehow he'd been able to get a one-bedroom apartment, a luxury, assigned to their family by the management. Thinking back, Leo imagined the negotiations, the promises, the bribes or cigarettes exchanged, the way things were procured when money meant so little. His father, too, had been able to see things from a distance.

But there was no one to check facts with. His parents were gone so soon after Fujian. As if his father had planned it all, as if he were preparing Leo for the fact of their deaths.

On the balcony of their hotel room that day, at eight years old, Leo looked out at the sea that stretched into the distance and met the sky. He could see the death of everything and everyone ever, stretching far behind and far ahead. What was the point? What was the point of it all?

He felt that same hopelessness four years later, when he scored the highest marks on the math exam among all junior high school students in Shanghai. If he was the best, that meant there was no one else, no one greater. If he was the best, then he was truly alone. His uncles and aunts cheered, stared at him in amazement, called their friends, shouted down the hall to let the neighbors know. But he was overcome with loneliness—and disappointment. Was he really as good as it got?

On a long bus ride as a young teen, to see his extended family during a Lunar New Year celebration, Leo told the younger of his two uncles about Stephen Hawking, about relativity. He had just finished *A Brief History of Time*; he was excited about it all, about the realm of knowledge that was opening to him. He remembered going on and on, without pause, for hours. The bus was a local shuttle, filled to capacity, the seats removed to create more space, a few farmers holding three or four chickens each on their laps. Nearly to their destination, the bus ran out of gas and sputtered to a stop. Leo understood vaguely what was happening, but he was also in the middle of telling his uncle about black holes and the event horizon, and he didn't want to pause. They—Leo, his uncle, the farmers, the chickens—got off the bus and sat on the side of the road, rubbing their palms together in the cold while someone came to replenish their gas. Leo continued. He was trying to explain what happens when two black holes collide, how they do emit particles (and how Hawking's pride had made him resist this truth!), the primordial black hole, its link to the fate of the universe. Leo's uncle nodded along, grunting, looking left and right for the damned gas truck. Leo bore into him, calling him—"Uncle, Uncle!"—to help him focus on the conversation at hand. The truck came rambling down the road. Leo and his uncle and the farmers and the chickens all got back on. In no time they arrived. As Leo and his uncle squeezed their way to the exit, everyone stared at Leo, as if he were an alien who had been speaking the whole time in a foreign language.

In college, upon the advice of his father's former boss to invest in apartments, Leo borrowed money from everyone in his family, from his father's coworkers, from friends. His father had always dreamed of a place of their own. Leo's two units in Gubei had sat empty for a number of years, but then, when the rise of real estate became something undeniable, and something everyone was talking about, his big uncle suggested renting them out. Property, rent prices were rising. Why not, even, transfer ownership to him and let him handle everything? The apartments had been purchased for so little, and today they were worth so much more. Leo was good with numbers. He didn't yet have a clear sense of value, of what money was worth, of what an investment was, but he understood the numbers, and he understood that this growth was something his father would have wanted him to have.

Leo found out all he could about the apartments and about investing in Shanghai. When not studying for his engineering degree, he researched the housing market. In those moments—when he visited his father's old company to chat with Boss Niu, when he read the newspapers for information about housing and district developments—he felt close to his father, he felt he was embodying his father. Soon, he was collecting rent off the two apartments. By then he was about to leave for Paris. He hired an assistant to manage his properties.

He was lucky. His assistant proved to be both savvy and kind. Over the years, Bibi grew the business. While Leo was in Paris, losing himself in physics, the shape of dimensions unseen, his number of apartments was also growing.

Bibi, now COO of their small real estate company, went for drinks with officials and developers; he got them blocks of apartments in a development in the city center, near Jing'an. When Xintiandi was announced, Bibi was there, picking up a few units. They could not compete with the big holdings, the companies with more money and better connections, but still, they were there.

By the time Leo finished his studies, he was very rich. The Shanghai of his youth—the bulldozing, clearing, demolishing, construction—it was gone. The city that had looked like an endless war zone, gone. In its place was an incongruous mix of shining, smooth glass buildings and stout blocks of shikumen brick.

. . .

All over Shanghai sat his units, speckling the map of the city. Apartments and families, pets and kids. Renters flowing in and out of their boxes, while the money accumulated. By law, he would own these places for seventy years. In truth he was a renter too; the government was the owner of all the land. He'd get out before the contract was up.

Managing homes, houses, where people ate, slept, and died. Renovation. Improvement. People late on rent. Negotiating rent. Breaking rent. Leo became bored with the details. He had no patience for Bibi's long meetings and phone calls.

But he and Eko had discussed a transition back to China after marriage. In a few years' time, they might leave Paris, start a family, explore new opportunities at home. In Shanghai he could find something worthy of him, something truly of scale, something that would last.

Before Eko walked out onto the aisle, her mother had called her a China doll, but not in a nice way. Why couldn't she just keep her opinions to herself? The music was ringing in her ears. She tried to match her steps to the rhythm, but it was too slow. And everyone was standing up and staring. She felt the prickle of sweat along her hairline and under her arms; the dress, she now realized with regret, was too big and too heavy, and she was covered in a thick layer of makeup. Eko was nearly there now and she hadn't fallen, no, she hadn't tripped; she looked over at her mother and saw—were those tears of happiness or sadness? Daphne had told her only once, in explicit terms, that

Leo was not the right one for her. She had said, "You don't have to go to China," that was how she had put it, and there had been tears of relief for a while, the two of them sitting in their car off Rue des Thermopyles. But then her mother had backtracked immediately—"Love is hard," she said—and told Eko that she and Leo were really alike in a way, well suited: "two big children."

But now it was made, the decision. And there were the good things, too, better than anything she'd ever experienced before: the kiss near the river, his hands on her dress, an olive-green silk so thin it felt like his warm hands were already touching her skin. And later, biking across the city, when she took one hand off the handle to pluck a passing flower from a tree and then she was falling—it was unstoppable—but there he was, right there, to catch her and the bike and her wrist, and it was incredible, really, how fast he'd moved. After checking for scrapes, he'd gone back later that night to get that exact pink flower from that exact tree. He'd put it in a black velvet jewelry box. And he told her, opening it up, that she was the loveliest, most reckless person he knew. She felt, just by being near him, that everything was going to be fine. She was that flower.

She was at the altar now and the vows were being read and then the officiant was asking, "Do you?" in Chinese and Leo said, "Yes I do," first in Chinese and then in French, and she said it too, "Yes I do, yuanyi," and then "Je le veux."

"You may kiss the bride." It was a light kiss, not like the kiss at the river. Maybe no kiss would be like that ever again, but even so, it was a very good kiss. Cheers from the crowd and her hand in his. So that was it, then. So this is married life.

. . .

With Eko standing before him, with the music ended, Leo felt the bubble dissipate. He fought it. He wanted to keep it: its magic, its serenity, its clarity. But he had never been able to choose when or where it would grace him. Time had slipped away. The officiant was asking him to say, "Je le veux, I do." And then Eko was saying it herself.

And then there were the photos. And the drinks and the handshakes and the warm palms grasping his shoulder. And the slow transition indoors, somehow everyone moving in without notice when the time came, when the aperitifs were gone. And the breaking down of the chairs.

Acknowledgments

Thank you from the bottom of my heart to everyone who has supported the making of this book: My agent, Stephanie Delman, at Trellis Literary, and Allison Malecha and Khalid McCalla. Sue Armstrong at C&W. Joey McGarvey at Spiegel & Grau, and Cindy Spiegel, Julie Grau, and the whole team. Hannah Chukwu and everyone at Dialogue Books. My mentors Liam Callanan, Joan Silber, Vanessa Hua, and Toni Nelson. Deb Allbery. My MFA cohort, especially Roseanne Pereira and Joy Deng. Mike Fu and Rose Smith. Anne Horowitz. Yuri Baxter-Neal, Lola Milholland, and Shaya d'Ornano. You've all helped this book grow so much, and I am forever grateful to you for sharing your brilliance.

Thank you to Lisette, for so many years of learning and shaping our dreams together. To Alyson McDevitt, my true friend in writing and in life. To my devoted *TSLR* family. To Peter Hagan for conversations on architecture and design. To my Shanghai village—Yeye, Nainai, and the ayis who've lovingly supported our household. To Alan, for making so much possible over the past thirty years. To

Claire, who knows me best. To my grandparents, whom I miss dearly. To my mother: you have taught me everything. You are my North Star.

To Hana and Max, my babies: you are my life's greatest joy. To Haidong, my loving, my beloved, my inimitable Shanghai man: I treasure every part of you. I love you to the end of time.

Notes

The quoted lines in "Born with a Broken Heart" are from the manga *Ghost in the Shell* by Masamune Shirow. "Stayin' Alive," a disco track released in 1977 by the Bee Gees, was quoted in "Hanami." The summarized facts about the hummingbird in "Torpor" were gathered from various internet sources on birds and nature. "The East Is Red," quoted in "Je Le Veux, I Do," was a national anthem of the People's Republic of China during the 1960s.

About the Author

Juli Min is the editor in chief and fiction editor of the *Shanghai Literary Review*. She was born in Seoul, Korea, and grew up in New Jersey. Min attended Phillips Academy Andover and Harvard University, where she studied Russian and comparative literature. She holds an MFA in fiction from Warren Wilson College.